A STORM OF PASSION

A STORM OF PASSION

TERRI BRISBIN

KENSINGTON PUBLISHING CORP.
www.kensingtonbooks.com

BRAVA BOOKS are published by

Kensington Publishing Corp.
119 West 40th Street
New York, NY 10018

All Kensington titles, imprints and distributed lines are available at special quantity discounts for bulk purchases for sales promotion, premi-
ums, fund-raising, educational or institutional use.

Special book excerpts or customized printings can also be created to fit
specific needs. For details, write or phone the office of the Kensington
Special Sales Manager: Kensington Publishing Corp., 119 West 40th Street,
New York, NY 10018, Attn. Special Sales Department. Phone: 1-800-221-
2647.

Brava and the B logo are Reg. U.S. Pat. & TM Off.

ISBN-13: 978-0-7582-3516-9
ISBN-10: 0-7582-3516-X

First Kensington Trade Paperback Printing: December 2009

10 9 8 7 6 5 4 3 2 1

Printed in the United States of America

ACKNOWLEDGMENTS

First, my thanks to Kate Duffy and Megan Records at Kensington for their support in my first project with them. It has been a wonderful learning experience for me and I've enjoyed working with them.

And, I would like to thank Jennifer Wagner and Cara Carnes for serving as my mini critique group when I wrote this book. Their input and, more important, their questions about plot, characters, and scenes were a tremendous help to me in making this story come to life. Thanks!

Prologue

The damp fog crept off the sea, moving onto the land and over the hills of Quinag like tendrils of sticky sea grass. It seemed alive even as it covered the dead of her village. The smoke from fires set by their enemies choked her and burned her eyes as she searched for someone, anyone, still alive in the destruction. Struggling through the hazy gloaming, Moira slipped in the mud and fell once again.

She pushed her hair out of her face and rubbed her eyes. Shoved into a hidey-hole by her mother at the first sound of the attack, she'd stayed as long as she could, resisting the urge to fight back, to stand with her father and brothers, to protect her mother and her sister. Now, they lay dead, their lives' blood draining out onto the ground in the center of their village. Unable to help them in life, she knew she must help them find peace now.

It took hours, but she worked into the night to find and drag the bodies of her sister and mother nearer to the burned remains of their cottage. She worked on and on, sometimes giving in and crying out her grief, especially when she looked on the battered and bruised face of her sister. Then only her mother was left to bury.

When Moira reached under her mother's arms to pull her into the hastily dug grave, her mother's hand twitched, scaring her and sending Moira scurrying back. Taking a breath, she crept forward and touched her mother's cheek, hoping against hope and sense that she was still alive, though she knew that her mother could never survive the wounds she'd received.

"Mam?" she whispered. "Mam?"

Then, a rasping, labored breath, drawn in and sputtered out of her, spewed more blood on the ground. Moira tried to lift her, but the hours of digging had left her with little strength now.

"Get away," her mother said, choking with each word. "They will return . . ."

Tears flowed down her cheeks as she watched her mother struggle for a breath and lose that battle. She did not ken how long she sat there, holding her mam in her arms, but the growing light of dawn creeping over the mountains to the east told her it was too long. She would be vulnerable in the light of day, a lone girl amidst so much death with no one to protect her. Gently, she laid her mother down and offered a short prayer for her soul, their souls, and then she ran.

Their enemy did return as her mam had warned, and she was able to avoid them only by squeezing under a decaying tree and hiding in the morass of roots and grass at its base. Moira listened to their words, and the only bit of it she could hear and understand was that they'd been sent by someone called *the Seer*. The soldiers spent hours in the ruins of her village, and then they left.

With hunger and thirst driving her, she waited for the sounds of their leaving to cease completely before creeping from her hiding spot. Stumbling through the forest, she stopped to drink from a stream and pluck some berries. So confused, so tired, and so heartbroken, Moira could not think of where to go or what to do. Looking around, she knew she must find shelter, for the sun was sliding down the sky toward the sea.

Gathering what berries she could stuff into the pocket of her skirt, she found the path that led away from the sea and toward the mountains. If she could follow the path through the mountains, she could find the village where her mother's sister lived. Surely she would take her in.

The final shock met her as the path rose to enter the first mountain pass, and she nearly buckled under the pain of it. If she had kept her eyes on the rocky trail, she might have missed it, but it was at that very moment when she looked up.

Her father dangled at the end of a rope, his body twisting in the winds. Moira's stomach clenched and heaved, forcing her to her knees. His eyes were gone, and his body showed signs of torture at the hands of his enemies. She crawled on, not daring to look back.

When she reached a place where she could not see him clearly, she stood, and—from someplace within, some strength she knew not of—a burning desire for vengeance rose. Clenching her hands, she offered not only a prayer for the soul of her father, but also one for courage and resolve.

She would find the ones responsible for this, and she would make them pay. It might take her years, it might mean more suffering on her part, but she would make someone sorry for the day they chose her family as their target. This man, *the Seer*, would pay with his life.

Her fingers dug into her palms, mixing her blood with that of her slain mother and sister. Holding her hands up to the sky, she spoke the words of a blood oath to the souls of her family and to any god listening.

"I will not cease until every drop of my enemy's blood is spilled or until I give my own in the trying. On their blood, I swear this."

Chapter One

Six years later

He didn't remember seeing her before, either in the keep or in the village or among Diarmid's people. Connor walked past the woman, but then turned back to face her. When the visions approached, with the power seething through his veins and the heat building throughout his body, it was difficult to think about much other than women. If she stood by his door, she was most likely sent there by Lord Diarmid and for one purpose only.

To sate his lust.

Connor smiled as he considered this one, surely sent to ease his needs. He leaned in closer and allowed his essence to envelop her even as he inhaled hers.

Arousal.

Fear.

And something more surrounded her, like the curtain of her brown hair. He inhaled again, savoring the female essence of her, and then he recognized the other scent that she carried.

Anger. A bone-deep, overwhelming rage that she kept hidden from others.

Startled by it, he tried to meet her gaze to ascertain its source, but she only looked away. No matter. She was for him. 'Twas always the way it worked—Diarmid sent them, the magic in his blood entranced them, and he pleasured them even as they did him. His appetite for the fairer sex grew as the power pulsed stronger and stronger and as his body prepared to channel the visions sent to him.

At first the wench did not react—she even shook her head as though trying to clear her thoughts—but when he held his hand out to her, she took it. As he guided her into his chambers he realized that she was not the curvaceous, full-bodied woman that the lord usually provided to him. He'd fallen into a pattern of selecting bedmates whose breasts and hips were voluptuous and soft and whose bodies could take his weight and height and length, and Diarmid had noticed quickly and provided them to him.

Instead, this woman was tall and strong, her steps nearly as long as his, and from the firm grasp of her hand, her body nearly as strong. Her body clearly had its feminine softness, but there was a leanness about her that spoke of an inner strength and purpose.

His cock hardened, his mouth watered, and his blood raced in anticipation of the lively bout of bed play this one would give him. The ones before always gazed at him in adoration and allowed him his way, but this one teased him with her seeming indifference and the mysterious scent of her skin. Would it taste different as well? Would her female essence taste different when he sampled that place of her own arousal? Connor smiled at the possibilities between them.

They entered his chambers, and he closed the door behind them, dropping the bar. Now that his interest and his lust were growing he wanted no one interrupting them. If he was lucky— and he usually was when it came to the females in his bed—it would take at least the whole of the afternoon to wear them both out from the passion that filled the air around them now. And to ease the torturous tension that grew within him as the visions approached.

Connor dropped her hand, but still she did not look at him. She peered around the chambers, better appointed certainly than the ones she was most likely accustomed to, and he stepped aside to observe her reactions. The plush rugs on the floor instead of woven rushes, the thick tapestries covering the walls and blocking out the coastal winds, and the carved wooden furniture that turned his rooms into a comfortable place must be impressive to those who lived in less-luxurious parts of the keep or village.

Hell, it rivaled even Diarmid's chambers when it came to comfort. And cost. Whatever the Seer wanted, the Seer got, be it for his comfort or his whim or his pleasure.

She stood, staring at the chair on the raised dais at one end of the chamber, the chair where he sat when the visions came. From the expression that filled her green eyes, she knew it as well.

Had she witnessed his power? Had she watched as the magic within him exploded into a vision of what was or what would yet be? As he influenced the high and the mighty of the surrounding lands and clans with the truth of his gift? Walking over to stand behind her, he placed his hands on her shoulders and drew her back to his body.

"I have not seen you before, sweetling," he whispered into her ear. Leaning down, he smoothed the hair from the side of her face with his own and then touched his tongue to the edge of her ear. "What is your name?"

He felt the shivers travel through her as his mouth tickled her ear. Smiling, he bent down and kissed her neck, tracing the muscle there down to her shoulder with the tip of his tongue. Connor bit the spot gently, teasing it with his teeth and soothing it with his tongue. "Your name?" he asked again.

She arched then, clearly enjoying his touch and ready for more. Her head fell back against his shoulder, and he moved his mouth to the soft skin there, kissing and licking his way down and back to her ear. Still, she had not spoken.

"When I call out my pleasure, sweetling, what name will I speak?"

He released her shoulders and slid his hands down her arms and then over her stomach to hold her in complete contact with him. Covering her stomach and pressing her to him, he rubbed against her back, letting her feel the extent of his erection—hard and large and ready to pleasure her. Connor moved his hands up to take her breasts in his grasp. Rubbing his thumbs over their tips and teasing them to tightness, he no longer asked; he demanded.

"Tell me your name."

He felt her breasts swell in his hands, and he tugged now on the distended nipples, enjoying the feel and imagining them in his mouth, as he suckled hard on them and as she screamed out her pleasure. But nothing could have pleased him more in that moment than the way she gasped at each stroke he made, over and over until she moaned out her name to him.

"Moira."

"Moira," he repeated slowly, drawing her name out until it was a wish in the air around them. "Moira," he said again as he untied the laces on her bodice and slid it down her shoulders until he could touch her skin. "Moira," he now moaned as the heat and the scent of her enticed him as much as his own scent was pulling her under his control.

Connor paused for a moment, releasing her long enough to drag his tunic over his head and then turning her in to his embrace. He inhaled sharply as her skin touched his; the heat of it seared into his soul as the tightened peaks of her breasts pressed against his chest. Her added height brought her hips level almost to his, and he rubbed his hardened cock against her stomach, letting her feel the extent of his arousal.

As he pushed her hair back off her shoulders, he realized that in addition to the raging lust in his blood, there was something else there, teasing him with its presence.

Anticipation.

For the first time in years, this felt like more than the mindless rutting that happened between him and the countless, nameless women there for his needs. For the first time in too long, this was not simply scratching an itch, for the hint of something more seemed to stand off in the distance, something tantalizing and unknown and somehow tied to this woman.

He lifted her chin with his finger, forcing her gaze off the blasted chair and onto his face. Instead of the compliant gaze that usually met him, the clarity of her gold-flecked green eyes startled him. Connor did something he'd not done before, something he never needed to do: he asked her permission.

"I want you, Moira," he whispered, dipping to touch and taste her lips for the first time. Connor slid his hand down to gather up her skirts, baring her legs and the treasure between them to his touch and his sight. "Let me?"

She shivered again and reached out to grasp his shoulders, steadying herself. She did not speak, but only nodded in acceptance. It took him but moments to tug her bodice free, pull off her shift, and loosen her skirt so that it fell to the floor. Standing only in her stockings before him, Connor hesitated only because he wanted to touch every place on her and could not decide which would be first.

Her mouth beckoned to him, so he lowered his head and covered hers with his. Sliding his hand into her hair and holding her close, he tasted her, slipping his tongue deeply inside and searching for hers. She opened for him, and he felt her body do the same. Her step closer forced her legs to separate, and he could not resist caressing her there. She gasped against his mouth as his probing fingers were met with wet, hot proof of her body's reaction to him. With his thumb against that bud of flesh that was most sensitive, Connor slipped one finger, and then two, deeper into the cleft and stroked in and out, drawing the moisture of her weeping body out to ease his way.

When her legs buckled and she stumbled against him, he lifted his mouth from hers and noticed the shallow panting in her breathing. "Ah, sweetling," he whispered, "can you feel what your nearness does to me?"

Connor took one of Moira's hands and guided it down to his hardness, never moving his other hand from its place between her legs. When she covered his cock and began to caress it, he could not stop his body from reacting. Arching against her, he thrust once and then twice, noticing that wetness seeped onto his hand between her legs with each thrust. In spite of any trepidation he had that this woman was somehow different or hesitated in being part of this, her body fell under his magic just like all the others had . . . and would.

He paused then and released her from his grasp, only to take her hands and lead her across the room to the chair on the dais. Climbing one step and then the next, he sat down on the wide, wooden seat and reclined against the back of it. Although big enough for two people to sit side by side, it was wide enough for one woman to straddle one man on its surface.

And that was his plan . . . until she fell to her knees before him. Crawling forward to place herself between his legs, he watched as she unlaced his trews and freed his manhood from its coverings. Connor tried to imagine the feel of what she would do, but none of his imaginings came close to the sheer pleasure of the heat of her hands surrounding his cock.

She worked his rod, surrounding its width with her fingers and entwining them, closing her circle with her thumbs. Then she began her magic, sliding that tight grasp up and down, from the head of his cock to its base, turning and twisting and sliding with each movement. His blood forced near to boiling from her bold caresses, he lifted her chin so that she would look up at him.

No innocent wench this one, for when their gazes met she leaned forward and touched her tongue to the wide head of his cock. He felt the jolt of it and with each touch after, as she licked from head to sac, never taking her gaze from his. Then, as though she knew her own power, she began to use teeth and lips and tongue on the length of him, nipping and licking and sucking up one side of him and down the other. Connor felt his control slipping, so he clutched the carved arms of the chair to keep from thrusting the length of him into her mouth and throat. Now, it was his breathing that was shallow and wild with need.

Without lifting her mouth from him, he felt her tug on his trews, sliding them from his hips and off his legs. She moved closer, which made her breasts tease the insides of his now-naked thighs. When she slid to the head of his rod and closed her eyes, Connor knew he would not be able to stop himself.

The wench opened her mouth and took him into it. The heat and tightness made him ache for release, but he would not give in to that yet. With her hands surrounding it, she leaned down, taking more and more of him into her, until he was deep in her throat and her lips nearly to the base of his rod. His head dropped back against the chair, and he reveled in the sensations of heat and liquid and flesh on flesh. Placing his hand on her head, he did thrust then, once, against the pressure of her hold.

Connor felt the squeeze of her lips around him and waited. When she slid down on him even further, he let out a moan of pure pleasure at such temptation. Her hands then slid down to lift and caress his sac until it tightened in her grasp. He was near to exploding when the need to plow her deeply and fully took over. He lifted her head from his rod and pulled her forward and up to straddle him.

"Come, Moira," he growled. "Ride me, lass. Ride me."

Connor lifted her to kneel over his thighs and helped her position over his cock. Then he reached between her legs to make certain she was ready for him. His finger met wetness, and her womanly flesh softened under his touch. He moved his hands to her hips and waited for her to slide down the granite hardness of his erection.

He gritted his teeth against the feeling of filling her tight channel and let her set the speed of it. Finally, when he thought he would stop breathing, she settled onto him. When his whole length was inside of her, she stopped, opened her eyes, and waited for his reaction. She shifted, and their joined flesh rubbed, each part creating more friction against the other, and he felt something release within him.

Something primitive. Something feral. Something that screamed at him to take her, to take her hard and deep and to claim her as his.

Something irresistible.

Connor wrapped his arms around her and pushed himself up from the chair. She lifted her legs and encircled his waist with them as he walked across the chamber to his bed. Still deep within her, he climbed onto the bed and then fell onto her, driving himself as far into her as he could. He felt her breath being forced out by the pressure of his body on hers and in hers, but he did not pause now.

Connor slid his hand under her bottom and lifted her hips from the bed, angling them so that he could move deeper inside. Though he wanted to slow down and savor every part of this enigmatic woman, his body ached with the urge to take her. As it tore through him, he moved faster and deeper, ignoring everything else but the exquisite torture of their bodies joining.

The need within him curled and tensed, tightening with each thrust of his cock into her. He felt the muscles of her womanly channel grab him, and still he thrust, pounding against her womb, his thighs against hers, flesh against flesh until he could not stop. She slid her legs up and down his, silently urging him on, urging him in until he felt her begin to quake around his rod. Her inner muscles tightened and quivered and spasmed, causing him to swell larger and harder and causing his sac to clench in readiness of his own release.

When that release happened, it was like nothing he'd ever felt before in his numerous encounters with unremembered women. Her body shuddered inside and out as she milked his cock, and he thrust one final time, filling her, taking her, claiming her, marking her with his seed. He spilled deep within her, resting his head against her breasts and listening as she moaned out her own peak, feeling the outpouring of heat and wetness inside her that mixed with his seed.

Once he regained his senses, he was panting and still within her body. Not wanting to separate, he realized that more than just the need to fuck had eased within him. For a moment, he'd felt a satisfaction that always remained out of his grasp. In that final second when his seed spilled, he felt a calmness and peace in his heart that he could not explain. Remaining still, Connor listened to Moira's racing heart, yet hammering within her chest.

When her heart and breathing slowed, he lifted his head to look at her. Repletion made her features soften, made her look younger and more relaxed. Although his cock was still inside her, he allowed her hips down to the bed's surface, and he moved up until he was level with her face. She'd not uttered a word other than her name. He knew nothing about her except that she was different from every other woman whose charms and heat and passion he'd sampled.

Her lips were swollen, but he could not resist the urge to

taste them once more. Leaning down, he slid his mouth across hers softly, so as not to bruise them. Then he claimed her mouth in a leisurely kiss, one meant to sooth and ease rather than to inflame. When his tongue touched hers and she shifted restlessly under him, he knew they had not ended their passionate encounter, but had only just begun something he did not understand.

His cock did, for it lengthened and hardened within her, regardless of his intentions or plans. And his attempts to go slowly and savor the taste of her and scent of her skin did not last either, for passion flared hotly, and he took her another time without pause, without hesitation and without understanding how it could be this way between them.

Connor was only able to slow down after a third and a fourth time, and only after he'd claimed her body and marked her not only with seed but with his mouth and teeth too many times to remember. And each time he reached his release and she screamed or moaned out hers, that same strange sense of peace filled him.

He tried to think on it hours later, when darkness filled the room and she dozed at his side under the warmth of furs and blankets in his bed. Spent from the hours of passion between them, Connor began to fall under the spell of sleep. And as his body relaxed next to hers, his breathing matching her slow, deep pace, he realized what that elusive feeling was.

Home.

When he was deep within her, stroking her desire and forcing them to that peak of satisfaction, his heart felt like it had found the home he never thought he would have.

She fought against the lethargy trying to claim her and waited until his breathing was slow and easy and she was certain he slept before trying to slide out of his embrace. The Seer never kept a woman in his bed for long; indeed, most never spent the night there, so she felt confident that he would not miss a body next to him. Moira slid quietly across the wide surface of the bed and down from it, walking slowly in the darkened chambers, trying to find her clothes and shoes without the benefit of lamp or torch to light the way.

In a few moments, she'd dressed and made her way to the door. Turning back, she waited to see if he woke before she tried to leave. Though it was never her intent to bed him, only to get into his chambers to see the lay of it and to discover a hiding place for use in her plan, she did not hesitate to allow him to believe she was there to see to his needs. And then, when she'd thought that taking him in her mouth would be the fastest way to get through it, she'd looked into his eyes and had been caught up in the web of his desires . . . and something more.

Moira had witnessed dozens of women approach him in the very same manner and end up in his bed and no worse for the experience. He drew them to him as flies to honey, and always just before one of his visions.

'Twas said that he was irresistible then, even enchanted. 'Twas said that no woman could refuse him. 'Twas said he was kind to the women he bedded, sometimes giving them baubles or a few coins to ease their way. She'd learned the truth of several of those rumors in the last hours.

Just as she'd learned early in her quest for vengeance that a woman with nothing had only one thing to barter.

Moira had no qualms over using her body to gain whatever supplies or information she needed. Surprised by how men lost their minds when a woman opened her legs or took their pricks into her mouth, she'd used it to find out the identity of the Seer and where he lived. More recently, it had gotten her a place to work in the laundry here and kept her fed and alive while planning her attack. The sex that had just happened between them was simply that. Currency of the fleshly kind.

Yet, as she made her way to leave him, she knew that for the lie it was. This had become something much different, more dangerous, than joining with a man to get something in return. If she'd been prepared for this unexpected opportunity, if she'd had her dagger with her when she went seeking a look at his chambers and kept her reason about her while with him, then her life's task would have been a joyful end to the spirited bed play between them.

Her body ached within and out, from their vigorous efforts, and even now the muscles in that place between her legs throbbed from the aggressive attention he'd given there with hands and mouth and teeth and prick. Tempted for one heart-stopping moment to crawl back into his bed and allow him his way one more time, Moira shook off the clutching feeling that surrounded her and walked to the door.

Sighing, she slid the bar from its brackets on the door and placed it on the floor next to it. It might be months before she got this chance again. Mayhap, she would never get this close to him, and her goal would be thwarted. Opening the door just a crack, she looked outside the chamber to see if anyone waited. Seeing no one, she crept out and pulled the door closed behind her. She leaned against the wall and took a deep breath. Exhaling slowly, she closed her eyes and remembered the last hours.

He was a challenging lover, demanding everything from her while taking nothing that she would not give, instead driving her to heights of pleasure she'd not experienced before. Oh, her body enjoyed the results of desire and lust, but she was always careful to never let it affect her mind or her soul or her heart . . . or her purpose.

Moira made her way down the long hallway away from his chambers, her head tilted down to avoid anyone getting a clear look at her, should she pass someone. It wasn't until she reached the small room she shared with several other women that the feeling of dread turned her stomach. Almost as though some veil or stupor was lifting from her, horror and shame covered her as she remembered her actions with the Seer.

What had seemed and felt so right just moments ago now screamed out its treacherous truth at her. Falling to her knees on the straw pallet in the corner she called her own, she doubled over in pain as she realized that she had done more than simply allow him to take his ease on her body. She'd enjoyed it and, for those hours, had lost herself in the passion he offered, never once thinking about her real purpose there.

Her stomach clenched and burned, and her chest pounded in pain as her body and will became her own once more and she knew the genuineness of the rumors about the Seer's true powers. He could ensorcell women into losing their abilities to think and choose freely. He ensnared her into his trap of pleasure and passion, and she'd gone willingly, never even fighting back or struggling, losing sight of everything important to her.

He plied her body with his kisses and his caresses and his forceful mastery of all things sexual, bending her will until she'd forgotten why she was standing outside his door. Worse, she'd revealed her real name to her enemy without thought of the consequences of such a revelation.

What power could he have that could make her lose the memories of her family's fates? How could she allow her body to betray her into reveling in the time spent wrapped in his arms, surrounded by his body and the comforts of his bed?

Falling onto her pallet and tugging her thin blanket over her shaking body, Moira sought the inner strength and focus that had kept her alive over these last six years. She ignored the aching between her legs that now served to remind her of the ecstasy they'd shared. She ignored the places on her skin that now wore the mark of his possession. Instead, she brought to mind the horrible images of her mother's and father's bodies the last time she'd seen them. Anger began to bubble deep within her, seething and pulsing until she gagged at its strength.

Now, the reason she sought the Seer was clear to her. He must pay for his part in the destruction of her family and all she held dear. He must lose his life in exchange for those he caused to lose theirs. And now, he must suffer for showing Moira a side of herself that she had never wished to see: the woman who loved life and wanted all the passion it offered. Because he tempted her with what could be but never would, he must not be allowed to live.

'Twas gossiped in hushed voices among the servants of the keep that he grew weary after each vision and disappeared into his chambers, sometimes for days, to recover. Now that she'd tasted his true power, she knew that his weak time would be the only safe time for her to approach him again. She would watch, from a distance, disguised and out of his sight, and wait for her best chance.

Turning onto her side and curling into a ball, Moira whispered her oath over and over again until sleep finally claimed her.

His blood for theirs.

Chapter Two

"I told you I wanted wine, not ale," he shouted.

Swinging his arm across the surface of the table, Connor swept the goblet with the offending drink to the floor. The metal cup bounced several feet, splashing the dark liquid over the table linens and the clothing of several guests, before coming to a rest. He just did not care. Several servants came running to both fill his request and clean up the mess he'd made. Angry yet, Connor settled back in the chair and drank the wine he'd finally been served.

His head pounded, the fierceness of the pain growing by the minute, it seemed. He'd had no rest for days, unable to quell the need in his blood and unable to find the one wench who'd satisfied him those months before. Now, his body burned and his head ached without respite.

Moira. Moira.

He could smell the scent of her, and his tongue remembered the taste of her essence at just the thought of her name. Even his skin ached to touch her again. And his cock stood hard and large as the memory of the hours spent with her flooded back. Reaching under the table, he tugged on his trews to loosen their hold on him.

Refusing to remain here where all could see his rage and do nothing to assuage it, he pushed back from the table, and with a curt nod to Lord Diarmid, he strode down from the dais and off to his chambers. Servants and visitors alike jumped out of his way, or he pushed them, as he covered the length of the main floor, climbed three flights of stairs, and walked down the hall to his corner chamber.

Two months had passed since he'd found her at his door, and he'd not had another moment of the peace or satisfaction of spirit or desire he found with her. His body ached for release, and no amount of fucking and no number of women could quench the desires that burned through him. And aye, he'd tried to drown the memory of her out of him, using any potent drink or concoction he could find, without success.

He pushed his hair back out of his face and searched the darkened corners of the hallway, praying and hoping like some lovelorn idiot that she would reappear and ease the torment growing inside of him.

Seeing no one, he raised his hand to push open his door, when it opened from the inside. Only Ranald, Lord Diarmid's spy and his attendant, stood there waiting for him. Pushing past him, Connor went to the table and poured a cup of the potent ale he kept there. No matter how much he drank, he could not rid himself of the memories of his time with Moira.

"My lord," Ranald said, bowing to him and stepping back. "I found her."

Connor stopped swallowing before he stopped drinking and choked as the ale poured into his mouth. Dropping the cup and wiping his mouth with the back of his sleeve, he crossed the chamber in two paces. He grabbed Ranald by the tunic, twisting it in his grasp as he pulled him up to face him.

"You found Moira?" he growled. "Where is she?" He shook the servant for not answering quickly enough, but when Ranald clutched at his throat—the one Connor was tightening his hold on—Connor released him and let him breathe. "Where?"

Ranald was not by nature a stupid man, and most likely he knew, from their time together as master and servant, that Connor was at the end of his control. Wisely, he took but a few quick breaths and answered.

"She awaits you, my lord. In your bed," he stuttered, pointing to the tall, wooden screen that separated his bed from the rest of the chamber.

Connor raced around the end of the screen and stopped before his bed. There, a young woman lay, naked and legs spread, opening and rubbing her womanly flesh, flesh that glistened in readiness for his pleasure. She had brown hair and green eyes, but a quick glance told him that was where the similarities ended. Rubbing his eyes with his hands, he shook his head.

"Get her out of here, Ranald," he ordered without looking.

"My lord," the girl said, her voice soft yet laden with the huskiness of desire. "I will do whatever you need. I can please you in many ways."

When the sound of her voice grew closer, he dropped his hands only to find her kneeling at the edge of the bed and reaching for his belt. He shoved her away and nodded his head toward the door without saying another word. Ranald came forward, draping a cloak over the girl's nakedness, and led her out, whispering instructions the whole way. From the glazed expression in her eyes when he first looked upon her and from her complacent manner, Connor suspected that his efficient, if incorrect, servant had drugged her.

He sank on the bed and held his head in his hands. These last eight months had been hell, pure and simple. His life was falling apart, and there seemed to be no way to slow it down. Diarmid, who had accepted—nay even encouraged—his eccentric and outlandish behavior, now looked on with a suspicious glint in his black eyes at his seer. Connor was not certain of the extent of Ranald's reporting to Diarmid, but surely the nobleman knew much about both the increasing power of the visions and their new and dangerous cost to him.

The only time the terrible cost had not driven him to his knees was the day after he found Moira and took her to his bed. He had no idea of why, but when the visions finished, the pain and burning had been bearable for the first time in months. He wondered if there was some connection; however, he had no way of knowing without her. And she had disappeared like the fog on a warming day, never to be seen or found in the keep or on the island.

Lifting his head, he heard Ranald moving around the chamber. Pushing off the bed, he walked around the wooden screen and stopped. Ranald stood by the door, speaking in a low voice with Diarmid, the lord of the keep, a powerful chieftain in the isles that lay to Scotland's west.

"My lord," he said, walking forward, out of the shadows.

"Connor." Diarmid nodded as he met him nearer to the door. "I would speak to you."

Diarmid's glance told Ranald to leave, and the man did so without hesitation. When the door was closed behind him Diarmid, a leader among King Magnus's many powerful earls, cocked his head and inspected Connor from head to toe.

"Are you well? You did not seem so at table," he began. "I know you chafe under this constant watch, Connor, but I . . . ."

Connor held up his hand, shaking his head at what was to come . . . again. "I appreciate your concern for my welfare, Diarmid, but there have been no attempts in the last two months."

With the power of Sight, he had become a valuable asset to this lord, and, in exchange for care, comfort, protection, and wealth, Connor served only him. Apparently someone wanted to stop that arrangement, and whether Connor or Diarmid's influence with both the Norwegian and Scottish kings and many other island chieftains was the true target, they knew not.

"My men have been searching for those connected to the assassins."

"Aye, I know that, but two months is longer than the intervals since the attacks began. I should be safe now."

"You and I both know that the effort was planned ahead and in concert with others, Connor. Though none of the three we captured talked before they died, I am beginning to understand and suspect that there is a web connecting them. A few more weeks . . ."

"I will go insane in a few more weeks, Diarmid," he swore.

Turning away, he sought the cup of ale he'd dropped. Ranald had cleaned up the spillage and set a new one there for him. Filling it near to the rim, he glanced at Diarmid, who shook his head. He drank most of it before stopping.

"Is that wise?" Diarmid asked.

"It is necessary, Diarmid."

"I thought that the women eased your pain before the visions. Is that not true now?" He could feel Diarmid's dark scrutiny. "Is there something I should know?"

Connor did not meet the astute man's gaze for a moment, trying to bring the pain that stabbed his head and the heat in his veins under control. It was worse, and it was growing even more painful. Although refusing the women who showed up at his door these last weeks seemed a good idea to him, his "gift" thought otherwise. It seemed foolish to him to continue to bed women when none could satisfy him, but the pressure building warned him of the dire results of such forced celibacy.

Like some cruel joke played by ancient gods against mortal men, each time he used the power of the visions, he suffered with repercussions he could not have imagined when the power first asserted itself within him. Now each vision of the past or the present or some unknown future brought devastating consequences: he was going blind.

Somehow he'd managed to keep the worst of it to himself. The effects lessened over days, but each time the power flowed, the blindness lasted longer and was more complete. The first time it happened, now just over ten months ago, it had almost seemed like his imagination rather than a real event. Then, each time, it worsened, and it now lasted for several full days, the cone of darkness around him larger and deeper with each occurrence.

And the power flowed more freely as well, stronger and stronger, both luring him and allowing him to see deeper into the past and further into today and beyond and drawing more women to him daily, while reaping its terrible price on him.

"The visions grow stronger, Diarmid, and so too do their effects on me. I suffer from pains in my head for days after being gifted with a vision."

"So that is the reason for your seclusion afterward? I thought," he said, walking closer and lowering his voice, "I thought that you might be losing your . . . gift."

Connor considered how to answer. Truth be told, he did not know the answer to that question. Only tales passed down could explain what happened to him. There was no one who knew exactly how his power worked or the reasons behind these more recent changes to it. Was he losing his gift? Of what value would he be to Diarmid if that happened? Taking a deep breath in, he realized the only prudent thing to do was bluff through it until he had more of an idea of what the situation really was.

"The visions seem stronger and come more often, as you know, Diarmid."

Of course he knew, for as the frequency and strength increased, he'd arranged for more of his cronies and potential allies to benefit from Connor's visions. When the portents changed and a vision approached, Lord Diarmid filled his keep with those whom he sought to influence and control and exposed them to Connor's powers. Though Connor could not completely control the choice of the recipient of his gift, he could feel when those requesting were true of heart—the one common element among those who received a vision in answer to their question.

"But these effects seem stronger and to plague you more viciously each time. Is there aught that can be done?" Lord Diarmid asked.

Find that damned wench! his body and head screamed out in silence.

"Nay, Diarmid. Nothing that I am aware of," he said, drinking down more ale. "Your healer has attempted every pain concoction she knows. Your priest prays incessantly for me, though for my demise or my improvement, I know not which. I have searched for years for someone who could tell me more of this gift and found no one." He rubbed his forehead again and squeezed his eyes shut against the pain. "I know of nothing else to try."

"And the girl you sought. You thought she might be somehow connected to this?" Diarmid's eyes darkened, and his face emptied of all expression, a sign he'd come to know in the years he'd spent here.

"Nay, Diarmid. She but provided me with several hours of vigorous bedplay, and I sought more of it . . . her," he forced out a laugh. "She had certain skills. . . ." He let his words drift off, allowing Diarmid, who also liked variety in his bed, to think what he would. "Better even than when I paid good coin for it. What better way to take my mind off the pain?"

Diarmid smiled then, and nodded. "I have my men searching for her, Connor. If she returns to the island or the keep, she is yours. . . ." Smacking him on the shoulder, Diarmid walked to the door. "First, at the least," he said then. "With such high praise from you, I will have to try her as well."

Jealous rage pierced him, tearing through his blood and making his jaws clench in possessive fury. But, to give Diarmid so much information about her importance to him was to hand the lord another weapon with which to control him. Something he knew better than to do, for Diarmid liked very little in life more than controlling others and making them dance to his tune.

"Find her, and you will learn the truth of my words of praise, my lord. Now, I would seek some rest," Connor said, opening the door for Diarmid.

"Have a care about the ale and wine, Connor. Should I send Ranald to you?"

"Nay," Connor shook his head. "His service to me this day is done. He can seek his own rest."

Diarmid stepped through the doorway and would have walked away, but Connor grabbed his arm and pulled him to a stop. There was one more thing they needed settled between them this night. Making certain no one lurked in the hallway, he spoke in a low voice.

"I will travel to my farm next week, Diarmid," he said in a calm voice. "Ranald need not accompany me."

"It is not safe for you to leave the keep, Connor," Diarmid answered, shaking his head decisively. "We will talk of this when the identities of those trying to assassinate you are known."

Connor stopped him when he would have walked away again. "I am not asking you this, Diarmid. I have been your faithful servant for years and have never given you reason to question my loyalty to you. I will only be gone several days, a sennight at the most."

Diarmid looked as though he would argue, but he crossed

his arms and nodded. "After the vision and with sufficient guards," he ordered.

Connor tilted his head, appearing to acquiesce for the moment. That battle could be better waged with a clearer head than he had now.

"My lord," he said, stepping back into his chambers.

Once Diarmid made his way down the hall, Connor closed the door and leaned against it as the pain flooded him. Trying to ride the waves of pain as they hit, Connor stumbled over to the large, wooden chest in one corner and opened it. After a few minutes of searching, he found the healer's latest brew and poured a good measure of it into his goblet. Filling it with sweet wine, he swirled the mixture and then downed it in two swallows. Connor walked over to the chair and fell into it, for the effects of the drug would begin soon.

The concoction began working in a few minutes, and Connor noticed that the pain receded a bit. He was still sitting in the chair, unmoving, when he realized that his physical needs, heightened now as the vision was but two or three days off, caused his body to emanate that essence that beckoned women to him. The smell of it, like something from deep in the forest, was more noticeable now than earlier—mayhap the pain blocked it from working?—and Connor knew it would take no time at all to be answered.

The sound of someone scratching lightly on the door at his back told him the first had arrived. Torn between his fleshly needs, accelerated now, and his desire for the only woman who'd made a difference, he took a deep breath and exhaled slowly as he began to experience more of the drug's effect. The pain moved further away from him, allowing the heat in his blood to spread. Erect and hardened, his cock knew the answer even if he struggled with the question.

"My lord?" the soft voice queried through the timber door.

Another breath, and more of the scent spread. And yet he took another breath before he gave in, deciding that celibacy was not the answer either.

What if he never found her?

What if waiting for her caused him to miss another woman who could make him feel the same things Moira had?

Mayhap the girl outside his door now, the one who had lain in his bed offering herself to him earlier, could drain him of the raging lust in his veins and give him respite from the pain, too?

He strode to the door, lifted the latch, and stepped away, pulling the door open as he moved. The girl entered, still wrapped in the cloak that Ranald had covered her in just minutes—hours—ago. With a motion of his hand, he sent her back to his bed, watching her long brown hair sway down her back with each step she took.

If he closed his eyes, it would feel the same. If he didn't taste her lips or the heart of her passion, he would never know. Connor pushed the door closed and followed her into his sleeping chamber. She'd stopped by the bed, and he moved around her, climbing onto its surface and sitting with his back against the tall, cushioned headboard.

"My lord, how can I serve you?" she asked, her voice soft and dreamlike. Her eyes, though green, were undefined and shadowed, not clear and challenging as the woman he wanted.

She'd not waited on his request; instead, she lifted his tunic and loosened his belt. Reaching into his trews, she took his cock in her grasp and then climbed between his legs, positioning herself as he knew she would. She paused and raised her head, waiting on his word now, and he nodded.

When she licked her lips and opened her mouth wide to accommodate him there, he tried to imagine someone else in her place. Her movements teased his hardness and made waves of pleasure pulse through it. Her hands were skillful as she massaged his sac, sliding her fingers around it, lifting it, and caressing it as she suckled on his rod.

He felt the pressure build in it and tried to remember the feel of Moira's mouth taking him in deeply. Connor knew his release was close, and he shifted, pushing farther into the wench's mouth. Her hair fell like a curtain around her, brushing his thighs and groin as she moved up and down again and again, pulling on his length until he felt his sac tauten and his release spew into her. She did not stop until every drop had been drawn from him.

Whatever feelings of pleasure he'd experienced waned quickly, and he sat there with a girl who wasn't the one he wanted between his legs, servicing him just as so many others had but with one difference now: the momentarily relief could not disguise the disappointment rushing through him.

But when she began to caress him once more, sliding those experienced hands over his thighs and belly and then down to his half-erect cock, he let her.

He just did not have the strength to fight the call in his blood. The visions were coming, and they proved his master yet again.

Chapter Three

The scene burst out before Connor and he was tempted to delay in his quest for the sheer enjoyment of such lightness and beauty. And clarity. The sky filled with huge white clouds. The sun's rays traced their outlines on the sea and ground below, barely able to keep up as they raced on the Highland winds. Following the coast, he searched for the cliffs and the loch that sliced into the land, making a path toward the higher mountain peaks.

As though a bird in flight, Connor sighted the trail that led over the mountains and followed it, on and on, until the castle came into view. Rough stone walls topped with a wooden roof, surrounded by another ring of tall stones. Now, he searched for the way in.

Flying lower and lower, he traced the route of a small stream and found its entrance under the walls. The location was unseen from the ground, hidden by an outcropping of rock and trees, but from his place in the sky, it was clear . . . and undefended. The perfect place to begin the downfall of the castle and its inhabitants.

"Follow the trail until it turns to the north. Then look to the south for a break in the forest and search for the stream that runs there. It will lead you to the secret entrance. Use it, and you will recover your daughter," Connor instructed.

His hand rushed across the slate creating a chalk map of exactly what he saw before him. The trail, the entrance to the forest, the stream were now all marked on the slate for the man to follow. He did not need to say that this man and his warriors would crush his enemies as well, for he knew that once the man was inside the keep, when he saw what had been done to his daughter, death and complete annihilation for those responsible would follow.

Even now, as he finished describing the vision and released the hand of the man who asked for his help, the scene was fading from his view. Connor handed the slate off to a servant waiting there and laid his hands on the carved arms of the chair. Clutching the strong wood beneath his palms against the pain he knew would come, he realized it was vital not to let anyone know the extent of it. Glancing in that moment around the large chamber, he nodded to his servant Ranald.

Ranald clapped his hands loudly, drawing the attention of all who observed Connor's use of the Sight. Ushering them out, Ranald waved off the attempt of the one requesting the vision to gift him with gold. So many tried, but Connor had learned the folly of accepting such payment a long time ago. With a nod of acceptance of the man's show of gratitude, he turned away.

He took in a breath and released it as the burning began. The heat filled his eyes like it filled his finger when he held his hand too close to a flame. Now, the blindness robbed his eyes of sight as the pain increased. Like white-hot iron pokers thrust there, the burning grew and grew. Fighting it long enough to allow Ranald to empty his chambers of those who came to witness the power of his gift, usually those whom Diarmid wanted to entice into his circle of allies, he held on to any vestige of control he had. As soon as he heard the door close loudly, Connor clutched his eyes and slid from the chair, down from the dais and onto the floor. His stomach clenched, and he heaved out bile as he writhed against it. Struggling not to scream, he curled up tightly and waited, praying it would end soon.

Minutes or hours passed, and the burning began to ease in his eyes. Connor remained on the floor, taking in deep breaths of air, trying to rid himself of the pain, but it was not done yet. A few more minutes, and he could remove his hands from his eyes. The burning was bearable now. Almost.

More time moved by as he waited for the pain to cease completely. This time it lasted longer than before. And it was more intense again, as though the respite two months before had never happened. Now, he waited to regain his strength before trying to stand, or even sit. Each time his recovery slowed with each use of his power.

When Connor could feel both the coldness and the hardness of the stone floor beneath him, he tried to sit up. His head pounded with dizziness, but he managed to get to his knees. Then, feeling the floor with his hands, he got his bearings of his position in the room.

Opening his eyes would do no good, for they were useless now and would remain so for days. This was the price of his "gift." Kneeling there, he pushed away all the thoughts of and prayers for release that plagued his days and nights and especially these moments after he used his power. There was no release, as far as he could discover, and nothing that could intervene in his descent into blindness. Connor fought not to wish that the recent attempts on his life would succeed and free him from all of this.

He heard the voices of those outside his chamber, some arguing with Ranald, others pleading. It would be to no avail, for until he could see, he could not have the visions they wanted, or needed, or begged for. Pushing his hair out of his face, he righted his cloak and sat back on his heels. The hallway would quiet, and Ranald would leave as soon as he cleared out those who still pled their case. It was as he was about to gain his feet that he heard the sound.

Someone was in his chambers.

Someone had witnessed his descent from Seer to blind man.

Someone was moving from one place to another behind him.

He turned his head quickly to try to gauge the intruder's location and his distance from him, but the first blow hit him then, a strong kick that shoved him to the floor once again. The dagger's entrance into his shoulder was quick and silent.

Connor grabbed for his shoulder and tried to call out, but the vision left him with little strength. Any sound he could make would be masked by the busyness and noise of those in the corridor outside his chambers. Rolling away from his assailant, he tried to make it to the door. Another kick to his ribs, and he collapsed on the floor.

Of all the ends to his life he'd considered, especially as the assassins had varied their attempts, murder by an unseen attacker was not one of them. Now as he waited for the death blow, he wondered what had brought this about, and why now. Was it another of the Fae's strange ironies? An enemy he knew not? The weight of someone pouncing on his chest ended all speculation, for he could not breathe.

With his right arm made useless by the dagger's wound, he tried to grasp with his left, but after another slashing wound to his forearm he lay helpless on the cold floor. Connor felt his attacker grab his tunic and slice it open down to his waist. He waited for death to come.

Instead, the attacker poked his bleeding wound and then whispered something he could not understand. A gasp, one that sounded strangely feminine, was followed by another whisper, and then he smelled the metallic odor of blood as he was touched again. This time something was smeared over his face and onto his chest.

"Who are you? Tell me," he gasped. He would at least know the reason for his death.

"Your blood for those slain at your word, Seer. Prepare for death." The attacker shifted, rising up as though preparing to plunge the blade with more weight behind it. "Open your eyes, and see who brings your death."

There was not time to explain the futility of it, and part of him wished he could look on the face of the one who would release him from the torment in which he lived. But knowing the horror that would be seen there, Connor clenched his eyes closed more tightly.

"Open them, pig," the order came again, whispered gruffly.

The dagger slit the skin at his neck as if to force him to obey. The voice was definitely a woman's; he could hear it now, even though she tried to hide it in the hoarse whisper she used. By God, they stooped to using women now. Was he so valuable to Diarmid and his enemies so desperate that they would draw a woman into their plans?

When he did not open his eyes, she did not delay, burying her blade into his chest. The searing pain of the dagger slicing through ribs and muscles wracked his body. He did open his eyes then, stunned at the feeling of his blood gushing out and soaking through his tunic and cloak. As he lost consciousness, he tried to see her face and let her see his.

The shrill scream pierced his stupor, but did not rouse him completely. She pulled the dagger from his chest, and still she screamed. Some part of him knew the horror she'd seen in his eyes and knew it was the source of her torment. Her cries drew attention from outside, and Connor was aware of the struggle as her weight disappeared from his chest and Ranald's concerned voice whispered to him to close his eyes.

Darkness followed then, with all manner of sounds filling it. Connor knew he was losing his battle to stay awake, but the questions about this woman and her involvement plagued him even this close to death. If he did not die, he wanted to know the truth. When he could, he forced the words out, giving Ranald one final order.

"I want her alive," he gasped, shocked at the amount of pain just speaking caused. "She is mine."

Chapter Four

The first two times he attempted it, he could see nothing, for the cloth placed by Ranald blocked his sight, as well as the view of anyone who would look upon him. The third time, the blindfold was gone, and a dull light broke into the darkness. Ranald spoke to him.

"Will I live?" Connor asked, as he felt Ranald's hand beneath his head, lifting it so he could sip at the cup now at his mouth. He tried to reach the place on his chest that burned and ached, but his hands would not obey him.

"You may, my lord. 'Twas a near thing though."

"The girl? Where is she?" The cup was tilted, and he was forced to drink and wait on Ranald's answer. "I asked where she is, Ranald."

His servant moved away for a moment, and Connor tried to pull himself up on his bed. Waves of pain stopped him from trying it a second time.

"They are holding her nearby, my lord," he finally answered. "Though I confess I do not understand why you are even concerned over the bitch. She tried to kill you!"

"Ranald? Is she alive?" He had a bad feeling about this.

"Perhaps, though in the five days since she attacked you she may have died. I have not seen her in that time."

Five days had passed? "Get her now," he ordered in as strong a voice as he could muster. "Now."

"Lord Diarmid has other plans, my lord."

The damn servant began walking away, intent on disobeying his orders and on letting the girl die. He knew Diarmid's methods and knew the men who would carry them out, and even with his attacker being a woman, they would show no mercy in their quest for information.

Though his liege, lord, and host, Lord Diarmid did not have the right to take her life while he still lived and ordered otherwise. Not while he needed to know the reason for the attack. And her identity.

Gathering his strength, Connor rolled to his side and swung his legs over the side of the bed. Ranald was there in a trice, cursing him for reopening wounds.

"Send word to Lord Diarmid that she is mine to punish. Tell him I live and will be very angry if he takes my right to punish the one who sought to end my life. Very angry," he said, putting his foot on the floor.

"My lord, you are not strong enough to leave your bed." Ranald tried to block his way. "Is your sight restored?" he asked in a whisper, so that no one else could hear.

"Nearly. Enough for me to find my way down the halls, searching room by room, until I discover where she is."

There had been many tests of wills in their past, and he'd won every one, even at great cost, so Ranald knew the outcome already. He backed away and bowed.

"Stay, rest, while I speak to Lord Diarmid."

Connor sank back on the bed and nodded. Truly, he did not have the strength to leave his bed, let alone his chambers. Once his head fell back onto his pillow, he lost consciousness once more.

Shadows shifted in his chambers, and whispers floated around him. Connor tried to focus his thoughts and open his eyes, but with his strength gone from the last contest, he could only lie in silence. It was possibly another day before he roused and felt clearly awake. The light, from both the braziers lit around his chambers and from the sun as it poured through the open window in the wall, told him that his vision was back.

It was different though, not as clear as before, and he was not able to see in the shadows. How many more times before he went completely blind? Would the Sight then vanish from him? Would the curse be lifted once the gift was gone? Whimpering in the corner drew his attention away from all the possibilities he faced.

Connor struggled, but managed to sit up and find the source of the noise. As he pulled himself to stand and edged closer to the corner of the chamber—damn it, but it was the one in the darkest shadows—the smell knocked him back. The foul stench gagged him, but Connor moved closer, now seeing a small heap lying on a pile of straw.

"Is that her?" he asked, knowing Ranald stood behind him now.

"Aye, though why you would bother with her, I know not."

"I do not need your permission or consent on this, Ranald. If you would rather serve another, I can speak to Diarmid."

The silence told him that Ranald was effectively quelled for the moment.

"Has she been fed? Given water?" Again, the silence gave him his answer. The odor and his own weakness kept him at a distance, frustrating him in his need to look on a girl brave enough and foolish enough to breach Diarmid's keep to get to him.

"Clean her and feed her, and then I will speak to her." Ranald began to argue, but ceased at his look. "I do not want her befouling my chambers with her smell. 'Tis a small matter, Ranald, not one that should cause any problem for you."

Connor made his way to sit in his chair, far enough away not to choke but close enough to insure that his orders would not be ignored. Ranald left the room, calling out to various servants in the corridor outside as he went. When he chose to be efficient, none could match his efforts, so Connor knew it would only be a short time before the girl was ready to be questioned.

A serving girl entered with some broth for him, and with her help he sipped at it as he waited for Ranald's return. Instead, one of Diarmid's burly house slaves entered, carrying two huge wooden buckets of water. The man did not wait for a tub. He put the buckets down and proceeded to dump one on the girl curled on the floor. She did not move much with the first, only coughed and shook, so he reached down and tore the garments she wore off. Then, before Connor could do anything to intervene, the slave threw the other bucket of water on her. The shuddering now was noticeable even from where he sat in shock.

Connor stood so quickly that he knocked the bowl of broth out of the servant's hands, and it bounced on the floor, splashing them both. He stumbled to the corner and tried to reach the girl, who lay unmoving now. Would he never discover her reasons for trying kill him? Why she would risk her own life to take his?

"Get out of here," he ordered the slave. "Send Ranald to me."

Ranald was only a moment behind his order and entered the chambers with three other servants. As Ranald helped him aside, they dragged the girl out of the corner, shoveled out the decaying straw on which she had lain, and tossed her back on the floor with a blanket over her.

"She has not long to live, my lord. Why waste any effort or concern on her well-being?"

"Because I ordered it to be so," he said through clenched teeth. He had never realized the mean streak in his servant before. "Now, get them out of here," he nodded to the others in the chambers, "and get her clothed."

Ranald waved the others out, but not before acquiescing to his orders for clothing for the girl. He wondered if a shroud would be needed instead.

His breathing became labored, and the chambers began to spin around him then. He'd moved too quickly, done too much and not enough. Connor fell to his knees and grabbed for the end of his bed to try to balance himself. Blood leaked through his tunic, and he could feel the tearing where stitches were being pulled from the skin. If he was not careful, he would end up dead without ever finding out who she was or why she attacked him.

But, the stubborn part of him would simply not give up. On his own life, or on hers. Curiosity won out, and he allowed Ranald to help him back to his bed now. He waited for his servant to go for more broth, and then he spoke, his words aimed at his attacker, words he thought would not be heard, really.

"It would have gone better for you if you had simply killed me."

He heard the scraping on the stone floor, as she shifted around in the corner. Surprised, since he did not think she was awake, Connor leaned up on his elbows and searched the darkened corner for her.

"Aye, a swift death would have been a blessing to both of us," he continued. "Now 'tis too late for both of us."

Darkness and light blended together into a blur for her, just as the waves of pain grew and receded, once and again, until Moira did the unthinkable and prayed for death. Her plea went ignored, and she forced another breath into her broken body.

She'd failed yet again and deserved to die for such failure. Her family's souls yet cried out to be avenged, and she would suffer the torments of hell for nothing. If only they'd killed her quickly, all of this would be over.

The cough surprised her, pushing its way from deep within her in spite of her efforts to keep it inside. It exploded then, and the thick, coppery taste of blood filled her mouth until she spat it out. Unable to turn, unable to brace herself against the onslaught of pain, Moira simply let go and melted back down into unconsciousness.

She knew not how many times it happened, but she felt the same pattern repeat itself many uncounted times until there was one moment of clarity in her mind. And, her mind clung to that moment and searched for more. The same tenacity that had kept her alive these last six years, through danger and starvation and other obstacles, now would not allow her to grasp the ultimate surrender to the pain and injuries.

Days and days later—she could not tell how many passed— a loud argument pierced her fog, and she feared more pain would come. Instead, Moira tasted some foul brew forced into her mouth, and then a blissful peace took control of her senses. Was this it? Was this the end of her suffering, the end of the quest that had given her purpose when she'd lost all?

More time passed—so confused was she by the pain and the darkness that she knew not how much—before she came to awareness again, but then the searing and tearing pain faded into something more tolerable. When she realized that the cold, hard stone floor beneath her had been replaced with a cot or pallet of some kind and began to recognize the comings and goings of servants and the pattern of life within the keep, she knew she would survive.

Whether from the potions given her or something else, terrible, ghastly images filled her slumber. Flames, like the very flames of hell, tormented her and pursued her as she ran through the keep. Demons, with horrible faces and fire where their eyes should be, ran after her, clawing and grabbing at her, then beating her and tearing her clothes. Moira ran and ran, but they grew closer and closer until she could only scream and scream and watch herself die.

Other times it was just the flames, like living torches, chasing her, nipping at her feet, with the tormenting heat growing stronger and nearer with every pace she took away. But every time, her screams were as useless as before. Her arms and legs seemed weighted, and, try as she might, she could not move.

Then Moira grew aware of more light and less darkness in the world that surrounded her. The pain subsided, and voices began to penetrate the silence of her thoughts. Sometimes stern and demanding, sometimes soft and coaxing, sometimes female and sometimes male. One day, Moira recognized the voice of the man she'd come to kill. The man whose eyes had burned with the very fires of hell. She forced her own to open a crack.

The room where she lay was not the large and spacious one he used for both his personal sleeping chamber and the place he called his visions. She'd seen almost all the chambers in the keep, but never this one. Moira suspected it was on one of the lower floors of Diarmid's keep. Since she'd arrived here, she'd crept through the passageways and hidden corridors of the stone castle, looking for her quarry and watching his movements and habits. Moira planned and prepared for months, knowing that the Seer was far too valuable for Lord Diarmid to let him live and travel unguarded.

Now, if her senses served her, he stood at her side, staring at her with those eyes that had burst into inhuman flames as he lay on the floor. Those eyes that had looked at her in desire and had watched her pleasure him throughout that strange yet wondrous day now so long ago. Not certain she could bear to see them again, Moira focused her gaze on his cloak and took a deeper breath.

"She is awake," the Seer said to someone else in the chamber.

A cool hand touched her brow then—not one of his, for she saw that he did not move. Then the hand moved to her cheek. Moira winced at the pain from the touch.

"I did not mean to add to your pain," said a woman. "The bruises run deep and will take a long time to heal."

Daring to open her eyes more, Moira looked above her and found the source of the touch and the voice. A young servant woman stood next to her, peering at her with a concerned gaze. Finally, Moira gathered her courage and faced her enemy.

His gaze burned no longer, but neither did it hold the compassion that the woman's did. Anger filled it now. Anger and something else she could not decipher. He took a step closer, and she steeled herself for the inevitable blow.

It did not come.

Instead he crouched lower, studying her face as though some clue was written there. Tempted to say something, anything, to break his contemplation of her, Moira fought the urge and lay silent. She was a prisoner now, and she understood what that meant. Torture to extract any information she carried that would help his lord continue his rule of terror over the local clans. The pain she'd suffered so far, for her attack on the Seer, was only a punishing prelude to what she would feel when they turned their efforts to keeping her alive while they worked.

Her courage faltered then, only for a moment, before she grabbed the shredded edges of it and tugged it harder and closer around her. Closing her eyes, she remembered the reason for this. The reason she would bear what she must.

Her family. Their bloodied bodies, strewn around their village. Her sister.

Under control once more, she met his gaze without faltering.

"What are you called?" he asked in a voice that was deceptively pleasant. Deep and resonant, she recognized the power there, power that had called her to his bed and power that emanated from him during his visions.

He did not know her! How could that be? Had he taken so many to his bed that each meant nothing and did not even garner memory to him? Then she realized that her face must be so badly beaten and torn that she did not look like the woman who climbed into his bed so easily.

She said nothing.

"I asked what you are called," he repeated, this time louder as though her hearing had suffered. His fists clenched and released as he waited.

"Connor," the woman said softly. A warning or plea, Moira could not tell.

Standing back to his full height, he crossed his arms over his chest, and then the right one fell to his side. She'd pierced the shoulder there, rendering his arm useless for now. Tempted to smile, she fought back the insane need to gloat at the damage she'd caused.

He could render so very much more.

"For the last time, girl. What are you called?" he asked.

Moira looked away then, the temptation to shout her name too strong to deny. He changed his approach then, demanding other information.

"Who do you work for?"

Startled by the strange question, her eyes darted to his, but she forced herself to remain silent.

"Why did you try to kill me when you knew you would die too?"

Ah, she'd known the consequences of her act, but her attackers had turned the quick death she'd expected into something else. Exhausted from just this short exchange, she closed her eyes and felt her body surrendering to it, inch by inch.

"Dara, when can she be moved?"

"Another day, Connor. Two at the most," the servant woman replied.

Through the corner of her eye she watched as he turned away and strode to the door. Dara followed him, twisting a cloth in her hands. Reaching out to him, she stopped him with her hand on his arm.

"And you still intend to see this through?" she asked.

The dread in her voice was so clear that Moira's stomach turned inside her. The fear within grew and taunted her until she could feel the sweat beading on her forehead and rolling down her neck. What could he have planned that was so gruesome the servant woman feared it? She must not ask. She must not beg.

"Aye. There is no choice in this. As I told the girl, it would have been easier for both of us if she'd only been true in her aim."

When the woman faced her with an expression of pity in her eyes, Moira lost her battle to keep the fear of what was to come at bay. Even the demons that chased her in her sleep were preferable to facing this. When her efforts to stay awake lost their strength, it was much easier to fade into the darkness.

And, she did.

Chapter Five

The day dawned bright and breezy, as many days had as summer progressed toward its end in the islands. Even the shackles on her feet and the guard who dogged her every step could not make her despair on a day like this one. Moira turned her face to the warming sun and breathed in the air. The tightness of the bandages wrapped around her chest kept her from taking a full deep breath, but at least this time she did not collapse into coughing.

Clutching the wooden stick under her good arm, she hobbled toward the main house from the barn where she was kept at night. The shackles that slid down nearly to the ground and the man set to watch her were unnecessary, for it would take many more sennights or even passages of the moon in her path across the sky for Moira to be able to run as she had before.

If she could ever run again.

These last few weeks had been their own kind of torture, giving her a chance to live and breathe away from the clutter and crowding of the keep with its cold walls and conspiracies at every turn. Here, on this farm, she had a glimpse of what her life could have been like if not for that terrible day all those years ago. The family who ran the farm for their lord were kind, though distant, in their care of her. Clearly torn between common decency and their loyalty to their master, they'd seen to her wounds and injuries and prodded her along toward recovery. Even in the first days when she still longed for death.

Now, her bruises faded in color and her scars no longer looked as pink and puffy as they had. Her legs ached constantly from several broken bones, but even that lessened each day. Standing up straight for a moment, she pressed her hand against her ribs and assessed the soreness. It was definitely less than yesterday. She tossed her head back, as the wind tousled her short hair—one of the other prices paid for failure.

Pol cleared his throat, and Moira realized she'd been dawdling. Positioning the stick beneath her once more, she made her way to the large manor house and whatever reckoning she faced. She entered from the back, into the large storage room on the main floor, and then followed Pol as he led her to the woman who'd summoned her. When they approached the stairs that led to the second floor of the house, Moira took a deep breath and prepared to climb them.

The door next to the stairs opened, and Dara motioned for her to enter. Pol stepped aside, and she followed Dara into a room that must have been used by the women on the farm, to gather. Dara pointed to one cushioned chair next to the hearth, and Moira gratefully sank onto its comfortable surface. Surprised when Pol carried a small stool over and lifted her splinted leg onto it, she nodded her thanks as he unlocked the chain between the shackles, giving her legs more freedom.

Dara sat near her, but she did not speak until Pol left the room, closing the door behind him. For a moment, Moira imagined this was what a guest felt like: comfortable, warm, and safe. At least, for now. Dara surprised her yet again when she held out a cup of tea to her. Taking it, Moira drank the warm, strong brew and allowed it to refresh her.

"Lady?" she asked, waiting to learn the true purpose of this encounter.

"I am called Dara, Ceanna," she replied, using the name Moira used when she came to Lord Diarmid's keep on Mull.

"Dara," she said. This was the woman who'd warned off the Seer from something he'd planned involving her. This woman had brought her to this farm and overseen her care for almost a month now. Shifting her leg on the stool, she waited for Dara to speak. From the shadowed expression on her face, it could not be good.

"Are you his woman?" Moira asked. "Or his slave?"

Dara blushed then, her face looking even younger than before. "Nay, Ceanna, I am not Connor's woman, nor his slave."

Moira shrugged, now that her curiosity was satisfied.

Dara looked away and cleared her throat before speaking again. Then, she leaned over and spoke in a soft voice.

"When Lord Diarmid's men took you from Connor's chambers, did they . . . ?" Dara's glance shifted away from hers, and the pause allowed her to think on the missing words. When she did not answer, Dara looked at her intensely. "You have not bled since you arrived here."

"I cannot carry," Moira said quickly. Though she'd planned her attack understanding what the consequences would be to her, picking a time just as she bled as she would be least likely to conceive then if things happened as she suspected they would.

As they had.

"How do you know that?" Dara asked in a quiet voice.

"Through enough years of living when it would have happened if it could have happened," Moira answered calmly.

Bairns were not for her, not for someone whose only purpose was living long enough to kill her enemy. She'd long ago resigned herself to it and no longer regretted it. Truth be told, she had not thought on it in a long time.

"You did not answer my question. Ceanna, did Diarmid's men . . . take you?"

A memory of Connor—carrying her across his chambers, filling her body with his, breathing her breaths and tasting every part of her—flashed through her mind.

He had taken her.

She closed her eyes, banishing the memory of it from her thoughts. What Diarmid's men did could not even be thought of in the same way and had meant nothing more than the pain it was meant to inflict.

"It matters not, Dara," she answered. Moira handed the empty cup to Dara as she slid her leg off the stool and pushed out of the chair. "I should return to my work now, if that is all you wanted of me."

Dara handed her the stick she used to aid her in walking, and she turned to the door.

"He's sent a message for you to return in a sennight's time."

A shudder she could not hide pulsed through her, causing her to lose her tenuous balance and stumble into the frame of the door. Dropping the stick, she grabbed for the door and righted herself.

Had she recovered this much only to be tortured and killed now? When the pain of her injuries was almost bearable and her strength was returning? Now? She turned to face Dara.

"He believes you must know something about the other assassination attempts," Dara said, her eyes filled with sadness, much like the expression Moira had witnessed that day in the keep.

"Diarmid?" she asked. Her voice cracked, and she was not embarrassed by the hitch as she repeated his name. "Diarmid summons me back?"

"Nay, Ceanna. 'Tis Connor that orders your return. Lord Diarmid has given Connor the first chance to discover what he must know before he turns you back over to his men."

Moira must have fainted, for when she came back to awareness of herself, she was sitting back in that comfortable chair with Dara and Pol both hovering close over her. She sipped the tea handed to her and did not try to refuse it.

Were the Fates laughing at her once more? Not content with the destruction of her entire family and clan, they now would not allow her efforts at justice. She had nothing to do with any other attempts on Connor's life—she concentrated only on her task and ignored all else that could distract her from her purpose. But this time, such ignorance would be her undoing.

And the poor timing of her attempt made it even more ironic, for it now caught her up in something bigger and more dangerous. If she had any humor left inside of her, she would have laughed. All these months and years of no life, no one else had seen to her needs, and now that she had been given a taste of what could have been, she must return to face her enemies and her worst fears.

It wasn't dying that she feared; it was that time before dying that made her recently healed skin crawl and made her throat dry. She'd been that close and had seen the weakness that had crept into her soul. Though a threat to no one, save the Seer, she would have to divulge too much to make anyone believe her and put others who had helped or hidden her in danger. Something she decided long ago she would not do.

"Your pardon, Dara, for keeping you from your duties," she said once she had finished drinking the tea. Moira put the cup down on the table next to her.

Moira shifted and began to stand once more. Dara and Pol backed away slowly as though waiting for her to fall. Grasping her stick and moving slowly this time, she made her way to the door without saying another word, for what could she say? Dara could do nothing to help her, especially while she herself served the Seer.

It wasn't until she'd nearly reached the barn, with Pol following a few paces behind, that Moira realized the chain had not been replaced on the iron shackles on her ankles. Fearing that to look at him would be to alert him to his error, she continued to hobble along the path, taking the same small steps that the chain had forced her to before. Uncertain of how long this small measure of freedom would last, she let the length of her gown drag along to hide it. Walking was ever so much easier without the weight and tug of the chain.

Moira paused in front of the door, hesitant to give up this time in the sun, but she accepted the restrictions placed on her and tugged it open with her free hand. Pol reached around to open it wider, and she walked inside, waiting for her eyes to adjust to the darkened interior. She stumbled as she misjudged the level of the ground, and Pol's strong grip kept her from falling until she had her balance.

She nodded her head, and he released her, as though such polite behavior was the usual way to treat prisoners. None of this made sense to her, and she feared it was part of a plot to allow her to believe she was safe. Then, just now as she regained her strength, they reminded her that her life was not her own.

Moira crossed the straw-covered floor to the bench where she sat to do whatever work was assigned to her by Dara or her husband, who worked this farm for the Seer. Pol lit the small lantern on the table as she placed her stick on the floor next to her.

It was a busy place, with cattle and a few crops, far from the intrigue of Lord Diarmid's holding, where he ruled in the name of Earl of the Orkneys and the King of Norway, both named Magnus. Though not of the families of most of the lords who owned lands here in the isles, Diarmid was powerful, with many influential friends, and he'd carved out his own little fiefdom, answering to very few, if any.

It was only when Pol left that Moira allowed her fears to

erupt. The news of her return surprised her, though she knew not why. She yet lived, she was certain, only to give them some information they thought she had on the other attempts on the Seer's life.

She had none to give.

Moira leaned over and rested her face in her hands. For six years, nothing had slowed her or stopped her from her pursuit of justice for her family. She'd given up everything, everyone, along the way to find this man and kill him. Now, he knew about her, he knew her quest, he had her in his control. Taking in as deep a breath as she could and releasing it slowly, Moira accepted her failure and realized something more important.

She was still alive.

Alive and healed enough to try again.

A bubble of hope formed in her soul at that thought. Surely, they would imprison her, but as long as she lived, she could try again. And she would try again.

Tilting her head, Moira smiled in spite of the pain in her legs and her face and nearly every part of her body, as the crushing weight of failure lifted from her shoulders now. Pulling the woven basket closer, she began to clean and sort the vegetables left there by Old Peg, the woman who oversaw the kitchens.

It kept her hands busy while her mind now turned to other things. There were plans to be made, for she must be ready when the chance came. Minutes turned to an hour or more as several possible plans came to mind. When the darkness fell and the call to the evening meal came, Moira was feeling better than she had in weeks and weeks. She would bide her time as she'd taught herself to do in the past and wait for her chance.

And when the fear about her future returned, as it did in that next week as her return to Diarmid's keep grew closer, she pushed it away and concentrated on the necessary things:

staying alive, gathering any possible weapons, and getting close to the Seer—close enough to strike him down.

This time, she would also make certain to end her own life just after she ended his.

The sun, as though sensing the bleakness she felt, stayed hidden. Clouds ran across the sky, obscuring any light and most of the heat, and swirling into shapes large and small as the winds pushed them relentlessly on. The small cart she rode in wobbled along the mountain path, moving closer and closer toward the sea, where the boat that would take her to her fate sat waiting.

Pol said not a word, though he'd looked as if he wanted to argue when the two men arrived last evening to take her back. Dara was none too happy, nor Old Peg, nor any of the inhabitants on the farm. A surprise to her, for she had tried to kill the man who owned their loyalty. Moira did not fight them. It would do no good, and she might end up in worse shape and be unable to take her last opportunity.

The cart creaked along, and she tried to balance herself on the plank seat. One man rode ahead and one behind, neither ever taking his gaze off her, as though she would jump down and run away. After much arguing between Dara and the men, the chain was left off, but the shackles remained at the ready for its replacement. Moira had no doubt that once Pol left her behind, the guards would use them.

She reached down and rubbed her leg. The aching itch grew strong within it, a sign of its healing, but she could not soothe it. Pushing her windblown hair from her face, she watched the shoreline come into view as they reached the final hill. The sun chose that moment to break through, and she lifted her face to its warming light.

"He tends to be a fair man," Pol said quietly. "Tell him what he wants to know, and it will be over quickly."

Moira turned to face him, unsure if he spoke of Diarmid or the Seer. She knew the words to be false about Lord Diarmid, for she'd witnessed his rough justice in her time in his keep and village. The Seer then?

She had watched him being treated as though he were royal for the power he brought to Diarmid. His every wish and whim were met, and anything or anyone he wanted was his for the asking. And all because his visions and words proved true and valuable for one such as Diarmid.

And cost countless lives of those unimportant in the schemes woven by more powerful or wealthier men.

Neither man was fair. Neither would stop until he had what he wanted, and if she suffered for it, it would matter to no one. And neither would allow her to live after her crime against the Seer.

"I can tell them nothing," she said.

Hers had simply been the last attempt and the one closest to success, but she'd not heard the slightest hint of others during her planning time. After spending the night in his bed those months ago, Moira had left the keep, seeking refuge in a small fishing village on the southern shore of Mull. Far enough to stay out of sight, close enough to continue her plans.

She noticed the sad glance Pol threw in her direction and hated the way it made her stomach clench. She owed him nothing and refused to allow some soft consideration of his opinion to matter. Well, she *tried* not to let it matter.

The path steepened, and she had to concentrate on holding on to her seat in the cart. When the ground leveled beneath them, she lifted her head and watched the shoreline and the small wooden boat grow closer. Since the ground was covered with grass and firm there, Pol steered the horse and cart almost to the edge and stopped. The two guards climbed down from their borrowed mounts and walked toward the cart.

Moira gathered her skirts and lifted her leg over the side of the cart, balancing on the better one as she moved to the edge. Leaning over, she grabbed for the stick she used to support her weight, but the guard got it first and broke it in two. Pol jumped down from his seat and rushed around to her, pushing the guard away and lifting her down. Once she gained her feet, Pol motioned for the two men to come closer and whispered furiously to them. From the glances thrown in her direction, she knew it was about their treatment of her.

It mattered not, for once in their charge, Pol would have no say, and there would be no one to stop them. Taking a deep breath in and feeling the tight support of the bandages wound around her chest, she tried to calm the fears that threatened and began to walk toward the boat. The firm ground turned to shifting sands as she neared the edge, making it difficult to move with any speed. Without the stick to help her balance, her walking became waddling as she lifted the splinted leg up and swung it forward with her hip before stepping on her stronger leg.

Moira focused on the pain in each step, and that helped clear her mind of the fear of what yet faced her. By the time she reached the water's edge, the men had quieted behind her. Turning back toward the hills, she noticed them standing and staring at her now.

Then Pol reached into the cart and took out two sacks, one clearly heavier than the other. As he tossed one to each of the guards, she heard the clinking sound of chains and shivered, in spite of her resolve. The other, lighter and silent, landed easily in the man's hands. Moira turned away and watched as the sun glinted on the water's moving surface, reflecting back at her and sparkling as though tipped with gold.

She eased her way closer to the water, trying to figure out how to get into the boat without swimming to it. One of the guards, without a word of warning, picked her up in his arms and carried her through the shallows to the boat. He dumped her in and tossed the lighter sack to her as he untied the ropes anchoring the boat in place and climbed into it. Moira winced when the metal links in the other sack clanged as they landed on the bottom of the boat at her feet.

All she needed was one good moment of opportunity, and she could die knowing her task was completed. All she had to do was stay alive long enough for one more attack. All she had to accomplish was to lull him into believing that she did not want his death and did not need it in her soul, and she could take him down once and for all.

Moira gathered the hood of the borrowed cloak and tugged it down around her head and face to block out most of the wind. Pol called out her name, and she turned toward the shore to see him waving to her. A strange impulse to call out words of thanks to him and for Dara pierced her then, and she fought against it. She spared only a nod for him, while words of gratitude and regret soured on her tongue, unspoken.

There was no time for such soft thoughts. She must prepare herself for the ordeal ahead and allow herself only to think on her plan. Last time, she'd been so surprised by what she'd witnessed in the Seer's chambers that she'd lost her nerve to end her own life before they could capture her. This time, she must be ready.

Closing her eyes, she blocked out the sounds of the gulls and the sun's light playing merrily across the waves to think only about the layout of the keep and how she could attain a weapon. Minutes turned to hours as the boat caught the winds in its sails and made its way around Mull to Diarmid's keep on the north coast.

"Keep yer voices down, ye bloody fools!"

They quieted and waited on his words. Standing in the darkened room, using their hooded cloaks and the shadowed corners to hide their identities, none knew many of the others. Except him. He knew them all, and he'd used their petty jealousies and fears to draw them into his plan to end the Seer's influence on Diarmid and Diarmid's influence on Earl Magnus.

"She returns on the morrow," he said, squinting into the shadows. "Did any of ye recruit her to our plans?"

"Bah," the tall one, Lord Struan, said, spitting on the floor. "No one would use a woman in something this important." Turning to those nearest him, he explained, "And a worthless bitch at that. She had a knife in her hands and no one to intervene, and she couldna even kill him. If ye expect more than the heat ye find between their thighs, yer expecting too much from them." He spit again, making his feelings clear to everyone.

"Ye brought her into the keep," he said to Gillis. "What know you of her?"

The younger man stammered at first, uncomfortable with the attention brought to him. "My lord, she just offered to warm my bed and . . . weel, all that goes wi' it, if ye get my meaning?" He paused and searched for an understanding gaze. At the soft laughter, he continued, "She said nothing about herself but that her family was dead and she sought a place to live."

"So there is no one to ask after her if she disappears?" the red-haired lord, Dougal, asked.

"Nay, my lord," Gillis said, shaking his head nearly as much as his hands did.

He waited and then asked again. He needed to be certain their plans had not been uncovered, by the stupid woman with her botched attempt or by anyone loyal to Diarmid.

"So, none of ye knew her or talked with her before her attack?" He watched as each man, other than the randy young one, shook his head; some whispered or mumbled their answers, but none acknowledged her. Turning to the door, he pulled his hood lower and gave his orders.

"Because we didna ken of her plans, doesna mean she kens nothing of ours. Either way, she could be dangerous to many of us. 'Twould be best, I think, if this one lost her footing on the stairs or got caught up in the frenzy of her welcome on the morrow. What say ye?"

He gazed around the room, meeting each man's look until all to a one had agreed. For something this simple, no specific plans were needed. No one man would be ordered to act, yet someone or other who understood his plans would, and the girl would be dead before she could be questioned by Diarmid's ruthless guards. Better to spill no words than to spill the wrong ones, even by accident.

"We meet in four days, after his next vision. Ye ken yer assignments," he said quietly. "Do not fail in this now."

Tugging the door open just a crack, he waited for the hallway outside to empty and then began to let them out, in groups of two or three so as to not draw attention to their gathering. When he was alone, he pushed back his hood and took in a breath.

Success was so very close now, and he tried not to laugh aloud at the thought. The Seer would be gone, and Diarmid's alliances would shatter, leaving him defenseless against his enemies. He did grin then, for the all-powerful Diarmid had no idea of how many were his enemies and how few were friends indeed.

Mayhap this woman was a tool to be used?

If she survived long enough to make another strike against Connor, both would be handled with her one blow. Diarmid would never know the extent of the plans against him until his own downfall played out before him. He would wallow in the false comfort her death would create, never even thinking that there was more going on behind and around him than one stupid bitch's botched and then successful attempts to kill his man.

He walked out into the hall now and pulled the chamber door closed behind him. Climbing the tower steps to the next floor, he sought his place at Diarmid's table, trying to keep the smile from his face.

If she died in some "mishap," he was safe.

If she stayed alive and tried to kill the Seer again, his plans would be in place.

No matter which, he would succeed.

Soon, very soon, the lands and titles and esteem in Earl Magnus's eyes that should have been his all along, would be.

And Diarmid and his bedeviled Seer would be dead and buried.

Chapter Six

Connor paced the length of the high wall around the keep twice and still could catch no sight of the boat that was overdue. Pushing his hair out of his eyes, he squinted into the midday sun and searched to the edges of the bay.

Nothing.

The guards sent to return her to the keep could have sailed last night, for the sky had been clear of clouds and filled with the moon's light as it waxed to its fullness. Even the seas had been calm, yet they'd clearly waited until today to bring her back.

Dara had a hand in this delay. Soft-hearted Dara, who had taken his attacker under her wing and cared for her when the girl lay near death. His own care had been seen to by Diarmid's healer, for only he could be trusted with someone of his importance to the overlord of Mull.

After one more circle of the perimeter wall, he shook his head and turned back to the stairway. His body was wound tight, and he'd not slept in days. Every sound made his head throb. Every step or movement reverberated through him. And every touch made his skin ache both in pain and hunger.

Another month had passed, and more visions were close. So

close he felt the ripples of power teasing his thoughts and pulsing in his veins, deep in his blood. Desire traveled there, too, ever seeking satisfaction, but his mind sought the one who had made a difference. At least, he suspected she had.

Instead, he would face the woman who tried to kill him. A laundry woman, a common servant among the myriad who worked for Diarmid, had almost killed him. Though Diarmid would have gladly executed her, Connor wanted to know why. Other near accidents and apparent attacks had been foiled and always the perpetrator had been killed, never leaving any answers for him.

Diarmid took it in stride as a part of being a man of power—other men wanted what you had. For Diarmid that meant power in the number of warriors at his call and allies who backed him. For Connor, it was the power of the visions, the power in seeing what had already happened or yet waited ahead.

He pressed his hands to his head, hoping that the roaring inside of it would cease. Some days, like this one, it was louder than even the roar of the storms that came off the sea to the west and pounded the coast. Some days it simply sat in the background, threatening to burst out without a moment's warning.

He rolled his shoulders, trying to loosen the tightness there and avoid worsening the pain in his head. Some clouds passed in front of the sun and dimmed the glaring sunlight, easing the need to squint so strongly. He wanted nothing more than to go back to his chambers and drown his pain in mead or wine again, but something deep within him forced him back to the wall to search the bay for signs of the boat.

Just like his self-control over the pain, the visions, and even his growing need for women in his bed, everything in his life seemed to be spiraling out of control. The visions that had fallen into a pattern over the last several years, now grew in intensity and frequency, happening now with the full moon's passing through the sky. The effects of them increased every time; he endured the pain and blindness for nearly a week now. The pulsing, growing lust in his blood grew more potent and demanding with every vision.

But because he did not know the origin of his powers, he had no way of telling how this would end for him, if this was leading to an end at all. Would his eyes finally burn out from the fires the visions brought? Would the pain and blindness be his punishment for some unknown transgression or misuse of the visions? Would he never calm the heat in his veins? Was there anyone who could tell him the truth of it or how he came to be so gifted?

Connor smacked his hands down on the cool, stone wall and gathered his control from within, allowing the winds to buffet him and soothe his frayed nerves. From here he could watch the villagers scurry from keep to town, Diarmid's warriors train in the yard, and even a few of the children who lived within the walls run freely around sheep and cattle being driven into the pens outside the keep. Life continued on, regardless of his questions or his pain.

And for some reason he didn't yet understand, Connor suspected that the woman who tried to kill him had more knowledge than he did about his past and his future.

The clouds moved once more, and a beam of sunlight struck a small object on the horizon, gaining his attention. A boat glided toward him in the distance. He did not move from his place there high on the walls as it grew closer and closer, finally stopping at the wooden dock near the main gate. Now he could see three occupants in it—clearly two men and a woman.

It wasn't until the pressure in his chest hurt that he realized he was holding his breath. One man climbed out and held out his arms as the other lifted the woman from the boat. Connor could see her wobble on the wooden platform and one man grab for her before she fell. He found his own hands clenching the edge of the wall. Releasing his grip on the cold stone and the breath he held inside, he fought the urge to run down to the dock to confront her. Instead, once he recognized the anger and tension bubbling inside, he called out to the guard at the stairs to have her brought to him in his chambers, rather than in the hall as planned.

Making his way down the tower stairs to his room, he tried to sort through the pressure plaguing his every step and every breath. Instead of sheer rage at her attempts to end his life, curiosity pulsed through him. His fists tightened and relaxed over and over again until he reached his chambers and entered. Ranald followed a few steps behind, aware, as always, of his every move within the keep.

"Lord Diarmid wants her turned over to his men for questioning," he said as Connor sat on the carved chair. "He said this idea of yours to keep her close is too dangerous."

"Tell Diarmid we have an agreement," Connor ordered. His clenched jaws sharpened his words. "When I am done with her, she is his to do as he pleases." He grabbed Ranald's arm as the man turned to leave. "But she is mine first."

The bow of his head was a reluctant one, but Connor knew Ranald would convey the words and the message to Diarmid. He glanced over at the newly placed spike in the wall and the chain attached to it. She would be kept here until he found out what he needed to know. The collar and chain were for his protection and hers, for Diarmid's displeasure over her attack was well known and his people would take action on their own with the confidence of his approval.

The commotion outside his door pierced through his thoughts, and he stood as the door opened, pushed so hard it slammed against the wall and bounced back. Connor stood as the two men sent to his homestead half dragged, half carried the woman in and brought her before him. Her cloak was torn, and he noticed blood dripping from her lip as she staggered a few steps.

He walked over to her, noticing the slats still encircling her leg and the way she awkwardly balanced herself.

"What happened to her, Ennis?" he asked.

"My lord, the crowd saw her and tried to . . . well, take her from us," Ennis explained, with a nod at the other man.

Considering that neither stood less than six feet tall and had the bulk and strength of seasoned warriors, the confession startled him. Had Diarmid arranged this to void their agreement? Or were so many so angered by her actions that they acted on their own? He thought not.

He watched as she raised a trembling hand and wiped the blood from her mouth. The hood of the cloak covered most of her face, hiding it from him. He remembered his last sight of her— so bruised and battered that he could not tell if he'd met her before or not. Other than this new injury, he wondered at her appearance and her identity. The name Ceanna and the fact that she'd worked as a laundry woman did not bring any particular woman to mind.

"Take off the cloak," he ordered, sitting down on his chair once more and preparing himself to meet his attacker.

Ennis grabbed the hood, dragging it off her head and exposing a mass of brown curls. He would have continued to simply pull at it if the woman had not tugged the laces and freed it from her. The cloak fell to the ground around her feet, and she raised her head to meet his gaze.

"You!" he choked out once he saw her face. He had crossed the distance to her before he even realized he'd stood. Connor searched her face for the truth, but there was none to see there.

"They said your name was Ceanna," he growled. So angry at her deceit that he could feel the blood pounding in his veins, he fisted his hand in her hair and tugged it so she would have to look up at him. "Is it?"

He thought she would remain silent, for it took her a long

time to speak, and though he could tell she struggled to stay on her feet, she did not fight his grasp.

"It matters not," she whispered in that voice that had haunted his sleeping and waking hours for months now.

Connor flung her into the guards' grasp and grabbed a cup of wine from the table nearby. Filled with rage and confusion, betrayal and disappointment, he drank it down and tried to regain control of himself. Caught between wanting to strike her down for her deception and wanting to throw her on the floor and slake his body's need for her, he ordered Ennis to chain her and leave. Not daring to watch, he walked back to his chair and leaned on the back of it until the men had completed their task.

He'd slipped up when he recognized her, for no one but he knew that Moira, the woman who had given him such pleasure, and Ceanna, the laundry woman who tried to kill him, were the same person. If Diarmid suspected it, he would not hesitate to use her in whatever way he wanted and to control Connor since he would know of his desire for her. When the door closed, he drank the last of his wine and turned to face her.

"It matters not to a dead woman," he said as he examined her from head to toe.

Because of her height and the short length of the chain, the only way she could stand upright was if she remained leaning against the wall. Even a step away would force her to bend to keep from choking on the iron collar. The heavy metal ring already scraped the skin of her neck, and there would be new bruises to join the fading ones soon. Her mouth still bled from whatever blow she'd received, yet her eyes burned brightly at him, as though daring him on.

"But if you want to live, you will give me the truth."

Moira watched as he struggled not to hit her and then as he turned away and let his men chain her to the wall in the corner of his chambers. He'd recognized her in an instant, but for some reason, he'd acted as though he did not know her name. Now, his men had gone, and they were alone. She wanted to meet him face to face and on her feet, but her legs trembled and threatened to throw her face down on the floor. The splint, its pieces of wood loosened by the jostling of the crowd on her way into the keep, hung in pieces around her leg, and she dared not put any weight on the healing limb.

Already the chain was stretched to its full length, and it gave her no room to maneuver. Soon, if the dizziness in her head told her anything, the decision on how to get down on the floor would be out of her control. Grasping the chain for support and to keep it from gouging her neck, she slid down along the wall, easing her leg straight out before her. The last foot or so was a rough drop, but at least she landed without more injury. Moira released her hold on the chain and shuddered as it clattered on the stone wall at her back.

He'd watched her every move, but never said a word. Now, seated and able to regain her breath, Moira used the edge of her sleeve to wipe the blood from her mouth and face. Someone in the crowd had shouted her name, and everyone had surged toward her. She felt the new bruises on her leg and the ones on her arms and shoulders, caused by the guards' tightened grip as they dragged her ever forward, beginning to throb even now.

Was that the worst of it then? She couldn't help shifting against the wall as the Seer stood again and walked toward her. On her feet, she was almost even to him and could probably fight off some of the blows to come, but on the floor, she was the perfect target for his strong, agile legs if he chose to kick. The journey today had taken any strength she'd managed to save out of her, and Moira closed her eyes so she would not watch the blow as it came.

"So, is it Ceanna or Moira?"

His voice was so soft and so close, it startled her into looking. He crouched down low, his arms resting on his legs, staring at her as he asked again. "You told me your name was Moira. Is it?"

Though she felt none of the strange compulsion to obey him that she'd felt during their bed play, she could not stop herself from nodding. "'Tis Moira."

Perhaps it was exhaustion setting in or simply a desire to be known as herself instead of the made-up name she gave to Gillis and then to everyone in Diarmid's keep. "Aye, my name is Moira." She slumped then, giving up the fight for now.

"You did not come to my bed a virgin. I did not mistreat you. I did not harm you. I gave you pleasure even as you saw to mine."

His voice and tone were level, almost pleasant, but she did not believe him to be harmless for a moment. She could tell he was trying to figure out her ruse and trying to determine the reasons a woman would come to him willingly and then try to kill him. The same battle had waged within her for days after their encounter, but she accepted it for the oddity it was in her life.

"You said my blood for those slain at my word, yet I know you not."

She met his gaze then, and his eyes gleamed. He remembered what she'd said just before plunging the dagger into his chest. Part of her wanted to scream out the truth of her family's destruction, but part fought to remain calm and not give in to the hysteria that threatened her now. Did he not realize the extent of his visions and the cost of them?

"Who died at my word, Moira? Tell me—make me understand why you tried to kill me. Why even now hatred pours out in your gaze at me when I have done nothing to you."

"Dozens?" she spat. "Hundreds?" The strength of her hatred overtook her control, and she spoke freely for the first time in years. "You reveal things that should remain hidden, and your words cause death. Greedy men, powerful men, men hungering for what is not theirs follow your instructions, your advice, your directions, and others die," she said. "They die without warning and without mercy." Taking in a breath and releasing it, she finally accused him of his unforgivable sin. "My family was killed at your word, Seer," she sneered.

Unable to breathe then, Moira waited for him to strike out at her. Instead, his reaction was completely unexpected: he flinched at her words, so slightly that she would have missed it if their gazes were not locked at that moment. Then he stood and walked around the wooden screen that separated his bed from the rest of his chambers and out, pulling the door closed behind him. All without a word or another glance at her. Still fearing the worst, she did not dare move for a long time. When no sounds entered his chambers, she allowed herself to lean back against the wall.

Surely he knew? He could not have parceled out the information gained in his visions and not know that someone stood to gain and another to lose from them. Diarmid had added allies to his cause using the Seer's powers, offering them to those he wanted to entice closer. None who had need could refuse such an offer.

One village leader wanted to discover his enemy's weakness. Another sought his daughter who'd been taken and held in hopes of forcing an alliance. And so on and so on, dozens, nay, hundreds of times since the Seer's powers had become known to Diarmid and put to his disposal. Moira had discovered that and more in her years of searching for him and the origin of his powers.

'Twas not possible that he could be ignorant of such things.

She leaned her head back now, at first putting too much pressure on a new lump on her scalp and then tilting her head until there was a less painful spot. The iron collar scraped her neck with every move and kept her in her place. Her leg, unused to such efforts as this day had forced, began to spasm and seize up in cramps. Her arms and back ached as the coldness and dampness of the wall and floor began to seep inside her.

Minutes and then hours passed, and soon darkness filled the chamber, the sun's light gone and the moon's not strong enough to illuminate the room through the small, high windows in the walls. At first, she tried to keep moving, to keep the cold at bay and to keep her leg from stiffening, but soon her only movements were the shivers that coursed through her, causing her teeth to chatter and her body to shake. Her cloak lay only a few feet away but was unreachable to her, and it taunted her as the chamber cooled without a fire in the hearth to warm it.

Then, her mouth and throat grew parched, her stomach began growling, and, worse, she'd had no chance since early this morn to see to other bodily needs, which now made her belly clutch in pain. Hours passed with no one entering his chambers, and she feared he'd planned it this way to force a confession from her.

Sometime in the deepest part of the night, he returned. He moved quietly, so quietly that she did not hear him enter the room. Only when he roused her with a gentle shake of her shoulder did she realize he knelt at her side. Moira rubbed her eyes to clear them and only then noticed a man standing back in the shadows. She shook so badly then that the Seer cursed under his breath and stepped back, motioning to the other with his hand.

"See to her, Breac," he said. He disappeared around the screen again before she could utter a word.

She wanted to fight back, but she was tired to the bone, in pain, hungry, thirsty, and more. And this hulking man, with long black hair and a nose that did not sit in the center of his face, was bigger in height and bulk than any she'd seen here at the keep and would kill her with one hand before she would be able to stop him. When he reached for her neck with both hands, she knew her death was at hand.

Chapter Seven

Breac's touch was lighter than she would have ever guessed as he unlocked the collar and lifted it from around her neck. Moira had not realized how much it weighed until it was removed. He tossed it away from her and began to poke and prod her from head to feet. Nothing got in his way—not her clothing, her hands, or her objections. Within a few minutes, he decided that the injuries of the day were not serious—no more bones had broken, and her split lip and the bump on her head would heal. His gruff manner eased her fears and, in many ways, reminded her of Dara's efficient way of treating injuries and pain.

Another servant entered the chambers, this one a woman, and she stood aside and waited for his orders. Once he completed his tasks, he nodded to the woman, someone Moira had not met before, who stepped in closer and helped her see to other more personal needs while Breac turned his back and waited. Then he lifted her as though she were a child and placed her on the Seer's bed. Within a short time, her leg had been wrapped tightly with clean bandages to hold the wooden slats in place and the various cuts and bruises treated with a foul-smelling unguent and dressed. Once Breac finished his attentions, the woman handed Moira a cup of watered ale and a bowl filled with a thick porridge.

She tried to fight off the exhaustion and the urge to sleep, but now that she was clean and warm and her stomach stopped growling, it was nigh to impossible. But, she lay in the Seer's bed now, and it was not her place. As she tried to sit up, Breac simply put a hand on her chest and pushed her back down. With no effort at all, he held her there until she could not keep her eyes open.

The next time she could open them, she discovered the Seer standing by the bed, watching her. Pushing herself up on her elbows, she pushed the hair from her eyes and cleared her throat.

"Breac would not allow me to leave," she explained. His expression did not change, so she continued. "I did not mean to fall asleep here."

It was then that she noticed the pile of blankets on top of her and the clean gown and tunic laying on top of them. Lifting the covers and pulling her leg to the edge of the bed, Moira moved to the side and slid off the bed. So focused on getting out of that bed was she that only the feeling of the fine linen sheets against her skin told her that someone had removed her clothing during the night. A modesty she never knew before caused her to reach for the gown that must be for her and tug it over her head. She tried not to wince against the onslaught of pain that happened as she moved.

His gaze never left her, but he said not a word as she pulled the tunic on next and then stood away from the bed to let the edges fall over her legs. He'd seen her back, now a mass of scars, the ridges still pink and new, and she knew bruises yet remained on many places on her skin. Always lean, now Moira could feel her ribs and the crest of her hip, as she smoothed the layers over her belly and legs, and knew she'd lost much weight since she was last in this room.

"Breac said you need a stick to help you walk, but I hesitate to give you something you could use as a weapon."

Moira looked at him now and noticed the dark smudges under his eyes and the bleak expression in his eyes. Had he not slept because she was in his bed? The thing she saw there that affected her, though, was the pity with which he looked on her now that he'd seen her naked. She needed no one's pity.

"I can make my way without one," she said, as she lifted her leg and swung it forward to show him. "And I will use what I can . . . when I can."

She lifted her face and hardened her heart against the despair she saw on his face. Despair and pain and anger and so much more that it nearly undid her resolve. This was not the arrogant, proud Seer she'd witnessed proclaiming his visions or the lust-driven, passionate one who'd pleasured her through that long day months ago.

Nay. This was an empty, tortured man. A man who did not know himself. Yet a man who held the power of life and death over her.

"Agnes," he called out as he walked away.

The same servant who had helped her last night came around the screen and assisted her once more. Efficient and silent, she took only minutes to see to Moira's needs and stand, awaiting his next command. It was not the Seer, but Breac who came to her then, a length of chain and an iron collar in his hands. She tried not to tremble as he approached, the iron ring open and ready to be locked around her neck again.

"I added some length to the chain so she can stand or sit now, Connor," he said in his deep, gruff voice. "I filed the iron so it will not tear her neck in two as she moves."

His plain explanation terrified her in some way she could not explain, and if not for his size and strength, she would have fought him. But making that decision and keeping it were two different matters, and Moira found herself clutching the rough wool of her tunic to keep her hands from grabbing at the collar as he surrounded her neck with it and locked it. Worse even was when he pulled the length of chain through a link in the collar and shackled her to the wall.

True, she could stand, but she could take but one step in any direction before the chain grew taut and the collar choked her. Sitting would be just as difficult as it had been yesterday, even more so since the slats were now tied tightly in place around her leg and there was no slackness to ease her way down.

Moira looked around and could see more of the Seer's chambers from her place in the corner. He stood between the chair and the screen, watching everything that happened, but said nothing else until both Breac and Agnes left. Then he walked back over to the bed, picked up the pile of blankets, and tossed them to her as he passed.

Clean clothes. Servants to see to her needs. Adjustments to even the chain that kept her prisoner. None of these things were the common way to treat prisoners, and yet he did them all.

"Why do you not just kill me and get it over with, Seer? Do you get pleasure out of playing with your enemies before you destroy them like Diarmid does?" she asked, in a tone bolder than she truly felt. "How long will you let me live?"

The chain rattling as she shifted onto her better leg was the only sound echoing through his chambers. He moved toward her so quickly that she stumbled back against the wall to get away.

"You stay alive until I discover the truth from you. But have a care, Moira. For if you do not give me the truth, Diarmid will take you from me, and under his care you will long for death many, many times before he grants it to you."

In spite of the heat of his body pressing her against the wall, she shivered as she remembered the punishment meted out by Diarmid's men. She did not doubt that she would long— aye, even beg—for death if he controlled her fate again.

What did he want to know? What could she tell him? Her attack and her purpose here was known, so what harm was there in answering his questions? She was about to tell him to ask his questions when the warmth pierced her. A dizzying heat and a smell she could not identify encircled her and flowed through her veins.

Moira noticed his nearness, the strength in the muscles of his legs as they pressed against hers. His hardness pulsed to life between their bodies, and her mouth watered at the thought of tasting it once more. She shifted to allow him closer, and he moved in, turning his body to cover more of hers. The enticing scent increased, and her head and thoughts swam in the musky, male smell that seemed to pour from him.

Her body remembered his caresses, the taste of his skin, and his essence as he poured forth into her mouth. She arched against him as the place between her legs grew wet and hot with the need to be touched and filled. And he would fill her there, and every other place he could, over and over until she begged . . . until she begged. . . . Oh, aye, she would beg him to . . .

She shook her head, pushing him away and trying to regain her senses. What had just happened between them? How had he turned her against her purpose again? Was she losing her mind after all these years of having such a focused plan? The air around her cleared as he moved back, and she took in several deep breaths to break free of that which confounded her.

"Did you put something in my food, Seer? You would drug me to gain the truth?" she asked, wiping her face with her hands and pushing her hair back. Her body yet ached for his touch, and her blood yet heated in readiness for their joining. "You know my purpose here: to kill you. My reason you also know: to avenge the deaths of my family. The only thing you do not know is how or when it will happen."

Moira could still feel the intoxicant, whatever it was, trying to gain control of her, softening her resolve and eating into her purpose, but she could force it away and she did. Whatever she planned on saying to him or he'd planned on saying to her was stopped when Lord Diarmid burst into the room.

"This close to your visions, I thought I'd find you planted deep between her legs by now, Seer," Lord Diarmid said with a terrifying leer at her. "Do not let the chain put you off. At least this way, you do not have to chase after her again."

He strode over to her, and she had no place to go but up against the wall. Taking hold of the slack in the chain, he pulled it up tightly, forcing her onto her toes to keep from choking.

"Has the bitch told you why she did it, or has she been waiting for me and my men to loosen her tongue?" Diarmid looked over at the Seer. "I think she liked it the first time with us and came back for more."

She tried to block out the raucous and lustful laughter that filled the chamber then, just as she tried to block out his fetid breath and the memories of the last time. None of that worked, and she waited to discover how quickly or slowly she would die at his hands this time.

Diarmid and his men spread out through the room, forming a wall between him and the woman. Connor waited for Diarmid to get past his first move of intimidation with her so he could find out the real reason for such an intrusion. Scaring her into pliability was only the beginning. But this show was for more.

Moira.

Ceanna.

The woman chained before him, who, in spite of her obvious terror at being in Diarmid's grasp, still looked like a warrior queen of old, and who had threatened him in the same minute that she'd begun to succumb to him.

Damn and hell! He'd not had time to question her more, to get something from her he could use to keep Diarmid happy and away. One glance at her told him she knew the gravity of the situation, for she'd lost all the color that rising passion and rising hatred had put into her pale cheeks.

He did not need ask what Diarmid had done to her a month ago. He knew their methods better than he knew his own gift, for they were clear and decisive: break down their victim, gain her cooperation or not, and then destroy her. Connor had watched Diarmid's enemies fall through such a pattern many times while in his time there, and he knew it had only been his intervention that kept her alive. And thwarted Diarmid's desire to destroy anyone who stood against him.

"We have an arrangement, my lord," he called out. Waiting for Diarmid to acknowledge his promise, Connor began walking closer, making his way between Diarmid's men and the wall. "I sent her away and let her grow strong enough over these last weeks to withstand my questioning. I fear she may not make it to yours."

Diarmid startled at his words, not those he expected from his usually docile Seer. "So, ye've learned from my methods then, Connor? You think you can break her down and find out her part in the other attacks?" Diarmid's black eyes narrowed. "Good for you, man! About time you learned how to deal with enemies and whatever minions they send at you!"

He dropped the chain, releasing Moira to her feet, and she staggered back, landing hard against the wall. "How long will you need with her?"

Diarmid's men relaxed back a pace or two, waiting on their lord's word to leave. Connor looked over at Moira and then smiled at Diarmid. Sliding his hand to rest on his still-erect cock, Connor made his point.

"Well, my lord, I have certain other needs that she will tend to before I am willing to lose her to your tender touch. What difference does it make if she lives a while more if she makes my life easier?"

He needed time to find out why she was so different from the others—that was no lie—but Diarmid did not need to know, nay could not know, that killing her was not necessarily in his plans.

"I cannot refuse a request put that way, Seer," Diarmid answered. "So what if she's not that other bitch you've sought for months. Use this one as you will since one cunny is just as good as another when there are 'needs.' "

Diarmid motioned to his men to leave, and they followed his order swiftly. Once they were alone, he turned back to Connor.

"We know how she got into the keep. Someone in the crowd yesterday recognized her and knew that she was Gillis's woman. We're searching for him now."

And he would die for whatever part he played in helping her. Connor understood the message, even when not spoken aloud.

Lord Diarmid nodded at him and strode out of his chambers, leaving Ranald at the door to close it. Before he faced her, he tried to bring his raging lust back under control. Only the panting, shallow breaths she took broke the silence between them. He went to the table and poured a cup of his strong wine and took it to her, forcing it into her hands and then to her mouth.

"Drink this," he ordered, guiding the cup until she began to swallow. "All of it." He took the cup once she finished it and put it back on the table.

Pacing back and forth, he sorted through his options. His long night of soul-searching, after her accusations made it impossible to ignore the consequences of his visions, had led him to one conclusion: he lived in a prison of his own making now—a comfortable one, a luxurious, privileged one—but a prison however he looked at it. And for years, he'd chosen not to look at it too closely. Content with taking the rewards of his powers—the constant flow of women through his bed, the wealth and lands given him by Diarmid, the servants at his call—he'd learned to ignore what could have happened to others affected by his power of Sight.

She said nothing, though more likely from shock and terror than from the wisdom of understanding her precarious position in the drama that played out around them. Connor poured another cup, this one for himself, and sipped it slowly.

Knowing his weakness did not for one moment lessen the desire pulsing through him or his need to seek satisfaction for the growing need within, but he fought to ignore it for now. But the power within grew and pushed out that scent again, drawing women to answer its call and fill his needs. He watched as she fought it, shaking her head and rubbing her eyes, even while he watched her nipples harden under her gown and tunic and her breathing grow labored and heated. Her head fell back against the wall, and she arched as though he touched her.

As she had when he'd touched her. He knew she would be wet and hot and would open for him—the scent at its strongest would allay any of her objections. His cock was ready, too, long and hard and eager to find her heat and sate its hunger for female flesh. Connor's head ached, and his body throbbed as he took a step toward her. Chained or not, willing or not, the power surged and would make it happen between them. Only the soft knock on the door stopped him on his path to take her.

"My lord?" a woman said through the barrier. "May I serve you?"

It was the young one, the one Ranald had thought was Moira, who stood there offering herself to his hunger. She seemed the most affected by his scent, and she always responded the quickest of any woman in the keep who felt the urge to couple with him. Connor knew that she would be naked under a cloak, her eyes filled with a dreamy vagueness and her body ready and willing for him to use as he pleased, as he needed.

He raised his gaze to the woman chained to his wall and met her eyes then. Clear and bright, they were, and filled with control and a bit of hatred. She'd thrown off whatever effects the scent caused again, as no other woman had ever done. Her expression told him she would fight him, and a pleasurable taking would become something violent and ugly between them.

He had never done that and never would.

Connor walked to the door and pulled it open, only a bit, but enough for the girl to gain entrance before he could refuse her offer. By the time he could say anything, she dropped her cloak as he had known she would and knelt in front of him. Her quick, skillful hands had his belt and his trews loosened and his cock in them in only moments. The loud gasp startled him back to the woman standing chained to his wall.

The woman he craved more than any other. The one who could control her own desires even when his powers surged, demanding her surrender. The one who could offer him an easing of the punishing torment after his visions left him blind and empty.

Connor peeled the girl's hands from his cock and tugged her to stand. Leaning down, he grabbed her cloak and covered her with it. Tugging the door open, he gently pushed her out with a nod to the ever-present guard to show her away. By the time he closed the door, Moira had slid down to sit on the floor and would not meet his gaze.

Having several women in his bed was not a usual way for him, but he had done it before and enjoyed it. Having Moira watch while another woman pleasured him, though, was something he did not want to do. The times he'd thought about her while someone else tended his needs left him feeling unsatisfied and never brought the level of satiation he needed to ease the urges within.

Connor leaned against the door and spoke to her, all the while slipping his hand inside his trews to gain some measure of relief.

"'Tis you I want, Moira," he whispered to her. "I searched for you after you left my bed, and none has been able to do what you did for me."

She stared at him as he continued stroking himself, seeking not pleasure as much as relief from the constant urgings in his blood. Closing his eyes then, he sought an end to the excruciating need that plagued him relentlessly, even while knowing that it would return to plague him again and again until his visions struck and drained him of everything good, leaving only pain behind. He exploded into his own hand, the act not bringing him anything but some moments of respite.

He cleaned himself quickly, knowing he must get out of there without seeing the disgust that would surely color her expression now after she saw how low he sank into depravity. Luckily, the bell for the noon meal rang, and he could answer its call and escape. Tying his trews and belt, he asked only one question of her.

"Was Gillis involved in this?"

She paused for a moment only. "Nay, he is innocent of my actions." Her voice shook then. "Can you help him?"

He did turn then to see if feelings for this other man were written on her face, but he found only worry there. "You are his woman?" he asked.

"Nay, Seer, I am no man's." She must have understood he was trying to find out what lay between them for she shook

her head and spoke again. "If you could help him, I would . . .
I would do what you need."

The offer was an empty one, Connor knew, for Diarmid
most likely had found him already. "You bargain so easily for
his life; will you offer me the same bargain if I spare yours?"

She did hesitate then, and he took her answer as no. Disappointment filled him, for he knew it would be no easy thing to
get her in his bed without her consent, and now, having heard
too much and seen too much, she would never give it.

Connor turned and walked out. He would learn what he could
about the fate of Gillis, but Diarmid's mercy would never extend
to a man who aided a murderess in gaining a place in the keep.
Gillis's only hope was if he were well away from Mull by now.

He turned in the corner stairway on his way to the noon
meal and waited for the man to catch up. As this man was one
of few he would allow to see his face and know his plans, he
could trust no other with the task at hand.

"Young Gillis has become a liability to us," he said quietly.
"Do you still have him hidden away?"

"Aye, my lord," the man replied. "As you ordered."

He'd known Gillis's identity and link to the woman Ceanna
would be revealed to Diarmid. Diarmid had a network of spies
and informants among his people and throughout Mull and
the isles that was unsurpassed by any other lord, be they earl
or king. Men who strove for higher than their place could always be counted on for such excellence in knowledge gathering and strategy. And his brother strove for much higher than
his birth should allow him to climb.

Now, it was too much of a risk to allow Gillis to remain with
his knowledge of their plot. Diarmid's torturers would get information from him, and he could not allow it to be their plans
that were revealed.

"I think Gillis must leave the keep now," he said, ordering the man's death as easily as he asked for a cup of ale with his meal. "Diarmid's men cannot be allowed to capture him alive. Do you understand, Ivar?"

"Aye, my lord. And the woman?" he asked.

Their plan to have the crowds do their work for them had failed, for Connor's men had expected such trouble and were prepared for it. They'd managed to get her to the keep with only some superficial wounds and nothing that would take care of her. Still, he thought she might be useful later, so he did not need to follow through with any other action against her . . . for now.

"Leave her to me, Ivar."

Ivar bowed, and their paths diverged as they reached the lower floor. He fought the urge to rub his hands together in unseemly glee at the turn of things; he would give in to such childish satisfactions only when everything was accomplished. Then, he would shout it from the battlements.

Diarmid is dead.

Long live Steinar, true lord of this isle.

Chapter Eight

The next several days passed quickly for her. Although he slept there in his chambers each night, she saw little of him during the days. Where he went and what he did, no one said, but he would arrive back well after dark and leave at first light.

The Seer also grew more and more agitated as the days passed and the visions grew closer, though he never asked to take her to his bed. She would spy him staring at her, lust filling his dark green eyes, and notice the heat in the chamber rise, along with that strange scent, but as long as she put her mind to it, it did not affect her as it had that first time.

Some items had appeared in her prison corner, a stool on which to sit, a comb and a woolen shawl, even another gown and stockings and a pair of shoes to replace the ones lost when she arrived here. Fairly strange, yet kind, treatment of a prisoner, but she accepted it.

Only Breac and Agnes were permitted in his chambers alone with her. For some reason, the Seer never allowed Ranald to be alone there. Moira knew he was Diarmid's man, but sensed some loyalty within him for the man he served.

They all called her Ceanna, and for now no one suspected

that she was the one sought out by the Seer as Moira. She wanted to ask him about that, but did not, fearing the answer she would get.

No word had made it into her seclusion about Gillis, so she could only pray he'd escaped Diarmid's rough justice and made it back to the mainland. His only sin had been to fall for her sad story and to give her a place to live and sleep. Her favors, such as they were, were not a good exchange for his life, which she knew he would forfeit on her account if caught.

The day of the Seer's visions arrived, with the fullness of the moon, and his chambers were transformed in a receiving room. The bed and the screen that separated it from the rest of the chambers were pushed closer to the wall to allow more observers to see the proceedings. Her few belongings were shoved under the bed and her stool taken away, forcing her to stand against the wall to watch. A guard had been ordered to stand at her side, and she recognized Ennis as he took his place there, forbidden by the Seer to leave until the chambers were cleared after his vision.

He'd eaten only at midday, she noticed, and had spent hours pacing around the chamber since then. Last month, she'd not seen this part of it, as she had been hiding beneath his bed until all was clear. The Seer spoke to no one as the crowd entered, first standing in the far corner, staring off at nothing, and then sitting on his chair.

Lord Diarmid arrived and escorted several men she knew not. He directed them to places close to the Seer's chair, so she suspected one of them would be the recipients of the vision today. He left them, walking in her direction, and not even Ennis would be able to stop him if he chose to approach her.

Which he did.

Moira tried to remain calm, but Diarmid played on her fears as only an expert could.

"Obviously, Connor has not followed my methods after all. You can still stand up straight."

She fought not to tremble before him.

"I told him how much you like the whip and cane while being fucked," he said in a low and ominous voice so only she could hear it. "I offered to show him how to make you scream and weep."

She turned her face away, but he moved nearer. Standing closer now and blocking his movements with his height and bulk, he pushed his hand between her legs and rubbed hard against her.

"See, over there," he nodded toward the door with his head, never taking his hand away. "They are so ready for you that they drool at the mention of your name, Ceanna."

She knew whom he meant and would not give him the satisfaction of turning to look. He pushed his fist in harder until she gave in and turned her head. One of the men made an obscene gesture with his hand, and the other laughed at it.

"I am told you are not pleasuring my Seer. Once he tires of your refusals, you belong to me."

"My lord?" Ranald called out then, surprising both of them with his interruption. "He is ready."

Diarmid dropped his hand and straightened his shoulders back, gaining his full height and looking every bit the warlord and master of the lands that he was.

"Seer, who would you speak to first?" he asked as he walked to the center of the room.

Moira let out the breath she was holding and fought to stay upright. Sweat poured down the edges of her face and down her neck and back from the reminder of what had been stopped that day. No matter how calmly she'd brushed off Dara's concerns about her condition after Connor's intervention, she would never survive what Diarmid's men planned to do to her next.

Rubbing the sweat from her brow with the back of her sleeve, she noticed the terrible shaking in her hands and clasped them together in front of her. She was such a fool!

If all it took to keep her in the safety, such that it was, of the Seer's chambers was for her to pleasure him, then that was what she must do. It would be no different than that time months before and no different than the dozens before him. That day in his bed had been nothing to fear and one she could repeat, once her leg healed more. Right now, she could not move with the ease she needed to repeat what gave him such pleasure before. Soon though . . .

Everyone grew quiet as, one by one, the men chosen by Diarmid walked up to the Seer and held out their hands to him. After hearing about this, Moira watched now to see how the visions would come. 'Twas the fourth man introduced to him that caused the change to happen. Luckily, she was tall for a woman and could see over most of their observers' heads to the raised chair where he sat.

His body grew rigid and then shook for several seconds before calming. The Seer's head fell back, and he mumbled something she could not understand, tossing his head side to side until he sat straight in the chair once more. Now he seemed to fill with an unexplained strength and vitality; his face radiated some force from deep within. But it was his eyes that changed the most.

Moira had seen the final step of this, when the fires of hell would engulf his eyes and they would burn without extinguishing for hours, but this was different and seemed to cause him no pain. The darkest part of his eyes changed and whitened, while the green circles resembled the strange green curtains of light that sometimes lit the night sky, flickering and moving as though alive. He grasped the man's hand tighter and pulled him close.

"What truth do you seek from me?" he asked in a voice not his own.

Moira shivered at the spectacle—some power not of this world was using him now, and she tried not to watch. But her eyes remained locked on him as he transformed yet again. This time, his face smoothed and appeared younger, without any sign of the torment or despair she'd witnessed there this last sennight. If she could believe what she was seeing, he began to resemble someone else, someone less physical and more . . . something other than human. She shook her head, not ready to accept what her eyes could see.

Ranald approached from his other side and placed a slate tablet on the flat arm of the chair and a piece of chalk into his hand. The man chosen now shook visibly as he tried to speak his request. It took him three times to get the words out.

"My lands are plagued by outlaws. They kill my cattle, steal my slaves, and destroy my crops. Tell me where to find them so that my lands will once again be safe."

The Seer raised his head and stared in her direction, though she could tell his human eyes saw nothing at all, for they were gone. The glowing ones looked far past her and even past this chamber now and the walls surrounding them, seeing with a power only bards spoke of in their stories of those touched by the Sith. Something otherworldly had touched the Seer and given him the ability to see the truth, wherever it lay.

The man came not from Mull, but from one of the smaller isles to the north. The Seer began to describe the lands and the coastlines, and then he told of caves hidden from view on the southern shore of the man's lands. His left hand moved over the slate, drawing a map as he explained the route the man must take to stay out of view and attack unseen. His right hand never moved from the man's grasp as he spoke of places the man, but no one else, recognized. It went on for some minutes, until the Seer released his grip and freed the man.

Moira waited for the next change, for by the time she'd crept from her hiding place he'd lost this otherworldly appearance completely. As she watched now, his face and body became his own, bit by bit, until the power slid away, leaving an exhausted man behind. When she squinted to get a better view of his eyes, she could not, for he closed them tightly and nodded to the man who thanked him for the information he'd been given.

Ranald stepped forward, at his side, and managed to clear the chambers within a mere minute or two, leaving only the Seer and her alone there. Even hating him as she did, knowing what would come now was not easy. He slid from his chair to his knees and crumpled over in pain as the terrible price of his visions hit him.

It seemed to last an eternity, pain tearing through his body and his eyes. She watched as he fought against it, not allowing himself to scream out the anguish so obvious to her. Moira bit her own tongue, trying not to cry out for help. Wave after wave, it struck him over and over. When she thought it finished, it began anew, longer this time than the one she'd heard here last month.

He rolled now on the floor, the expensive rugs softening some of the hardness beneath him, every part of him spasming, as he clutched his head and then pressed his palms against his eyes as though it helped. Once he opened them as he struggled, and the strange green light filled the room. Moira threw her arms up around her head to block the sounds and sight of his suffering and slid down along the wall until she sat with her good leg bent, leaning against it to protect her face from the scene before her.

His struggles lessened, and the sound of him fighting the pain ceased, leaving only his body on the floor in the middle of the room. She raised her head and watched as he took in one hitching breath after another. Minutes passed before his breathing eased into something less strained. Still, he kept his eyes shut tightly and his hands pressed against them.

Finally, he quieted and lay unmoving on the floor.

Now it was her time to force a breath or two into her own body, for the tenseness of watching him suffer was like nothing she'd ever experienced before, and she hoped to never experience it again. This was not the way she pictured the vision happening or the aftermath of it. It wasn't until she lifted her face that she realized tears poured down her cheeks.

She cried for the Seer.

Nay! She could allow herself no sympathy for the man who caused the massacre of her family and countless others.

Moira dashed away the tears and tried to find her anger and her hatred. Instead, all she could draw from within was pity. Pity for a man cursed, not blessed as she first thought. Cursed by something he could not control and tortured as its price.

Damn him for making her feel anything for him! She'd lived for too long without those other feelings clouding her thoughts and distracting her from her one purpose, and she'd be damned if she would soften now because he suffered. He deserved to suffer this and more for what he'd done.

Rubbing her face with her sleeve to remove any sign of her tears, she watched as he pushed himself onto his knees and then onto his feet. Wobbling and staggering, she thought he would fall more than once before he gained some sense of balance.

"Ceanna?" he whispered, turning toward one side of the room and then the other.

She shook her head, unable to say a word in reply.

"Moira?" he asked again, tilting his head to one side and waiting for her to speak. "Can you hear me?"

"Aye," she finally answered. He lifted his head and looked around the chambers as though he could not tell where she was.

"Speak again, Moira," he pled in a low voice. "I cannot find you."

Her head shook on its own as she realized the reason for it. Denying it did not make it a lie, and when he opened his eyes then and she saw the terrible burning there, she knew the darkest secret of all.

The Seer was blinded by the visions he conjured!

She must have gasped for he began to walk toward her, hands spread as he tried to get his bearings. He did not know how close she was or what lay in his path, for he tripped on the edge of a table and landed hard into the wall. When he would have walked into the screen, she called out to him.

"Seer," she said. "The screen lies in front of you."

He nodded then, seemed to know where he stood, and then eased his way along the screen until he found the end and stumbled to the bed. Guiding himself along the edge, he climbed on it and lifted a piece of wool left there by Ranald.

Stunned by all of it, she could only watch now as he tied the strip around his head, hiding the truth of his burning, blind eyes from anyone who might enter. He did not lie down as much as he collapsed on the bed, and she feared, nay thought, he might have fainted from the pain. It was only his hoarse voice that told her he was yet awake.

"Moira . . ."

He said it once and then made no more sounds at all.

Connor could sense her terror rather than see it or hear it. No one, not even Ranald, had seen the full aftermath of the visions since it had become this bad. He did not know if she'd realized the extent of the punishment his body took, but she'd heard it last time. This time, she witnessed the entire process.

First she was witness to his weakness of the flesh and now to the weakness in his body and soul.

His strength seeped away, and he could do nothing but lie silently and try to let sleep take him now. He would have laughed at the irony that struck him about this situation: he finally had her in his grasp and could not raise a finger. The visions burned the sight from his eyes and the desire from his blood, and it was the only time his body was at peace.

Except when he was deep within her.

Had it been just a dream? Had he only imagined that the pain and burning had lessened after he'd worn himself out on her body, or had it truly been different three months ago? What was her part in this, and did she hold the truth of it even now?

If he listened, he could hear her labored breathing now, from the place in the corner where she was chained. She was not unaffected by what she'd witnessed. Who could be? Not even the cold-hearted assassin she tried to believe she was, or the one she tried to make everyone believe she was.

Finally, the pull of sleep and a welcomed respite gained strength, and he followed it.

Chapter Nine

He did not move for more than a day, then barely as the servants and Ranald tended to him. She looked on in a kind of shock as he recovered from the visions. Moira was not certain she would ever forget what she'd seen. Yet, if the past indicated the future, he would go through it again when the moon reached its fullness in a month.

She shuddered then, nearly losing her balance as she stood silently while he spoke to Breac for the first time since collapsing on his bed two nights before. How did he yet live if she'd attacked him at his weakest? Was her aim so misplaced that she'd not pierced his chest after all? He should be dead, and here he was, surviving another dreadful vision.

His gift must include an inhuman ability to heal as well, she suspected. 'Twould make sense—if the Fae gave such power with such a terrible aftermath of pain and suffering, they were contrary enough to also give the ability to withstand it, too, so it would not end too soon.

If one believed the stories passed down about the Fae and their dealings with humans.

After seeing the changes and the power surge through him

as the Seer had his vision, she believed it. In her search, she listened to many storytellers share their wisdom about the otherworldly inhabitants of the sacred woods and glens of the Highlands of Scotland and the isles surrounding it. Even Mull had its share of standing stones and other places whispered to be the gateways to the land of the Sith or the Fae, as they were called in many lands.

She'd seen too much and learned too much more to ignore the existence of such powerful beings. She only had to remember the Seer's face during the vision to know the truth—he was touched by the Fae.

And yet, he seemed to be unaware of it. Had no one told him? Had he never sought the truth? Strange, that the one who wanted to end his life might know more about it than he did himself. She would keep her information to herself until she knew the best way to use it.

The next several days passed quietly, with the Seer spending more and more time sitting up or moving around his chambers. The blindfold remained in place, but she saw no hint of fire when it slipped down from his brow, exposing his eyes to her. Instead, she saw only black there, no color even in their depths. And the blindness remained.

Moira was amazed at the change in him now. Gone was the agitated, angry, lust-filled man she'd watched in those days leading up to the visions. Gone was the arrogant, irritated one who demanded everything from everyone around him. In his place was a different person. And, although she heard her name mentioned over the course of the next few days, he never spoke to her directly at all.

She spent most of her time sewing and mending, for Dara had sent word of her skill with a needle and thread and Agnes presented her daily with a pile of tunics, gowns, trews, stockings, and other clothing that needed repair. As long as there was light in the room, she put her hands to use and kept her mind on those tasks, rather than on the one that brought her to this place.

And she healed. Her leg grew stronger, the bruises on her neck and back faded, and even her courses arrived and ended in that week, as though it were a sign that she had made it through the worst. Being chained to the wall and not seeing the sun or breathing the fresh air bothered her more day by day, but she was alive and still had a purpose before her.

A week after the vision, as she waited for Breac's arrival and the removal of the splint from her leg, Moira noticed the sun's light making a path along the floor toward her. The windows high on the wall only received direct light for a short time each day, and now it approached. When it was cloudy outside and the winds roared, she did not miss it so much. But on a day like this one, when the sun grew bright and warm, her body ached to be out in its warmth.

Edging her way to the farthest spot the chain's length would allow, she felt the warm place on the floor where the sun heated the stones. Biding her time, she watched as that small circle moved inch by inch closer. Then, when it seemed at its closest, she leaned as much as she could bear against the collar and tried to place her face in its path. Closing her eyes, she waited for the heat to touch her.

"What are you doing?"

Her stance so unbalanced and her position so precarious, the soft question startled her into losing both. Trying not to fall with her full weight against the collar, she twisted and would have slammed into the wall if he had not caught her in his arms.

When she gained her feet, she stared at his face and his eyes. The were no longer completely black; a hint of green had reappeared around the centers.

"Can you see now?" she asked.

"Enough to wonder if you were performing some sort of suicide ritual. I have heard of such things in the old religions." He released her and stepped away, squinting back at the place where she'd stood. "Ah, you were trying to reach that small patch of sunlight."

Moira did not admit to her weakness; 'twas bad enough he'd witnessed it. "I try to stretch and move so my leg does not seize up."

"By hanging against the collar with your face tilting sideways? Interesting."

She knew he did not believe her, but it mattered not. She would not try it again, for to be so close and fail was too painful. Reminded by his very presence of her other failure, Moira stepped back to her stool, gathered up the garments there, and sat down to work on them.

"You are not comfortable talking to people, are you?" he asked. Now he leaned against the end of his bed and watched her sewing.

"I have nothing to say," she replied, once more hesitant to acknowledge the truth. She'd been on her own so long, keeping her own counsel, that the common chatting among family and friends, even simple acquaintances, was foreign and difficult for her.

"I think you have much to say, Moira, and it is time for me to hear it." He stood and walked closer, dragging a stool as he came. "I do not favor force in my interrogations, as Diarmid does," he began, as he sat on the stool and faced her. "I have my methods."

She shuddered then, unable to control it, for it was her body's response and not her mind's. Taking and releasing a breath, she dropped the tunic on the pile of garments and readied herself as best she could for his challenge.

"If not force, then what do you favor, Seer?"

"Connor," he said softly, meeting her gaze. "My name is Connor."

"The Seer," she added, resisting his attempt to have her use his name. "A changeling some say, placed with a human family by the Sith after your mother's passing. Others claim you walked out of the standing stones as a boy, without knowledge of your name or your past. So many stories are shared about you that it is difficult to choose the right one."

He flinched, surprised by her words. Truly, he was a mystery. There were stories of all kinds about the Seer's origins, and each one, she suspected, held a grain of the truth.

"The Seer came to Lord Diarmid's attention just past six years ago, and you have been in his employ since then, trading your visions for wealth and protection."

"For someone who has had little to say, you know much, Moira. How came you by this information?" He stood then, crossing his arms over his chest and pacing back and forth in front of her.

She hesitated to explain herself to him, especially since the entire reason she had discovered all she could about him was to find something useful in killing him. As long as she remained chained to the wall during the only time he seemed vulnerable, his death was out of reach to her. Moira stared at the floor, trying to decide how to handle the Seer's interrogation.

"I will offer you a trade then to loosen your tongue."

She knew it would come to this, and she was prepared to barter her body to protect herself. She exhaled and nodded at him to continue.

"One hour in the sun for what you have discovered about the Seer. Continue to answer my questions, and it could be longer."

She stared at him as though he was insane, and in some ways he believed he might be. Almost seven years of trying to understand the power he had, how it worked, what its limits were, and this woman seemed to hold more facts about him than he knew himself. And after spending his adult life searching for his past, he might now have the one person in his grasp who could tell him more.

Her eyes widened, and she nodded before he thought she would—her pattern was always to hesitate. She must think there was nothing to interfere with her cause in telling him what she knew, or else she planned on deceiving him with falsehoods. Either way, it gave him a bargaining tool to deal with her.

"Breac," he called out before she could change her mind. "Bring her." Connor took a cloak of his and tossed it to Moira. "Put that on and keep the hood up."

"My lord," Breac began to argue, "this is foolhardy and dangerous."

"You know the spot, Breac," he answered, walking to the door. "The guards know I am not to be disturbed if there with a woman. None will look closely at which woman accompanies me."

He waited only long enough to be certain that Breac would obey him, and then he began the climb to the battlements. His sight was still weak, but his eyes were almost returned to their normal appearance. He followed the walls around to the corner he preferred and nodded to the guards. Stepping into the shadows there, he waited with a sense of anticipation unlike he'd experienced before.

He had searched for his past, his parents or family, during those first years with Diarmid, but he knew now that Diarmid had simply ensured that he found nothing. With few contacts other than those appointed by Diarmid, Connor had no choice but to give up. Since then, he'd gained some who were loyal to him, but any search would draw Diarmid's attention or that of his wide net of allies.

He heard the scuffling of feet and watched as Breac came out of the doorway with Moira tucked closely at his side. She limped along, rushing at Breac's pace until they reached his place. He motioned Breac off a bit and waved to the guards, his signal that he expected privacy. No one would dare interrupt the Seer while he took his pleasure on a woman there. The guards turned their backs and remained at either side of the walkway.

"Stay close, Breac," he said, when the man seemed to object. Breac nodded and walked a few paces away, also turning his back.

Connor stayed in the shadows—it hurt his eyes less than being in the direct sun—but he nodded to Moira then. "You may remove the cloak now."

She shed it like a flower dropping its petals: The top fell away, exposing the loose and wild curls of her hair, first. Then she pulled the laces, and the cloak fell to the ground, puddling around her feet. Then, she blossomed in front of him.

She lifted her face and closed her eyes and let the sun beat down on her. The winds driven by the seas tousled her hair, but it was so short it never covered her face. He watched as she turned into the winds and stood unmoving as they buffeted her, tugging on her tunic. He thought she smiled, a thing he'd never seen her do before, but it was fleeting and gone before he could say aye or nay.

He allowed her some minutes of quiet before he began asking his questions. "How long have you searched for me?"

"Six years," she answered.

She could not have even been ten and eight years yet, which meant she'd been just a child when she set out to destroy him.

He tried to think back to some of his early visions. He'd had no control then, no sense of how to choose the recipient or how to guide the flow of the Sight. There were no rules then, only madness and chaos.

"When was your family . . . when?" he asked. He watched as a tear rolled down her cheek and expected her to refuse, but she did not. The tear was the only sign of her being affected by the questions.

"Six years ago, Seer," she snapped. "I heard the men who destroyed our village speak of you. How you had guided them to us and given instructions about our deaths."

"You escaped. How many others went with you?"

She turned then, away from his gaze, and leaned against the stone wall. He saw her shoulders shaking and knew she was remembering that time.

"None, Seer. I was the only one out of my family to escape your death sentence." She turned, and he saw the hatred back in her eyes. "Ask your questions about your past, not mine."

For now, he would allow her to guide the revelations, but he would discover her past as well. "Where did you hear the stories you mentioned before? The ones about being a changeling or foundling?"

"In a small village near Kilmartin in Argyll. A wise woman there told of a woman who'd found the place where the faeries are most vulnerable and captured one to do her bidding. The wise woman confided in me that she thought it was the other way around, that the fairy—a tall, handsome one with pale hair and dark eyes—had caught the woman."

Did he believe such tales as these? The faeries were involved? "A tale to be sure, but it could not be true," he said, shaking his head. He thought he might be trying to convince himself, since it made more sense than other explanations.

"You have not seen yourself during one of your visions, have you, Seer?" she said staring at his face. "Has no one told you what happens when the visions approach?"

He had not. Some mumbled about the change to his eyes, others about his voice, but Diarmid controlled those permitted in the chamber, and he could approach none of them with questions. "Nay. I do not remember it once it has passed," he admitted. "But how is this connected to the magic of the Fae?"

"You become someone, something else during your visions. Your eyes glow as though on fire, your face changes to someone else's, someone younger, and your voice is not yours. You spoke in some other language at first, though I know it not," she explained. "You wrote your instructions with your left hand, though I have only seen you use your right one. Surely these are all signs of . . ." Her words drifted off to allow him to make his own conclusions.

"All he has ever said was that it was a special talent," he whispered. Diarmid controlled far more about his life than he'd realized.

"Was that before or after he provided you with everything you ever needed or wanted?"

The sarcasm in her voice was clear, as was the fact that he had joyfully not looked too closely at the beneficence of Lord Diarmid in those early years. Then he was too dependent on the luxuries and the wealth and the lifestyle he'd come to know.

"It is known throughout the isles that Diarmid has someone who helps him to gain power over his enemies and to entice others to his side. Most think it is his spies, providing dangerous information that Diarmid uses to assure compliance. Very few get close enough to meet his Seer or avail themselves of his talent."

"Yet you discovered this truth. On your own. How did you learn so much about me?" he asked. Diarmid apparently kept the truth of his puppet quiet. How had this woman, this girl, found it out?

"I had reasons to seek you out, and it did not take long to learn the right questions to ask and the right men to ask them of." From the way she emphasized *men*, he understood her methods before she spoke of them. "Men lose their minds when a woman offers to lift their skirts. Or please them in some other way. Once I found the men who had the information I needed or who could help me in gaining entrance to places made difficult to enter, it was not hard."

Connor searched her face, realizing that she had been very young when she began her search for him and had made her way through most of it alone. Because her family was dead.

Because of him.

Because when the visions first started, he did not know enough about them or the people Diarmid brought forward or the true power of his words. He'd learned only this past year how to let the power seek out those who needed help or had good intentions and not those who were simply greedy or hungry for their neighbors' lands or possessions. But before . . . he let out a breath.

So many lives changed because of him, while he sat here in luxurious oblivion, drinking his fine wines, enjoying the attentions of a myriad of women who sought only his pleasure, and allowing Diarmid to benefit like a parasite from his gift.

Because of him.

The silence grew between them now, for Connor was not certain he wanted to hear more about himself from this woman who sought vengeance for the loss of everyone dear to her. He met her gaze and saw pity there, and he did not like it.

And now? What path was open to him now? From the signs, his gift was burning itself and him out with each successive month. The blindness, not gone yet, lasted nearly two days longer than it had last month. The pain and torment grew stronger yet again.

The vision itself was more powerful than any before it—the clarity and reach had shocked him as the vista of the man's isle opened before him and he soared over it. Though he remembered not many of the details of it, he could still taste the sea air and smell the extensive marshlands he'd witnessed as he'd flown over the coast.

Now what would happen?

He did not remember asking it aloud, but she shook her head. "I know not the answer to that. Some told me that you are not gifted, but cursed, and unless you discover the reason, there is no way to remove it from you. Another said that it will reach its peak after seven years and then fade away over the next seven, for seven is a sacred number to those who give powers like this. And another said . . ." She stopped then and shook her head. "It was only an old tale; she probably twisted two together and is wrong," she explained.

"Tell me the rest of it," he urged.

"Three is the other number sacred to the Sith. One old woman said she heard that there were three boys born to the woman who caught the faery and that all three were cursed in the same way."

Connor reeled back, leaning against the cold stone wall and trying to get his balance. He'd never dreamt that he had family. No one ever mentioned the possibility of brothers. Did they yet live? Had they a similar talent and curse? "Where are they?"

She shrugged and shook her head. "I know not, for only one old woman repeated that part to me, and I had no interest in searching for the others. I only sought the Seer."

Hundreds of questions raced in his thoughts, and he was about to ask her another when the noise near the doorway caught his attention. A number of men rushed through the door, with Diarmid in the lead, and he knew she was not safe here now.

"Breac," he called. "Hold her over the side of the wall," he ordered as he moved closer to her. "Moira, do not fight him, or I cannot guarantee your safety."

Now more than ever, he wanted her alive to find out more. He could not risk Diarmid breaking her to find out about other plots against him. This was too important.

"No, please, Seer," she began to beg as she backed away. "I answered every question you asked. Please, do not . . ."

Her voice drifted off as Breac lifted her from her feet and held her headfirst over the battlements. She clutched the edge of the stones, trying to grab on to something that would keep her from falling over to her death. Then she simply screamed loud and long, for it seemed as though her death was at hand.

Diarmid ran to where they stood and called out for him to stop. "Here now, Connor. I did not think you meant to toss her to her death. I have other plans in mind for her when you finish."

"Nay, my lord. She is a worthless liar and will not give me the answers I want. Even now she refuses," Connor bluffed.

Breac shook her, and she begged him again. "Seer! Please!" she screamed.

"One more chance then," Connor crossed his arms over his chest, praying the farce worked, and nodded to Breac. "Bring her up."

She shook so hard, Connor feared Breac really would drop her, but he placed her on her feet and she clutched the wall to stay standing. There was no color in her face, and she breathed in loud, shallow gasps.

"Did you have anything to do with the other attempts on my life?" he asked in a stern voice.

"Nay!" she cried out. "I know nothing about them. Truly," she sobbed.

"Did Gillis know of your plans?" he asked.

"Nay! He only helped me find a place to live here in the keep. He knew nothing else . . ." Her voice grew lower and her breathing more labored. She reached out to him, in a plaintive gesture, and he shook her off.

"Where is Gillis now?"

Diarmid interrupted before Moira could say a word. "That is what brought us here, Connor. One of the guards saw him running up the stairs, and we followed. We were not in time though," Diarmid finished.

"Not in time?" Connor's stomach began to tighten. He knew he would not like the answer he was about to hear.

"I thought he ran for the battlements, but he must have gone in a different direction," Steinar, Diarmid's half brother said.

A guard called out to them, and the word was as bad as he suspected. "They found him at the bottom of the stairwell, my lord."

The guard said no more, but they all understood that Gillis was dead and could neither confirm nor deny Moira's claims now.

The sound of her choking made him turn, just as her eyes rolled up inside her head and her body crumpled in a heap at his feet. With a nod of his head, he ordered Breac to take her back to his chambers. Once he'd carried her off, Connor turned to Diarmid and Steinar.

"Did she tell you anything else? Her reasons for trying to kill you?" Diarmid asked. "Where she is from?" Connor now suspected Diarmid had kept much more from him than he ever considered in the past.

"Only what you heard here. I have just recovered enough to begin questioning her this morn."

"Do you believe her?" Steinar asked. Diarmid narrowed his gaze and waited on Connor's response.

"I do believe her. About this man Gillis. I do not think he was part of her plans," Connor said.

"He ran from my men. That says something," Diarmid added, as he exchanged a glance with Steinar.

Connor simply nodded, never saying what they all knew—

anyone, guilty or innocent, would run from Diarmid's men, for all on the isle knew what they were capable of doing.

"I think I will continue her questioning when she revives," he said, as he turned and began to walk away. "I will inform you of anything new I learn, my lord."

Connor did not let the weakness within show while in front of Diarmid or his half brother, but once inside, he leaned against the wall and tried to catch his breath.

She'd added yet another reason why he had to keep her alive now. Besides the physical need for her and the need to find out more about what had happened to her family, now he needed her to find out the truth about his own past and the limits of the prison in which he now lived.

As he made his way down the stairs toward his chambers, he wondered if either of them would survive long enough to try an escape.

Chapter Ten

The darkness of the hallways was soothing to his eyes after the bright sunlight on the battlements, but it was more difficult for him to see in it. Though several people greeted him as he walked past them he could not see who they were, unless he could look at them directly. His sight was improving by the hour, but would not return to normal for another day or so.

He nodded to the guard standing at his door and entered. Breac stood by as Agnes tended to the still-unconscious Moira, who lay on her makeshift pallet in the corner. Tempted to have her placed in his bed, he was waved off by Breac, who had other ideas about how to treat her now. Connor watched and waited until they'd finished with her.

She lay unmoving, barely breathing, on the thin layer of blanket-covered rushes. Breac had placed the chain back on the collar before stepping away.

"You can remove that, Breac," he said. "She is no danger to me."

"You charged me with your protection, my lord, and hers. Let me do this my way," he replied, in a tone that said he would not allow Connor to interfere now.

Connor paced the room once, twice, even a third time, and still she did not move or make a sound. "Agnes, should you try to wake her?"

Both servants looked at him with exasperation in their gazes before turning back to the woman. Minutes passed and more without her making a sound or moving. The sound of Agnes's soft voice was the only way he knew when she'd roused.

Though both Breac and Agnes warned her to remain on her pallet, Moira struggled to her feet with their help. The rare breeches in her self-control—momentary outbursts, only seconds at a time—had not prepared him for the woman who met him now. Once she realized where she was and saw him watching her, she lunged for him with enough force to push both Breac and Agnes away. Only the length of the chain stopped her steps forward.

And only the first time.

Like a wild animal that would gnaw off its own foot to escape, she threw herself at him, and against the iron collar that kept her from reaching him. The collar dug into her neck, choking her and causing blood to flow with every attempt she made, but it did not stop her. She screamed for him and lunged again, was pulled back by the chain, and then lunged again. Breac regained his footing quickly and would have approached, but Connor overpowered her and pushed her up against the wall, using his body to pin her there.

While she tried to scratch and tear at him, he slid his leg between hers to control her kicking by trapping her legs within her gown and then took each of her hands and held them high over her head against the wall. She bucked and pushed with her body, trying to dislodge him, but, even weakened, he was stronger than her.

"I am no better than you now, Seer," she snarled at him, using her head to smash at his face. "Are you pleased that I share in your guilt now?" He quickly repositioned, taking both hands in one of his and leaning his forearm across her throat to keep her pinned there. "He was innocent of this, and now his blood is on my hands," she screamed.

"His death was not your fault," he whispered, trying to calm her. "His fear of Diarmid drove him to it."

"He had nothing to fear but his knowledge of me," she cried out. "If I had not used him, he would yet live. I am no better than you now," she repeated, shaking her head and crying openly. "An innocent died because of me. . . . I spilled the blood of an innocent."

Then she cried, but in a silence so eerie it made his heart hurt. He eased his arm away from her throat and lifted his weight off her body slowly. The anger and fight drained from her quickly now, leaving only horror and despair in her eyes.

"How do you live with the pain of it, Seer?" she whispered, as her body slid slowly down the wall until she hit the floor and gasped for air.

Connor stepped away without answering. In truth, he'd never thought on it until her accusations just days ago. How would he live with it now that he knew the cost of his gift to others, who were innocent and yet caught up in its expanse? If the pain of one tore at her like this, what would the dozens or hundreds or more cost his soul if he thought on it?

"See to her, Breac," he ordered softly.

Though Breac approached with caution, Moira did not seem to even be aware of them now. She closed her eyes and continued that silent weeping, her shoulders shuddering and shaking against the stone wall. Breac crouched down and motioned for Agnes to come closer now.

She would have discovered Gillis's fate in time. There would be no way to keep it from her, and the shock would have been the same. It was just watching her torment as she suffered the same realization he had at her words.

Innocents died because of him, and now because she sought him.

In many ways he wished he could return to the days of mindless rutting and drinking and enjoying everything that the exercise of his gift brought to him. The days of not recognizing the prison in which he lived. The days, not so long ago now, of accepting as the truth that he was as powerful and important as Diarmid made him believe.

He let out the breath he held and watched as Agnes cleaned the blood from Moira's neck and shoulders. The chain clattered with every movement, and Connor realized they really were alike, for he was as tethered to this place and this life as if a chain locked him here.

Diarmid's call came at midday.

The man who called forth the vision last week had returned, victorious over the outlaws plaguing his lands, and a feast was to be held in the hall to celebrate it. Diarmid's allies, as well as those considering joining him, would be present and, of course, Diarmid's Seer would hold the place of honor. He knew there was some jealousy among Diarmid's men that he, who'd never raised a sword in battle for their lord, should have such a high place at his table and in his regard, but that came from those not privileged enough to know his true value to Diarmid.

Steinar had been the worst: his begrudging acceptance was long in coming, and even now, five years after his accession as his half brother's heir, there was no trust between them. Sometimes though he preferred Diarmid's direct but brutal approach to Steinar's secretive, more devious one. At least you did not have to guard your back with Diarmid; he attacked straight on, without subterfuge.

Well, with some subterfuge, he guessed, when it related to him. He suspected Diarmid had known much more about him, and for longer, than Connor was even aware of. Curious now, he would try to find out just how much Diarmid knew about his past and his powers.

He dressed in his best: the richly colored tunic with the cloak over his shoulder, held in place by the large gold pin. Around his neck was another long gold chain, a token of Diarmid's esteem, though provided to Diarmid by one of his chosen few. Connor could take no gold or jewelry directly from someone who had benefited from his gift, for the pain on accepting such a thing was worse, in those early times, than the torment he suffered now after his visions. But, if Diarmid provided it as part of his care and esteem, the pain did not occur.

Again, was it some strange curse that caused such a thing to happen and forced him to become dependent on someone strong and wealthy enough to act as his . . . pimp? He stumbled as he realized the truth of his relationship with Diarmid. In many ways it was no different from the whoremaster who oversaw his stable and controlled every aspect of the women's lives and their livelihood as well.

He turned the corner and entered Diarmid's great hall, in which every possible inch of space was filled with some or another person Diarmid sought to impress or influence. Looking over the crowd, he nodded to those who noticed him first. Then Diarmid saw him and called out his name, pointing everyone's attention in his direction.

Uncomfortable now with the adulation he'd come to expect after his visions proved true, Connor understood what bothered and worried him the most now: if his gift disappeared tomorrow, of what value would his life be to Diarmid and those around him? He'd conveniently never considered such a thing, but these last several months, with their disturbing changes, forced him to face it. Making his way to the front, he climbed the few steps up to Diarmid's table, where only the most privileged sat.

"Connor," Diarmid called. "Come and sit here in the center of my table so that all may speak with you."

He forced a smile and sat where Diarmid directed, feeling part of a farce. He didn't remember feeling that way until just months ago. Before, he'd enjoyed it for the pleasure and privilege it brought him.

Now, he saw the hollowness and falsity in it: each man there vied for the morsels Diarmid would throw his way, firmly caught in his web of power. He'd barely sat down when the man next to him grabbed his arm.

"My lord Connor," he began. " 'Twas just as you described to me, to us." He nodded at Diarmid. "Lord Diarmid's men accompanied me back to my lands and routed out my enemies." He lifted his cup in salute. "I pledge my fealty to you, Lord Diarmid!"

Connor accepted the acknowledgment, but he did not know the man's name. "I do not remember meeting you, sir," he explained. "What is your name?"

"I am Anakol of the North Island." Looking from him to Diarmid, Anakol frowned. "You do not remember?"

"I have very little memory of the days of the visions," he said. "And less of the people involved." Turning to his other side, he decided it was time. "Is that not right, Lord Diarmid?"

"Aye, it has ever been so with his visions," Diarmid agreed swallowing a mouthful of ale and nodding. "Since they began."

Luckily, Anakol was inquisitive and followed with a question of his own. "How long has the Seer been under your protection, my lord?"

"His visions began almost seven years ago," Diarmid said, slapping him on the shoulder. "And they grow stronger each time."

"And when did I come to your attention for the first time, my lord? You have never shared with me how you came to know of my visions?" Connor asked, drinking his own ale then and smiling.

Diarmid was well ahead of him in drinking the potent ale he liked so much and began telling the tale Connor had heard before. This time, he gave heed to the small details he'd ignored all those other times.

"An orphan, you be, Connor," he said, nodding somberly at him. "A foundling over in Argyll. The couple that found you on their doorstep raised you as their own and came to Mull to live with the wife's family." Diarmid drank again. "Good farmers, they were."

They had died just after Connor came to live here with Lord Diarmid. Strange that he had never thought of that before.

"They said that when you had seven years, you began to tell them things that would happen and you were right!"

"When I was seven?" he asked. "I do not remember that at all."

"Nay, you were but a wee child then. It happened again when you were ten and four. Surely you remember that?" he asked.

Connor laughed then. "That I do remember," he looked at Anakol. "I announced that our neighbor's daughter would give birth to a boy."

Anakol shrugged.

"No one kenned about her carrying yet, until I told them," Connor explained.

Diarmid laughed, too. "I'd heard stories of such a gift as this, and when his parents made his ability known to me, I decided to bring him here and have him tutored in writing and reading and in numbers. When he reached twenty and one," Diarmid placed his hand on Connor's shoulder in a gesture that anyone watching would take as fatherly, "his gift made itself known to him and us."

Why had he never realized it before? The first vision at seven, the next at ten and four, and then the full power of sight at twenty and one.

Seven and three are numbers sacred to the Sith, Moira had revealed.

Diarmid shook his head as though he'd just figured it out as well. "This is your seventh year of visions, Connor. Soon they will reach their full strength. Imagine your abilities when that happens!"

It had been accidental in timing, but he met Steinar's gaze across the table as Diarmid uttered those words and beheld a hatred so strong it shocked him. As fast as he'd seen it, Steinar pulled it back within himself and presented an amiable smile to him.

Anakol, still impressed at being the one who received the benefits of the Seer's power, added his own good wishes. "To seven more years of visions such as these!" he said loudly.

He would unchain Moira and give her his own dagger if he had to face seven more years of this hell. He could not say so, though; instead he nodded and drank the rest of his ale. Soon, the food was served: great roasts of beef and mutton, along with loaves of bread made of the finest milled flour, wheels of cheese, sauces to cover the meats, and more dishes than he'd seen on Diarmid's table.

"From my bounty," Anakol explained, "to Lord Diarmid's table, in thanks for his help and his protection."

Connor ate some of everything offered in the feast. Anakol leaned over as he reached for a cup of wine and spoke in a low voice to him.

"Diarmid told me of your request, and I willingly obey," he said, bowing his head.

"My request? Remind me of it, Anakol."

"He spoke of the need to appease your appetite of the other kind. Two of my daughters will be sent in less than a sennight to ease your pain."

"I cannot offer marriage, Anakol, and would not insult you or your honor with less," he tried to refuse graciously, the shock of this undermining his control.

Anakol nodded once more, unaffected by such a claim. "It will be their honor to serve you, Lord Connor, for as long as you have need of them. It is a fair exchange for the lives of their family."

In about a sennight, he would rage like a ravening beast, fucking any woman Diarmid sent knocking on his door. He knew it, Diarmid knew, and apparently Anakol knew it as well. His attempts to resist that call in his blood increased his pain and agitation until he wanted to throw himself off the battlements to escape it. Or drink herb-laden wine that could calm it for a few hours.

If Anakol had not spoken so frankly, Connor would never have known that this was how Diarmid kept his supply fresh. An arrangement made without his knowledge, but in his name. One that provided the endless, nameless bodies he needed.

Another sin laid on his soul. Innocents of another kind whose blood he would shed. And fool that he was, he'd managed to never see the truth or look too closely in his time of need or wonder what became of them when his interest waned.

It took hours to complete the feast; course followed course, wine and ale flowed, and no one in Diarmid's keep left without a belly full of good food and strong spirits, all at Anakol's expense. Except Connor, for his appetite had fled upon hearing of Anakol's daughters.

Finally, sometime after night had fallen, the hall began to clear, and Diarmid dismissed him with a wave of his hand. Content to be away from it, Connor walked out, delayed only by a word shared here or there on his way. The guard nodded as he entered his chambers.

He listened to the silence as he stepped into the room. Agnes sat sleeping in a chair near the corner, but Breac was gone.

He'd seen one and then the other in the hall tonight, taking their meals and returning here, as he'd ordered, to keep watch over Moira until his return. He shook Agnes's shoulder gently to wake her and sent her back to the chambers she and Breac, the only servants here who were loyal to him, shared. Connor closed the door and dropped the latch.

The light of the low fire in the hearth threw shadows on the walls, and he walked over and crouched down in front of her. She'd not moved much since he'd been here last, except that she slouched down against the wall and had drawn her knees up and rested her head on them. Spying pieces of wood near the door, Connor knew that Breac had removed the splints from her leg.

In the darkened corner, he could not tell how badly she'd damaged her neck, but she wore a clean gown and tunic. He moved quickly and as quietly as possible over to his bed, pulling off his own tunic and trews and placing the gold chains and pin back in the wooden strongbox where he kept them. He lay under the bedclothes, enjoying the ease of one of the very few nights when the need to satisfy his lust did not rule his body and soul. Come the dark of the moon, the growing power would stir the lust in his blood and make a calm night's sleep impossible for him.

But, this night was made for sleep.

An hour or so later, he was still awake.

Moira's words about the stories of his past and Diarmid's version of his life, as well as his own memories, swirled around in his thoughts until he thought he would go mad. He sat up, with the intention of finding some wine to soothe his way to sleep, when he heard her for the first time.

Sounds she would never make awake—whimpering, crying, and muttered words begging for . . . something—echoed through his chambers, tearing at his heart and twisting his gut until he stood before her. He tilted his head, trying to hear her words, but then she began to weep, the sobs welling up from deep within her and shaking her body as they escaped.

Even though he knew her intent was his death, even though he could feel the place where her dagger had plunged into his chest, and even though he understood that she sought vengeance from him, Connor found he was unable to ignore the pain he heard and saw in her. Though not intentional on his part, her downfall was his fault; his words had caused the destruction of the life she should be living. Uncertain about what it all meant, he only knew he needed to offer her some comfort for the pain she suffered now.

He went to the headboard of the bed and took the leather cord from it. The key slipped in quietly, and the collar fell open. He lifted it from around her neck and let it drop onto the floor next to her. She did not rouse until he slid his arms beneath her legs and around her back and picked her up off the floor.

"Seer?" she asked in a voice hoarse from screaming. "What are you doing?" He leaned over and placed her in his bed; then he climbed in with her and arranged the warm blankets and furs over them.

"I am going to sleep," he answered, gathering her into his arms and turning her onto her side. Leaning his head on hers to keep her still, he waited for her to settle. The last thing he expected was for her to speak.

"The night you found me at your door," she said softly without moving. "What did you do to me?"

He tried to think of a way to explain it to her, but she spoke again. "'Tis said you cast a spell, a love spell, on any woman you want to draw to you, Seer."

"It is something that happens before the visions, Moira. The power grows within me and causes my blood to surge with lust. It also casts a wide net and attracts any willing woman to my bed."

She turned in his arms then, facing him. Pain yet filled her gaze, and her face showed the tracks of many, many shed tears. "And the women, they do not object to this? Does your power make them forget themselves?"

He frowned then, and she lifted her hand to his brow and touched it. 'Twas the first time she had willingly touched him without intending to kill him.

"Did you forget yourself? You were here with me, you felt the power, you smelled the scent my body uses to call women." He leaned up on one elbow and searched her face for the truth. "Ah, but you seem to be the one woman who can resist it. It did not overpower you that night or the other time it happened."

She met his gaze then, and he knew she was remembering the night he brought on his own release while she watched. Then, she closed her eyes, and he wondered if her strange questions were at an end. But they were not.

"Make me forget myself, Seer. Spin your magic spell and make me forget," she whispered.

"Moira, you need to sleep," he said, trying to turn her back away from him.

"I need you to make me forget the things I learned today. I beg you, make me forget."

The desperation and the pain in her voice drove him to the insanity of trying to stir the desire that the visions forced into his blood. And, if he thought on it, he wanted nothing more than to lose himself in her body and forget his own sins for a brief time. "We will both face more sins on the morrow, Moira."

"For now, Seer. Just for now. Take my thoughts and memories from me."

Chapter Eleven

He knew he could bring it forth; he'd done it before when he was foolish and full of himself and had no idea of the torment it would later bring him. Closing his eyes, he began to breathe deeply and think about the feel of her skin, the taste of her essence, the smell of her arousal, the sounds of the moans and gasps she would make as he took her and the sight of her face as she found that moment of physical ecstasy. Soon, the earthy smell began to pour from him, surrounding them both with the scent of pleasure.

"Ah," she whispered, taking in a deep breath and then another. "'Tis your scent that does it."

He watched as she inhaled his scent and felt the heat in his body rise. More scent escaped, and this time she did not resist its call. As she moved in his embrace, his body responded to her nearness and growing arousal. He'd searched for her for months, even trying to find what they'd had with other women, but now she was here and willing and had placed herself in his hands.

Slipping his hand between the edges of her gown and tunic, he gathered them up and slid them higher and higher, past her thighs and hips, until he could touch her there, in the place where she would give off her own scent and he would answer its call. Her body responded to him, but would she go through with this? He pressed one finger in between her legs to test her readiness and found her dripping in wet heat.

"Moira, open your eyes," he whispered. Her legs relaxed instead, and he smiled, touching her now with two fingers. She arched against his hand. "Your eyes, Moira. Open your eyes."

Leaning back so that the light of the fire lit her face, Connor could see only a frosty white where the gold-flecked green should be. With another breath and more scent flowing, her eyes turned completely white, and he knew that Moira was lost and the woman in his arms was his now without question or hesitation . . . or choice.

He tossed back the covers so that he could undress her, and she moved restlessly against him as he did it. His cock stood hard and large, his desire for her spiraling out of control in a way he'd not experienced before. His body knew the pleasure that would be between them this night, and he felt everything in him tighten in anticipation as he finally laid next to her and brought her naked body to touch his.

Having a care for her injured leg, he lifted it up onto his hip to steady it and to open her to his touch. She lay quietly there, letting him caress and stroke her legs and the place between them as he wanted to.

One finger then two, in and out, softer and rougher, slower then faster until her body spread open more. He turned his hand and used the back of it against the swelling folds, heating them with his caresses and waiting for her to open more to him. When she spread herself wider, he slipped in three fingers to fill her and tease her until she swelled and began to rub herself against him. Then he whispered to her.

"Touch me, Moira." He guided her hand up to wrap around his shaft. "Touch me."

As she encircled it with her fingers, he leaned over and

kissed her mouth, tasting her lips and then sliding his tongue inside to plunge as he would soon do with his cock between her legs. He moved down, all the while enjoying the feel of her hands working him, imitating his hands as she moved hers harder and then softer, slower and then faster. When he reached her breasts, he licked one nipple and then the other, teasing them with his teeth and grazing them with the edges until they became taut and hardened for him to suckle. She gasped at each pull and tug on them, arching against his hand each time and tightening her grasp on him.

He wanted to be inside her now—he needed to fill her and take her and feel that moment of home that he'd ached for since their last time together—but he wanted to give her what she needed first. He rolled her onto her back and climbed between her legs. She whimpered as she lost hold on his cock, but he soothed her with his mouth, kissing her breasts and down her belly. Sliding down until he lay flat between her legs, he kissed the inside of her thighs and on the crest of her hips and across her belly, smiling now as she writhed beneath his mouth.

Spreading her legs, he slid his hands beneath her and lifted her to his mouth. She gasped and tossed her head from side to side as he tongued the folds there, sliding in deeper and then higher to find the bud that would make her scream in pleasure. He licked around it, teasing it from its folds until he could suckle on it as he had the tips of her breasts. With his hands beneath her, he used his thumbs to open her and hold the womanly layers apart for his further exploration. Rubbing some of the wetness from within her down into the crevasse between the globes of her bottom, he stroked against the puckered opening, using her wetness to ease his way inside.

Her body arched again, but with his thumb inside her he pressed down and stroked, using his fingers to make her cleft weep. Sliding deeper inside both places, he watched as her body responded—her legs tightened, her breasts swelled, her face and skin grew flushed, and her core throbbed against his hand even as the muscles of her ass tightened around his thumb. She lifted her head and looked at him with those vacant eyes, her body no longer her own but under his control.

"Seer," she whispered once more before letting her head fall back.

He paused and lifted her legs over his shoulders and tongued her again, sliding over the folds, over the engorged bud, nipping at it and licking it until he took it in his mouth and sucked on it hard. Her body bucked then, but he did not stop. Stroking in and out of her ass, he used his mouth and teeth and even his chin to press against her and bring her, force her, to the edge of release. Her taste drove him mad, and he continued touching, stroking, pulling, tugging, licking, and biting on her sensitive folds until she arched and arched and then spasmed against his mouth, falling over the edge where he'd held her into that mindless release she'd begged for.

She moaned as the pleasure took her, and he waited, with his thumb still pressing and stroking and his mouth tasting the essence of her satisfaction, until the strongest waves passed and her body shuddered with the next and the next and the next. As the tension in her body eased, he slipped out of her, lifting his head and moving back until he could kneel between her legs. The musky scent of her arousal and the glistening place between her legs spoke of her body's readiness, and he waited for hers to be the only smell between them.

Moira looked down and watched as he climbed over her. Though she ached and craved more of his touch and the oblivion he'd given her, she could feel her head clearing and noticed the tiny ripples of pleasure pulsing through her body, from her breasts to her core. He let his hand graze over the hair between her legs, tickling and enticing her with one touch.

He leaned down then and kissed her mouth, the musky

taste of her own release on his face. She licked his mouth and lips and chin, watching him shiver as she opened her mouth widely and sucked his tongue. His prick lay hard between them, resting in the wet folds and rubbing there as he moved.

Moira felt every touch now as he caressed her again, teasing the tips of her breasts and making her arch against him by twisting her nipples between finger and thumb. Gasping at the pleasure, she knew oblivion was gone, and she had to face giving herself to him without the benefit of the nothingness his scent brought the first time.

"I want you to remember," he said, rubbing his face against her breasts, chafing the sensitive skin there and making her throb inside. "Forget everything else, Moira, but remember this."

She wanted to say no. She wanted to resist or try to lose herself and her guilt once more, but he would not give that to her this time. He reached down and spread her open, placing the thick head of his prick at the opening to her core.

After watching him abstain from the other woman and knowing how his blood burned as he gave off his scent, she waited for him to plunge into her womb and take his long-withheld pleasure on her. Instead, he eased inside her, inch by excruciating inch, drawing back, and then a bit more and a bit more, until she grabbed him with the inner muscles of her woman's channel and, placing her hands on his hips, drew him into her.

Fully. Completely. Until there was no space between them and she could not ignore or forget what he did to her. She held her breath as he pulled himself back out and began his torturously slow pace again. She was ready to beg for him to take her. Deep. Hard. Fast.

"I do not wish to hurt you, Moira. Let me go slowly," he said against gritting teeth.

She wanted to erase all who had gone before him even while he tried not to hurt her. "You will not hurt me, Seer. You have eased the way; now enter."

He did then, just as she'd asked. He thrust in until he touched her womb and then slid back, not leaving completely but not inside enough. Then he thrust deeper and did not pull out as far. Again, he filled her completely with his length and girth and began to move relentlessly against her. She felt the tension grow throughout her once more and let her body enjoy the friction and the resulting wetness that eased it.

She felt the tremors within just as she felt his prick grow harder and his sac tighten as it slid against her folds. Opening her legs and tilting her hips, she took him, all of him, and tightened her muscles to hold him firmly. He resisted, sliding out against her grip, only to drive deeper the next time. He was close now, and she watched his face as he released within her.

The warm spray of his seed began and filled her as he pumped in and out. Her body held onto his prick, drawing out every bit of release until he lay spent on her. She waited for him to remove himself from her. Instead, he remained there, deep inside her body, gathering her under him so that he still covered her.

Something was unusual this time. There had been a moment the first time they joined, even the other times that same day and night, when a spark ignited and a flash of something unknown existed between them. This time she felt as though she'd been watching it happen without it truly touching her soul. Had he noticed the difference?

Warm from his body covering her and exhausted from the terrible day of disclosures and weaknesses laid bare, she felt herself drifting off to sleep as they were. But he had to know the truth first.

"It meant nothing, Seer," she whispered, already halfway to sleep. "Simply scratching an itch." He raised his head then, staring hard into her eyes as he shook his head in reply.

"Nay, Moira," he said, dragging out her name in a way that made her feel his mouth on that place between her legs once more. She tightened her legs together as he whispered to her. "Nothing between us can ever be simple."

The Seer rolled her onto her side then, slipping out of her and making her feel empty in a way she did not want to feel. Curling up behind her, he surrounded her with his body, and soon she felt him relax into sleep's grasp.

Tired beyond measure, she let it come and take her, praying the oblivion she needed would be found there. And when it wasn't and her sleep was torn apart by the faces of the dead and the voices of the betrayed, he held her tighter and whispered her name over and over, like the chant of a wisewoman calling forth the spirits to guide her.

Or like the Seer, weaving his webs and casting his spells.

The sounds of the keep coming to life began just as the first sign of dawn's light crept into his chambers the next morning. He knew, because he had not slept at all through the night. Thoughts plagued him, and confusion haunted his attempts to rest. And worse than those, the sounds of the dreams that captured Moira during the dark of the night made it impossible to sleep.

If he had to lay a bet about her, Connor would gamble his gold pin that yesterday was the first time since her family died that Moira allowed emotions to cloud her path or rule her decisions. So strong was her control over them that he could almost feel the barrier she'd built to keep them tightly enclosed while she sought out only one thing: his death.

Looking over at her as she slept peacefully for the moment, he thought on what he knew about her. If she was, as he suspected, nigh to ten and eight years old, it would mean that she had watched her family massacred before her eyes when she was about ten and two.

Six years of pursuing him. Six years of living alone. Six years of using her body to pay her way to this keep and to gain her chance to kill him.

She was the worst of his sins he had to face.

The others before her were nameless, faceless victims of his visions, ones like the latest ones on Anakol's isle whom he would never recall and never remember because of the way the visions occurred.

Moira's destruction was on his soul—if not because of her need to avenge the lives of her loved ones, then for the sin of forcing her return here to Diarmid's keep. A return because he needed answers. A return that exposed her to worse danger than she'd already faced here. A return that forced her to see the emptiness and futility of her life's purpose now that it was known there. Worse, now he needed the release and the relief her body could give him as the days until the next vision became fewer.

He felt more guilt over bringing her here and exposing her to danger than he did about his need for her. He pushed it away for now, for he had less choice in this situation than she. He never asked for this power to be bestowed on him. He may have enjoyed the results, but 'twas never his choice.

When he was a child, the life ahead of him had been clear: he would follow in his father's path and learn to work the farm they owned, never dreaming that Fergus was not his father and a different life awaited him on Mull.

Moira shifted, drawing his attention for a moment, but she showed no sign of waking yet. He put his hands behind his head and watched her sleep.

The changes in her from the first time she shared his bed were striking. Her hair was the most obvious, for Diarmid's men had cut it off after they caught her. Dara told him she tried to repair the different lengths left by trimming it all short. Her skin bore marks of her punishment, for a scar ran the length of the side of her face, near her hair, and her nose showed signs of being broken and placed back in its position.

The worst of it he'd felt and not seen, for the darkness covered the scars on her back and shoulders and legs from the beatings she'd received, but his hands could feel them as he touched her. He'd gotten a glimpse of them when she climbed naked from his bed the first day here, but not enough to tell the extent of them. Her leg was broken when she had been kicked by her captors after she would not answer their questions, as Ranald had reported to him. If he'd lain unconscious for one more day and had not intervened when he had, she would have been dead.

As he would have been if something had not stopped her from continuing her attack.

Another part of the puzzle he would have to find and sort. The other thing plaguing him this morn was that something was not the same between them during this bout of bed play and the last. Was it because she came to him under his influence and not her own as she had the first time? Was it because she seemed unaffected when he took his pleasure and entered her overwrought body? For whatever reason, the release he received was pleasant, but not the satisfying one from before. Would he never be able to enjoy a woman's favors without using his power to bring her to him?

She mumbled something in her sleep. A name? A place? He leaned over to listen when she said it again.

Quinag? Was that a place or someone's name? He had access to Diarmid's maps, so he could find out.

Seumas Mac Neacail. Her father or brother? A Scot's name to be sure. Not a Norse one like so many in the isles, but he knew not if it was from the mainland or another of the isles to the south.

Moira rolled to her side and curled next to him, not touching him but so close that she could. Connor noticed her thinness, now so apparent that the bones of her hips and ribs were prominent where womanly softness had once been. She'd lost much flesh after she'd been beaten.

He closed his eyes and realized that he could not allow her

to be harmed again. He wanted her alive and well. He wanted her in his bed. He wanted her to forgive him for his part in her family's deaths. He wanted to take the pain from her eyes and the sorrow from her soul.

Most of all, he wanted to give her her life back.

All of it was impossible or nigh to it, but before his end, he wanted to make certain that she would live. If it made reparations for a few of his sins, then it would give him some peace as he faced the uncertainty of his own survival.

When next he looked at her, she stared back at him. Not certain which Moira would greet him, he waited and watched as she became aware of her place in his bed.

Her throat burned and her neck stung from the collar tearing into her skin, but otherwise she felt uninjured. Physically at least, for she doubted if she could ever remove the stain from her soul now. Moira slid her arms under the clean linen sheets and enjoyed the warmth for a moment more before pushing back the blankets and furs and climbing out.

Her leg, now unsupported by the wooden slats, felt weak and ached, but she tested it under her weight and walked to the other side of his bed to find her clothing. The Seer said nothing; he simply watched her from his place in the bed, as she picked up the gown and tunic tossed on the floor next to him. Her skin tingled from the coolness in the chambers, for even in these summer months, the winds off the seas kept the stone keep cool. And this room was even colder, as there was no way for the sun to warm it.

"Wait," he said quietly, as she shook out the shift Agnes had given her to wear next to her skin. "I have asked for a bath."

The shift would be too wet to wear if she tended his bath in it, but she did not want him staring at the scars on her back. Putting it over her head, she tugged it on, hiding in some small way the damage wrought to her body when she failed to kill him.

"The water will arrive shortly. Why are you dressing?" he asked.

"I can wash you in my shift," she replied. "Or do whatever else you wish while you have your bath." She only just realized that he probably would want her to pleasure him while in his bath. Though after the disappointing joining she'd given him in his bed last night, she thought he would have called for that other girl to serve his needs.

"The bath is for you, Moira," he said. Sitting up, he sorted through the pile of clothing on the floor for his trews. "Agnes did her best to clean up things yesterday, but I thought you might like one this morn."

His eyes, now back to their full deep green color, were somber, and she did not see lust in his expression. This was such a different man than the one she'd watched for months here. 'Twould seem that the days between vision and the new moon allowed him some measure of peace and normalcy. His outbursts between new and full moon were legendary here, as was his appetite for women during that time—just as he'd explained last night, from what she remembered he'd told her about it.

"For me, Seer? Why?" she asked, damning herself for asking as soon as the word escaped her mouth. "Your care of prisoners who continue to try to take your life is not what I expected."

"I have decided to keep you."

"Keep me alive? But for how long?" she asked again.

"I said I am keeping you," he repeated, climbing off the bed and walking toward her.

Naked in the light of day, his size and shape were formidable. His body began with broad, strong shoulders, ones more expected on a warrior, not a courtier as he was. His chest was hard and muscular, and those muscles continued down onto his belly and thighs. A light sprinkling of pale hair covered that chest and belly and narrowed and darkened as it reached below his waist. His prick and sac, hung low and relaxed between his legs for the first time since she'd encountered him, gave a thorough hint of his size when erect.

As men went, his body was better than most she'd seen. She looked away and glanced back once more. Truth be told, his body surpassed any she'd seen so far. The determination in his eyes scared her, and she backed up a pace or two, trying to keep some distance between them. She'd not pleasured him last night as surely he expected of her, and men, especially those not satisfied, could turn nasty in an instant. He reached out for her, and she put up her hand to stop him.

"But why? I am prepared to . . ." she began, but could not say the words.

Until yesterday she was prepared to die for her failed attempt on his life. Through the beatings and the rest, she prayed for death. She returned here knowing it would mean, either immediately or at some near time, her death. And discovering that Gillis died because of her certainly made her deserving of it. But when Breac held her over the wall and she faced death, not knowing at what moment the Seer or Diarmid would order her thrown to the ground, Moira had discovered that she wanted to live.

"Die?" he asked, as though reading her thoughts. "I think you were, but things have changed. You have changed."

He lifted his hand and stroked the side of her face, and she tried to remain motionless beneath his touch. Such kindness was foreign to her. No one had shown her kindness without wanting something in return, and she knew he was no better or different from those in the past.

"Not as much as you might think, Seer," she said, stepping away from his touch. "I still want your death."

"Bold words from someone in your situation," he said, following her step away with one of his own, closer. He used the back of his hand this time, and she fought the urge to close her eyes and enjoy it. "I think part of you still wants someone to pay for the deaths of your family, but I suspect the other part of you is beginning to wonder about my role in it."

"Your words condemned them, Seer. That much I will never, can never forget!" She pushed his hand away and put the bed between them. "I will try again," she promised, though the words did not strengthen her commitment the way she'd hoped.

The knock on the door interrupted any reply he would make, and he ordered her to stay with a motion of his hand. He walked to open it, and she heard the sounds of his bath arriving. While standing out of sight next to his bed, she spied his eating knife on the floor next to the bed. It must have fallen from his belt as he undressed the night before. Not as sharp or as long as she wished, still it could . . . kill a man if used well.

Grabbing it up, she waited for the noise to cover her actions and then tossed it onto the pallet in the corner, praying it would land in a spot out of sight so that she could hide it later. Praise the Almighty, it did! Then she stayed as he'd ordered until the bath was delivered. Just as the last buckets were brought in, she looked over to see two men peeking around the screen at her.

"I thought Erlend said he kept her naked and chained to his wall," the taller one whispered.

"Look there, there are the chains!" the shorter one said. Then they both caught sight of her and looked to each other.

"You have duties to see to," the Seer called from nearer to the door, and the men turned away and quickly left the room. The door was closed, and she heard him drop the latch. "Come now, Moira," he said quietly.

She peeked around the screen to find him standing next to the largest wooden tub she'd ever seen. It stood filled halfway to the rim with steaming water, and several other buckets sat off to the side. A sheet was draped across and covered the bottom.

"Naked and chained," she said, repeating the men's words.

"It adds to my reputation here, you see," he said, walking toward her. "When my needs grow uncontrollable, you will be there, naked and ready."

She shuddered, damn her weakness, for they were close to Diarmid's words, too. "That is why you will keep me alive then? To use when the madness strikes you?"

He was close enough to her now to grasp her wrist and draw her to the tub. Lifting the edge of the shift she'd placed back on, he tugged it up until she raised her arms for him to remove it. "Get in," he ordered.

The Seer watched her every movement, and she noticed that his prick responded as she stepped into the steaming water and the sigh of pleasure echoed across the chambers. He grew thick and hard, and she waited for his next demand. Pleasuring him was a fair exchange for the comfort of a real bath.

"Sit down." His voice was throaty with desire, but he did not approach. Instead he walked to his chair and sat in it.

She bent over and used the sides of the tub to support herself as she sat down in the water. She'd not felt the comfort of this kind of hot water in . . . years, usually being the second or third one in if a tub was available to the servants at all. When she finally rested on the bottom, she slid under the water because the tub was so large! It took her a couple of minutes to find somewhere to place her feet to keep from going under the water's surface, though it did feel lovely.

"I am keeping you because I need you."

His words, spoken softly, carried the tone of need mixed with desire. "I am willing to tend to your needs, Seer. A bath like this is more than fair payment for pleasuring you." She shook her head then. "Though I do not understand why you would agree since I could not please you last night."

He leaned forward as though to stand and shook his head at her. "Last night was for you. You needed . . ."

She interrupted him. "It will not happen again," she insisted. It had been an aberration. Unable to confront the guilt and the hatred at herself for wanting what she could not have and for becoming no different than him, she lost the battle to keep her emotions under the tight rein she had for so many years. "I know what you like. I can please you."

"You cannot accept kindness, can you? Too many years of fighting your own battles and plotting your own course in the world," he said as though he knew the truth about her. It was too close, very close to the truth, and she did not want to deal with it now. Too many emotions still lay too close to the surface, and she needed to pull them back in before they destroyed her or got in the way of her purpose.

He stood then, and she realized she'd not washed herself yet. Leaning over the side, she saw the small crock of soap and reached for it. She'd spent too long in the water, and he must want his turn before the water cooled. Moira lifted herself over the side and grabbed at the soap and the cloth, but missed both and fell back into the water.

"You do not want me to probe too deeply into your life, do you, Moira? That is one way we are not the same."

He reached over and took the washing cloth and dipped it into the soap and held it out to her. Moira accepted it without meeting his gaze and began scrubbing her arms and then her shoulders, neck and face. Her bad leg was loosening up in the hot water, and she bent it up and back until it moved smoothly.

"This," she nodded at the bath, "means nothing. That," she nodded at the bed behind the screen, "means nothing, Seer. I will kill you for what you've done."

Chapter Twelve

He took the cloth from her and, ignoring her threat, lifted one leg from the water. She had to grab the sides of the tub to keep her head out of the water. "It may mean nothing to you, but it means something to me. You see," he said, letting her leg slide back into the warmth, "I've slid down so far into letting the visions, and the powers and the needs they bring, rule my life, that satisfaction has eluded me for some time. Oh, I love to fuck," he said with a wicked laugh, one that made her body throb, "and the release is pleasurable, but . . ."

He washed the other leg and placed it back in the water, motioning for her lean up. Caught up in his explanation, she did so, baring her back to him. Moira waited for his reaction, but he did not hesitate. Scooping more soap onto the cloth, he began to move in swirling motions across her shoulders and down her back. The movements were so soothing she could have fallen asleep at that moment.

"Until I found this green-eyed woman standing outside my chambers and learned her body and spent a day and most of a night pleasuring her and being pleasured by her, I did not realize how much I had been missing with my mindless swiving of any woman I could bring to me."

She found breathing difficult as he described what had happened between them. And waiting for his hand to move lower across her back and lower yet caused her body to ache as she remembered that day. It had been about passion and more. That spark between them. His endurance and the heights of pleasure reached. The way her body begged her to stay in his bed in spite of everything that could not be. He stopped then, and she almost leaned into his hand to make it move again.

"I am keeping you until I discover why it was different with you." He moved the cloth again now, and she took in a hitching breath, shaking her head.

"I am keeping you because you know more about me than I do myself, and I want you to trust me enough to tell me." The warmth spread at his declaration, even while she tried to keep his words from sinking in too deeply. It could not work. There could be nothing between them other than hatred.

"I am keeping you until I find a way to make you forgive me for what I have done to you."

She shook her head harder then and began to pull away from his touch and from his words. "It cannot happen. There can be nothing between us." She would repeat it as many times as it took for him to realize the truth . . . and as many times as it took to convince her wayward heart and soul, for they wavered now under his assault.

"Lean back," he ordered, softly, but she understood he would be obeyed in this.

She leaned back, lounging almost against the end of the tub, and waited for his next touch. He moved an empty bucket behind her and crouched there. After pouring some water over her hair from another bucket, he rubbed soap through her hair and massaged her head with the fingers of one hand while cushioning her head on the other.

Moira felt the water lapping against her breast with each stroke of his hand through her hair, teasing the tips of them as surely as if he used his mouth there. Even the thought made them tighten and ache with each kiss of the water against them. She shifted, trying to hold herself either higher or lower to avoid such a feeling, but his hands held her in place.

He rinsed the soap from her hair and helped her to stand, the warm water sluicing over her skin and trickling back into the tub. His care did not end there, for he tucked her into a warm drying cloth and lifted her out of the tub and onto her feet. "Go, stand by the hearth as you dry, or you will catch a chill."

Certain that he wove another kind of spell around her, she followed his instructions, watching over her shoulder as he climbed into the tub and washed himself. She realized that the tub was long enough and wide enough to fit his large body and that it must have been made for him.

Anything for the Seer.

Moira dried her hair, taking only seconds to squeeze the water from the curls and rub it quickly with the cloth. Turning around, she watched as he spread soap up and down his arms, his legs, and his torso before rinsing it off. When she expected that he would stand and show her his erect prick, he instead leaned his head back against the side of the tub and closed his eyes.

He lay there quietly, not moving in the water, which must be cooling by now. Strange that he did not take the first bath in it. Moira dried off her arms and legs, and drew the drying cloth across her back and bottom before finding the shift she'd worn and pulling it back on. Unsure of what to do next, she caught sight of his eating dagger on her pallet.

Keeping a watch on the Seer for any quick movements, she eased her way over and picked it and her gown up together. Sliding the dagger under her palm and covering it partially with the sleeve of her shift, she knew this was her chance. She was looking for a reason to approach him, when he called out to her.

"Could you wash my hair, Moira?" he asked.

Her hands began to shake as she took one step and then the

next and the next toward the tub. She tried to smooth out her breathing, saying the calming words in her mind as she positioned the dagger so that her thrust would be the strongest. With his head leaning back, his neck was the perfect target, and it would not take much effort to slice open his throat.

Only a few feet stood between Moira and the one thing she needed to do, but her body refused to take that last step. He deserved to die for what he'd done, she reminded herself, but the words were hollow now that she was learning about the man. She did not know how it had happened, but the words that had always worked to shore up her resolve failed to do so now, and she could not convince herself that he did indeed deserve to die.

"Strike hard and deep," he said softly. "Do not hesitate as you did the first time."

He knew!

Yet he did not move or try to stop her. She took the last step and stood over him, stretching out her hands, putting all her strength behind the hilt, preparing to strike him.

The door to the chamber crashed open, but she stayed where she was—holding the dagger just above his head. Breac came running but stopped as he realized that she could kill the Seer with one stroke now. Moira tried to steady her hands when he began to give Breac instructions.

"If she does this, Breac, kill her cleanly and quickly. Do not let Diarmid get her again." She gasped at his words and stared into his eyes. "Breac? Do you understand?"

"Aye, my lord," the big man responded.

Then the Seer said nothing more, just stared back at her waiting, waiting for his death. The shaking in her hands became trembling throughout her body as the thought of killing him became real.

"Damn you to hell, Seer!" she cried out, flinging the dagger aside and collapsing to her knees. "Damn you."

Breac moved first, picking her up in his strong arms and dragging her back to the corner. With one arm around her, he lifted the collar and began to place it on her neck.

"Breac, let her be."

"My lord?" Breac continued to restrain her against the wall. "She was going to kill you."

"Breac."

"You need to stop thinking with your cock and begin using your head, Connor. Else you'll be dead before you even hear them coming at you."

She did not fight him as he locked the iron collar on her neck or when he attached the chain once more. She huddled there against the wall, holding the gown she never put on, and watched as the Seer climbed from the tub and approached her. Holding his hand out to Breac, he waited for the key. Then he unlocked the chain and collar as Breac complained about the decision.

Confusion ruled her thoughts then, for she'd had the perfect and probably last chance to strike at him—and she'd even had a weapon in her hand—yet she could not kill him. Worse, instead of regretting her inability to carry through, her heart felt glad of it. The heart she'd hardened against everything in life and especially against him. The heart that was torn apart as she watched her family die and that now betrayed her and them.

She could not listen as Breac and the Seer argued and finally Breac left them alone again. How had the Seer known she would try to kill him? And more, how had he known that she could not carry it through? Had it been a trap he placed, leaving his dagger for her to find? He sat down on the pallet next to her, leaning his naked body, wrapped in only a drying cloth, against the wall and pulling her closer.

"I would tell you a tale I am certain you have not heard before, Moira. Mayhap it will help you accept your change of heart."

"I . . ." she began, stuttering and uncertain of what she wanted to say. He took her hand in his and entwined their fingers. It felt so strange to be this close to a man and not be readying him for sex. Did he know that?

"When I had twenty and one years, the visions came. Diarmid already had me here, tutoring me in writing and reading and numbers, for if not his seer, I could be his clerk. He would get some use out of me, either way. Before they left me with him, my parents, the couple that raised me, told me that my birth happened on Samhain Day, and it was approaching."

She did not know this part, for all her information was about before or after his visions happened, not about his first ones. "Samhain? An auspicious day for the Sith and the others who inhabit their lands outside of time," she said.

"Now that I think back on all of this, I should have known or suspected the origin of the visions, but I did not. The first one struck me by surprise, for a man visiting Diarmid grasped my hand in greeting and it began." He laughed then, remembering it.

"Diarmid thought at first that I was having a fit, and he tried to pull the man free. But when I spoke in that voice"—he looked at her, and she nodded—"he knew it was something more.

"I did not recognize the tie to the faces of the moon until months later. I did not know how to control it at all then. Diarmid brought people around me, and it would happen the same as the first. Nearly a year later, I felt as though I could decide who received a vision, and began to concentrate on those in the chambers who needed the truth shown to them or needed help in some way." He paused and let out a breath. "Diarmid still brought those he wanted under his influence, but I could feel my way then."

"Why tell me this?" she asked.

"Because, I think that if my vision led to your family . . ." he skipped over saying it then. "If your family died about six years ago, it happened during those first few horrible, uncontrolled visions. 'Tis not an excuse, Moira—I cannot excuse what has happened—but I offer it in explanation. Your family did not perish because I wanted them to. I just did not know enough about controlling this power within me to keep it from happening."

Her throat tightened and burned then, as tears threatened to spill. The reaction came so quickly she could not stop it. All these years, her belief that this man had set out to destroy her family had been a lie. She'd built her hatred on lies, on ignorance of the truth about a young man with a powerful talent he could not control.

Still, many years had been spent nursing her hatred, and it was difficult to simply let it go on his word. What better way to destroy her than to make her lose her purpose? Now her heart and mind warred over his words.

"I wanted to tell you that, so you can consider whether it was through ignorance or intent that your family died. And I want you to consider if living and living well would be the better revenge than losing your life as they did."

The Seer stood up and walked over to his trunk and took out clean trews and a tunic and put them on. "I am expected at table for a morning meal. Agnes will bring you food. I want you to eat all of it."

Startled yet again, she could only watch as he prepared to leave. Then she remembered that the chain hung loosely on the wall, not attached to the collar or to her.

"If anyone enters, stay over in the corner as though you wear it. The guard will not allow anyone entrance except Breac and Agnes."

"Does Ranald not question that you keep him out?" she asked. Everyone knew that Ranald was his . . . keeper, reporting back to Diarmid anything he thought the lord should know and anything that would result in a reward.

"I pay him well enough to ignore certain things, Moira. He enjoys the importance and attention he gets by attending me during the days of the vision and in the aftermath. He knows his place."

'Twas not her business to contradict him about the manservant, whom everyone in the keep knew provided diversions of another kind to Diarmid's half brother. And who gained what he wanted by using the Seer's name when he made his demands. How had this man survived in the dangers of Diarmid's world without knowing what he was or who truly stood at his side?

"God protects the fools and the innocents," she mumbled under her breath as he left the room.

With her world tilting and changing moment by moment before her eyes, she did not know which one he was . . . and was not certain she wanted to know.

Connor walked down the stairs, smiling then, for his body was in a condition that was not usual for him. Only in these days, before the new moon began, could he imagine what sex was like for other men.

Connor wanted Moira—his body could ready itself in an instant if she'd give a signal of her willingness—but he could ignore the desire, too, and focus on things other than fucking until he or the woman in his bed could not walk. So unlike the two weeks that followed the new moon as it grew to fullness. During those weeks, his desire would burn uncontrolled and ever-present in his blood, until the visions emptied him of lust and sight.

For now, he would enjoy it and try to understand why it was different with her and what part her consent and willingness played in it. Connor arrived in the hall after everyone was seated and after Diarmid and his guests were served. Striding through the crowd, he climbed the dais and found his chair waiting for him. Anakol was nowhere to be seen, but another stranger sat next to him.

It had begun.

For the next several weeks, Diarmid would bring in visitors to meet him, men who had questions and matters for the Seer's talent. Connor would indicate to Diarmid which men should be included in the gathering in his chambers before the day arrived, and Diarmid would invite them. He could never tell which man would be "gifted" until he grasped his hand that day, but certain men caused a reaction in him that he knew was an indication of someone of true purpose.

If he had time, if he did not think the power was going to leave him at the end of these seven years, he would try to control and direct it even more. But now, with so little time and with the visions becoming stronger each month, he feared he would lose what little guidance he had in the situation if he changed the manner in which he prepared for that day.

Diarmid set the tone for their discussions, keeping them general to ascertain this new possible ally's opinions about various leaders and his role in the power structure of the isles that now belonged to Norway, without objection from the King of the Scots. All of it would help Diarmid decide if this man was worthy of his interest.

Before Diarmid could leave the table, Connor turned to him with his request. It was time to begin gathering as much information as he could about the pattern and substance of the visions, which would hopefully tell him what the next several months would bring.

"My lord," he said to Diarmid as the men began to leave. "May I have a moment of your time before you seek out your duties?"

"Of course, Connor," he said, drawing him to one side of the dais. "What do you need?"

"You have kept a record of my visions since the beginning, have you not?" he asked. He tried to keep his tone light and almost disinterested.

"Aye, I have."

"I would like to examine those records, if I may," he said.

Diarmid looked around them to make certain no one over-heard their words on something as important as this. "You have never asked to see them before, Connor. Why do you wish to see them now?"

Connor decided that honesty was probably best right now, and the least dangerous path. "You mentioned to Anakol about the patterns of seven years, something I'd not realized before. I know that the visions are changing now, as my seventh year of this gift approaches, and I would seek knowledge from those records about any other patterns in them. To be prepared for the increase in their strength and clarity, if nothing else."

Diarmid stared at him, considering this request. He should have no reason to refuse him, but Diarmid could be contrary sometimes.

"They are in my outer chamber with the rest of my books, Connor. Ask Ranald for his help in finding any particular one," he finally gave permission with a nod. "And Seer, let me know if you find anything interesting in them."

"Of course, my lord," he said, bowing his head as Diarmid turned away, called out to Steinar, and followed him out of the hall toward the yard where their men would train today.

With a sense of anticipation growing within him, Connor decided that he would go directly to Diarmid's chambers and seek out those records. And he would examine the maps of Scotland and the surrounding isles to see if Quinag was a place, as he suspected. He wanted Moira to trust him, and mayhap if he found out something from Diarmid's records and shared it with her, she would begin to open up to him about her life and what she knew of his.

Five hours later, he suspected more than he could share with her, but he knew where she'd come from on her long journey to avenge her family.

Chapter Thirteen

For the second day in a row, the sun shone brightly on the island. But for the first time, she could walk its path around his chambers and let it warm her skin as it moved across the room. It came through only one window that was shuttered during the night and opened during the day to let the fresh air into the room. As she felt the warmth on her face and closed her eyes against the brightness, she realized that her entire world had changed in the last day.

Agnes had appeared twice with a tray of food for her, and she'd eaten it all, as the Seer had ordered her to do. For the first time in her memory, her belly felt full, and hunger did not follow her around every minute. In spite of the absence of the chain tying her to the corner, she chose to sit there and work once again on mending and sewing, for it helped her to sort through her confused thoughts. Moira may not have been chained, but she was still a prisoner and in danger from many sides if she left the protection of the Seer's chambers.

Breac was there to oversee the removal of the tub, but then Agnes stayed the rest of the time that the Seer was gone. And he'd been gone for hours now, since right after his bath. The sun had crossed the sky heading to the west, so it was well past midday, though there were still many hours before dark at this time in the summer.

She watched the two servants exchange quiet words several times before realizing it: Agnes was Breac's woman. No wonder Breac always whispered words of warning to her when he left. He feared that in his absence Moira would turn her rage on his woman. Once she realized their connection, she noticed many more personal things about the way they spoke and even touched, for Breac rarely walked past the woman without making contact or a gesture of some kind. She'd missed it all these days and was fascinated by it now that she knew.

Her mother and father had done those kinds of things, too. Her father reaching out to stroke her mother's cheek as she cooked. A touch on his arm as she passed him in the village. They always . . . Moira reached up and wiped the tears that came silently now. She'd never thought on those memories before either, for they did not give her strength. They made her soft and weak, and she could not afford to be such things.

If Agnes noticed the tears, she did not speak about them; instead they sat in silence, each working with their hands as the hours passed. Moira took advantage of her new freedom to walk the length and width of the room several times when her leg ached, and it eased the pain and tightness there. As the day passed, Moira grew curious about Agnes. She knew not how to approach it, so she just blurted out her question.

"You are Breac's woman?" she asked, darting a glance at Agnes, then staring down at the mending on her lap.

"Aye, Ceanna," Agnes replied softly.

But she said no more than that. She was forced to ask more questions to find out what she wanted to know. "Have you children?"

Agnes put her mending down, and a sad smile lay on her face. "I had children, but they were taken from me . . . Breac and I are too old for that now."

Moira did not understand her answer. "How long have you been married to Breac?" she asked.

"We have not had the blessing of a priest, Ceanna."

'Twas not an unusual occurrence between men and women. Arrangements were made between families, and permission was only needed from their chieftain or village leader. Priests were not always available to those who had not money to pay for them.

Moira found that knowing a little made her want to know more. "And your children? They were not Breac's?" At first, she thought Agnes would not answer, but she did after a few moments.

"My husband decided he did not want me anymore, for he had found a rich woman in our village who wanted him. He put me aside, and when I would not leave, he had me beaten," she said softly. She did not speak of her children, but only of her own fate.

"I beg your pardon, Agnes. I did not mean to . . ." If Agnes had been married, no priest would have blessed her union with Breac while her husband yet lived, no matter the reason, no matter that it was not her doing.

"'Tis many, many years since then, child," she answered, that sad smile back in place. "Breac found me and took me in. I have been with him since."

Moira had seen other women like Agnes during her six-year search that took her all over Scotland and to many of the isles. Only the wishes and desires and needs of men mattered, and women were the ones who bore the burdens. But Moira had grown up in a village and in a family where marriage was the way of things, and her parents had been happy together.

She blinked away the gathering tears and stood to walk around the room again. Nothing could be as it was before. Now, memories of the good kind, times with her mother and father, her sister and brothers all flooded back. She'd managed to keep them all under control from the time she left her aunt's home until just yesterday, but now they overpowered her and burst forth, and she felt emotions she'd long buried.

Her sister Eibhlin had nearly ten years then and loved to run by the sea. Her brothers Cailean and Dòmhnall, the twins, rode as well as their father and were two years older than her and close to manhood. Their betrothals to two girls in the village had just been announced.

She had buried their lives as surely as she'd buried their bodies that day long ago. Now, it seemed important to remember them, to keep them alive in her thoughts and in her heart, where now there seemed to be more room for such things.

Could the Seer be right that living and keeping her family alive in her memories was a better way to avenge their killings than to let them slip off into oblivion? She knew about the lives of her grandparents through the stories told of them by her mother and father. If there was no one to speak of her or her family, the memory of them would die as surely as they had.

Turning back to the woman who sat quietly working, she decided that someone must know about them if she did not live to tell.

"My name is Moira, daughter of Seumas and Grainne of Quinag," she offered quietly. The feeling of speaking of something so personal, so guarded in the past, made her stomach ache.

"Not Ceanna?" Agnes asked.

"Nay, my name is Moira. I only . . ." *became*, she started to say but changed her mind, "used Ceanna because it was too painful to remember."

Agnes looked at her and then stared more at her face. "You are the Moira he searched for?" Moira sat down and nodded. "He was like a madman, searching every room in the keep, checking every woman here, to find you."

"I do not understand why he did that. He has taken many women to his bed and will take many more," she said with a shrug of her shoulders. "It meant nothing."

Agnes offered a smile then, not the sad one from earlier, but a womanly one that spoke of secrets known. "He never asks a woman her name when he beds her. In the years I have served him, he could not tell you the name of one." Agnes brought the fabric to her mouth and bit off the extra thread above the knot. "Only yours."

"But why? What do I offer him that others have not before? Some bed play? A place to bury his prick in and seek a moment or two of pleasure? Any woman can offer him that," Moira admitted.

Then she remembered that spark of something else between them and wondered at it.

"I think that's what bothers him the most. Whatever happened between you two made him realize that the others had not mattered."

"So he but seeks the answer to that and keeps me alive?"

Agnes laughed then, and Moira felt stupid, as though she missed some important detail.

"Oh, child, I do not think he knows what he seeks. And if he knows, he does not admit it to himself or others." Agnes smiled at her then and reached out to touch her arm. "I suspect that you made him question things about himself and his life in a way no one ever did before. I think he *hopes* that you can give him other answers."

"But I know nothing. I have nothing to offer him that he cannot find elsewhere with any other woman," she argued, but Agnes shook her head denying it.

"From what Breac tells me, you know more about Connor than anyone else, save mayhap Diarmid, who shares nothing."

"The Seer," she corrected. "I know only the Seer."

"But if you have put aside your need for vengeance against *the Seer*," she began, "will you be able to help Connor, the man?"

"I will see to his needs," she said, offering the only thing she knew how to do for a man.

Agnes looked as though she had other counsel to offer, but shook her head and stopped for a moment. In that moment, Moira missed her mother so much it stole her breath. There should have been times like this with her mother, who could have answered her questions and guided her in making decisions about her life. Instead she sat here talking with the servant woman of the man responsible for her mother's death.

"When Breac found me and took me in, I thought he only wanted a warm body in his bed and it was all I had to offer him. I was wrong then, and mayhap you are now?"

She would have answered, but the door opened and the very man of whom Agnes spoke entered. She watched as he carried in another tray of food and placed it on the table, and then as he looked first to Agnes and then at her. Agnes met her gaze and smiled, a blush now creeping into the older woman's cheeks and making it very clear to her that there was much more between these two than sharing a bed.

"Come, eat as the Seer ordered," Agnes said, rising from her chair and walking over to the table. Lifting the cloth from the tray of food, she smiled. "He convinced the cook to send you one of his favorite sweets."

Moira walked over to see what the cook had made, when Agnes clutched her hand and pulled her closer.

"You have suffered much more than I did, child. Worry not and give yourself time to heal." Though Moira would like to believe that Agnes spoke of the injuries to her body, she allowed herself to consider that her soul and her heart were more the matter of the woman's advice. With a nod that surprised her, she turned to the tray on the table.

A concoction of golden baked dough, sugared fruits, and cheese lay under the cover, steam still rising from its surface and giving off an aroma that made her mouth water. Breac reached into his pocket and brought out a spoon for her, but there was more here than she could eat alone.

"Are there more spoons here?" she asked, wanting to share this treat with them. "There is enough for the three of us."

She did not miss the glance exchanged between them and did not examine the reasons behind her offer too closely yet. Breac nodded and retrieved two more from the wooden box on the Seer's trunk. Soon, the tasty treat was gone, and her stomach was filled again.

The afternoon moved on, the sun dropped toward the horizon, and Moira waited on the Seer's return to his chambers.

Connor returned to his chambers only to change out of his soiled clothes and into clean ones for Diarmid's table, barely exchanging words with anyone but Breac inside and Ranald, who waited with instructions outside his door. After deciphering the records of his visions for hours, he'd sought some relief by training in the yard with Diarmid's men. Though he never used his skills in battle, he could wield a sword or bow as well as any of Diarmid's warriors and enjoyed stretching his muscles and working out with the men.

The evening meal brought two strangers to Diarmid's table and lasted longer than the evening before. The waning moon showed less than a quarter of its face in the sky this night, warning him of the beginning of the madness that led to the visions. With this month's full moon coming near the end of the month and September's closer to that, it meant that October's full moon would fall on Samhain and the twenty-eighth anniversary of his birth.

He shuddered now at all the connections to the Sith and their history of stealing human bairns and replacing them with changelings, of consorting with human women, of their powers and their gifts and their curses. It was not going to end well—that much he felt in his soul. He did not expect to live through whatever happened and needed to make arrangements for those he was responsible for to see to their safety and care.

It was long after nightfall by the time he returned to his chambers to find the scant light on one lamp and Breac resting in his chair by the door. Rousing him, Connor nodded to him and sent him off to his room.

He spied the remnants of a meal on the table and hoped she'd eaten her fill this day. She needed to regain some flesh on her bones and her strength, and a full belly was the first step.

Walking around the screen, he found Moira asleep on her pallet. He leaned over and tucked the blanket around her shoulders as he passed her on his way to his bed.

After using the water in the basin to clean his face and hands, Connor blew out the lamp, undressed, and climbed into his bed. He settled down to sleep, tired from his work with the sword today, but it eluded him for some time. He'd just closed his eyes when he heard the noise. He shifted in the bed, trying to appear asleep so that he could jump out quickly, when she whispered in the dark.

"Seer?"

He could just make out her form standing next to his bed. Lifting the blankets, he moved over to allow her in beside him. His cock responded, and desire surged in his blood as he felt her naked skin next to his, though not with the desperation that would choke him soon. This was a man desiring a woman, a woman who had just climbed in his bed. Connor smiled in the dark, waiting for her to settle at his side.

"Breac said you trained with Diarmid's men today."

Her soft words startled him then, for it had not been her custom to initiate talk between them. She answered his questions reluctantly or he could goad her into it, but this was something new between them. "Aye, I did." He laughed softly as he turned to face her. "And they pummeled me like the novice I am at swordplay. When there are sometimes weeks between my work with them, I lose strength in my muscles and become winded easily."

There was a hesitation, as though she struggled to find words to say. "I watched you work with his men. You did not look like a novice to me." He laughed once more, trying to determine if she was complimenting him or telling him the truth.

"Breac brought some of the healer's oil. May I ease the pain of your hours of practice before . . . ?"

She did not specify before what, but they both knew how this would end. His cock surged at her words, anxious for any touch she would give, and his voice cracked as he accepted her offer. "Oh, aye," he said.

She slid from the bed, and he heard her moving toward the hearth and back to take something from the table next to his bed. Then she tugged the bedclothes down and out of her way. His cock sprang up.

"Turn over and put your hands under your head," she ordered. He moved quickly and positioned himself as she said.

The oil was hot as she drizzled it along his shoulders and arms and down his back. Not hot enough to be painful, but hot enough to soothe the pulls and strains of overdue exercise. When she used her hands to spread and massage the balm over his skin and into his sore muscles, he swore he let out a groan of pleasure. His cock surged against the bed, waiting for her touch there. But she moved slowly, working her strong hands over his arms and across his shoulders, applying more of the oil to his back.

The soreness from overwork eased in the muscles beneath her touch, but others increased in a different sort of ache he anticipated her soothing later. The strokes down the backs of his thighs and lower legs became stronger, pressing and releasing, moving down along the bones and back up to his arse. She did not ignore that either, her hands rubbing and pressing, relieving the tightness in every place she touched.

His muscles relaxed, and his head spun from her attentions, or maybe from holding his breath as she moved her hands over his skin. Then without a word of warning, she climbed over him, resting on his arse and sliding on the oil she'd rubbed there. Her legs gripped his hips as she reached up and worked the oil into his shoulders.

But all he could focus on was the heat between her legs as she sat over his arse. She lifted, and her legs slid along his hips as she moved. She rested back, and her legs slid once more. It was driving him insane. Just at the moment he decided he could take no more, she ordered him to turn over.

He eased up, letting her ride the movement and his body as he turned until he faced her. The torture increased because now she sat astride his cock. He inhaled deeply and let it out, trying to keep from thrusting into her as she reached over for the bottle of oil and poured it on his chest. Her hands moved over his chest, spreading it up on his shoulders and down onto his belly. Her slippery fingers grazed the head of his cock as it lay caught between their bodies, and he gasped at the sensation.

The smell of the herb-infused oil permeated the air, and he breathed in the scent of it as she teased his nipples and the sensitive skin on his stomach. She moved down until she sat nearer to his ankles and worked more oil into the skin of his thighs. As she poured the oil down the length of his legs, she spilled it over his erect cock and her own thighs, and his cock surged as he thought of the feel of her hands on it.

She massaged his thighs, having him raise each leg so she could encircle it, much as she had his rod that first time. When she'd finished working on each leg, she used the oil to slide her way back up his legs and position herself on his thighs again.

"Where did you learn such things?" he asked, his voice hoarse with desire now.

She did not answer until she wrapped both hands around his cock and spread the oil with her hands and fingers from head to sac. "I stayed with a man who liked such things."

If he'd expected remorse or some softer reaction about it, he should have known better. Moira had whored to live while he'd whored to live well, and he thought that she accepted her life better than he accepted his.

"I like it as well," he whispered as he tried to stay coherent instead of losing himself to it. "Do you?"

"I would please you," was her only response.

He wanted to show her that it could be more than just payment for her food or her clothing or her yet remaining alive in his protection. Connor reached down and held her hips. "Straighten out your legs," he said, guiding her to a different position over him.

When he could reach her legs, he smoothed the oil down her thighs just as she had, mimicking her caressing strokes and hoping to ease the pain in her bad leg, stopping just before he touched the mass of curls at the junction of her thighs and listening to her breathing become affected by his touch. At least she did not try to fake her state of arousal while they did this. He lifted one leg higher to rub down to her feet, and she lost her balance and slid off him completely, losing her grip of his cock. Her body luckily landed in the middle of the bed rather than on the floor. Connor laughed then, for in spite of her seriousness, it was funny and unexpected.

"Will I have to tie you on?" he asked, as he lifted her back over him.

This time, he eased back to sit against the wooden headboard of the bed and moved her closer to him. With his knees raised, he kept her there. Now he retrieved the bottle of oil and poured some on her chest, spreading it first with the back of his hand and feeling her arch against it. He took the tips of her nipples between his finger and thumbs and rolled them until they tightened in his grasp and her body bucked on his. She slid against his cock once, and then twice, and he'd had enough.

Connor lifted her and placed her over his cock; the slipperiness of the oil on their legs and his cock let her settled on him quickly. Once there, she tossed her head back, and he pulled her closer and kissed her face and her neck, gently rubbing his face down and using his tongue along her skin. He wrapped her in his arms; their chests rubbed over each other's, making her nipples harder as she moved against him.

Circling his legs behind and around her, he pushed into her and listened as she exhaled in time with his thrusts. He liked having his hands free, for he could hold the globes of her arse in them and urge her higher, or forward, or faster. She seemed to enjoy the movements, for he felt her woman's channel swell and tighten around him. He leaned away only far enough for him to slide his hand between their bodies and found the part of her that hardened as he did.

She gasped as he touched her there, separating her nether folds and rubbing her until she ached even more. Moira wondered when he would take control over this, and now he had, for he began to move deeper and harder with her, filling her and making her want to reach that mindless moment when all control was lost and only passion existed between them.

In spite of her lingering doubts, in spite of years spent hunting him down, Moira found that his kindness made her question everything she had believed until this moment. He pressed harder, and she released the moan she fought to keep in. He lifted his head then and gave a laugh, a pleasant one that made her want to smile.

This was good between them.

Regardless of all else, this was good.

"Kiss me, Moira," he whispered, as he moved his mouth up her body, kissing and suckling his way over the tops of her breasts, over her neck to her mouth.

She opened to him, and he took her mouth in a heated kiss. He turned his face, tilting back and forth, tasting and touching until she could not breathe on her own. His exhales were hers, his movements were hers, his pleasure was hers.

His prick grew harder within her, filling her more, and she

felt the ripples of her release begin inside. He cursed and then lifted and rolled with her body until he was on top and thrusting relentlessly into her.

Something deep inside tightened and ached and throbbed, and every movement of his flesh against hers teased and tickled until she could only feel it . . . feel him. But the best of it remained just out of her reach. He leaned his head against her shoulder, lifted her hips, and plunged in until he touched her womb.

Withdrawing until she whimpered at the emptiness, he thrust back in forcefully and then out again. He moved faster and harder and deeper against her until she could not breathe, and everything in her came loose. She held on tightly, her arms around his neck as he pushed her to that place she sought, and then farther still.

Her body shuddered and shook as he continued, deep and hard. Her legs tightened and clutched at his, her core felt molten from the friction inside, and the muscles there spasmed around him, bringing on his release, too. He arched into her, and she lost herself and her doubts and her fears to the bliss that filled her body and soul. He emptied into her, and the heat of his release warmed her deepest flesh. A moment later, they both fell back, replete and satisfied.

She could not move, so he did, climbing off the bed, finding something to clean the oil away from their still-slick flesh and then gently wiping her skin until it was removed. After he wiped the rest from his skin, he helped her to the center of the bed and laid next to her in the silence of the night.

"Was that your power?" she asked, when she could put her words and thoughts together again.

"Nay, that was you and me," he replied.

That was her biggest fear now, that he had not only touched and controlled her body just then, but her soul and her heart, and it had come to pass. After years of keeping them separate and safe, she'd begun to lose them to the man, not the Seer, in only a matter of days.

Chapter Fourteen

"He treats her more as leman than criminal," the man explained to Steinar. "She is not chained and lives in his chambers like an honored guest, eating the finest foods, doing no work except servicing the Seer's needs."

"The Seer protects her from Diarmid as well, my lord," said the second one. "When Diarmid wanted to question her last week, he refused to allow it. Diarmid sputtered and yelled and turned red in the face—you know how he does that," he nodded at the others, "and the Seer stood there and refused."

At just that moment, the Seer and his bitch walked out of the keep and waited by the door. He could not see the woman's face, hidden as it was in the hood of her cloak, but everyone in the keep knew that the Seer put his cock in only one woman now, so it had to be her.

"Be gone now; here comes my brother," Steinar said, watching Diarmid's approach. "Gather whatever knowledge you can find and bring it to me," he ordered as they turned heel and left.

"Steinar," Diarmid called out. "I need six of your men to accompany Connor."

"Six men, Diarmid? Where is he going, and when?" Steinar asked. The usual destination was the farm on the south side of the isle, reached easiest by boat. Though Diarmid believed it to be owned by a childhood friend of the Seer, Steinar had discovered that Connor bought the land and paid for the buildings and cattle and animals to stock it, in truth making it his though it was held under another's name. "And for how long?"

"Wherever he tells them to go and for however long it takes," Diarmid barked back at him. "And when I give you an order, brother, 'tis not your duty to question the reasons for it."

Tired of being the one who carried out every whim or wish of the damned Seer, Steinar crossed his arms over his chest and shook his head. "You let your pet order you around as though he was lord here," he snarled. "Who is the master, and who is the whore?"

'Twas a mistake to allow his anger to gain control of his words, for Steinar never saw the punch coming. One moment he insulted Diarmid, and the next he lay in the dirt with Diarmid standing over him. Hatred surged through his veins as he climbed to his feet and brushed the dirt from his back.

"Six men. Now," Diarmid repeated, never even waiting this time for Steinar to acknowledge the order, for he spat on the ground and walked away. "As long as he serves me faithfully, I will humor his requests," he called back to him.

Steinar nodded to the man who stood as his second in command. Though Steinar's company of fighting men was a quarter of the size of Diarmid's, he would gamble his life that they were better and stronger than any Diarmid would put in battle.

"Godrod," he said. "My brother wishes to have six of my men escort the Seer this day. Choose the others and lead them yourself."

Godrod bowed and would have walked away to carry out

the orders, had he not stopped him with a hand on his arm. "If the opportunity comes, take it," he said, meeting the soldier's gaze. "At whatever the cost."

The man nodded in understanding and ran off to gather the others needed. Steinar trusted that Godrod would never do anything that could be traced back to him, but he knew that if the situation was right, he would do what was necessary.

Steinar remained to watch the Seer approach Godrod and explain his task to him. The soldier took two of the men and left ahead of the others, while the Seer mounted a horse, pulled the woman up behind him, and followed the others out of the gate.

Godrod would give him a full reporting when they met that night, so in a short time, he would know more than Diarmid did about the Seer's plans this day. In the meantime, he needed to speak to the men Diarmid had invited here for next week's visions and plant some seeds of mistrust there for his use later.

Connor held her tightly, gathering her arms around his waist and controlling the horse with his legs. Other than the cloak and her gown, there was nothing between them as they rode out of the gate and away from the keep. He'd paid Ranald an exorbitant amount of gold to aid his efforts in getting Diarmid's permission for this outing. Feigning the madness that was usual right after the new moon, with its shows of temper and anger, worked well even when he did not feel such things now.

When he'd returned to his chambers two days before and found her standing on the table that she'd pushed over against the wall so that she could look out the small, high window at the sun and the sea, he knew he must find a way to get her outside before she broke her other leg or worse. The plan this day came about from a casual comment Agnes made, revealing that she knew more about Moira than he did.

He'd been surprised to discover that she'd entrusted her

true name and origin to Agnes. Moira had told Agnes about living near the sea and her love of being outside in the cool, salty air. From the maps he'd found in Diarmid's collection, he knew that Quinag was a hilly peninsula far in the northwest of the Scottish mainland.

Now, they rode to a small inlet that he'd found a few miles away from the keep when he first arrived here. Other than the sea, there was only one path into it, and it was surrounded by the high cliff walls. A perfect place for so many things. It faced the south, so today's sunlight should warm the small beach and the shallow waters caught there on low tide. Squinting up at the sun's position, he estimated their arrival there as the tide was at its lowest.

She shimmied closer to him, cinching her arms tightly around him, afraid, she'd finally admitted, of riding on horses. Boats she did not fear. Carts or wagons, neither. But getting her onto the horse's back just now had taken cajoling and pleading and a bit of threatening, too. He did not expect a smile from her, but he knew that her expression would lighten when she saw their destination.

They climbed into the hills and rode south until he could see the edge of the cliffs ahead of them. With a nod to the guards ahead, he guided the horse to the trail that led down to the beach. He heard her gasp as they made their way down the steep path, but soon they reached the bottom and it leveled out. Connor felt her head buried against his back and waited for Godrod and his men to finish searching for anyone or anything dangerous to him. Once the soldiers followed the path away and left them alone, he reached back to loosen her grasp.

"You are cutting off my breath, Moira. You can let go now."

He managed to ease her hold enough to lift his leg up and over and slide off the horse. He took hold of her hands and pulled her off and into his arms.

"Open your eyes and see where we are," he said.

He watched her face as she did as he told her. He held her facing the sea, and she turned in his embrace, taking in the water and the beach and the cliffs behind them.

"We are alone? Where are the soldiers?" she asked.

"Godrod and the others wait above for us. We have until the tide turns, which should be in about three hours."

She almost smiled then; he watched as she caught herself and nodded at him instead. He sensed it was close for her, but she still kept up her guard in the light of day. Today, with the outing and the information he had to share with her, he hoped that would change.

He took off the leather sack he carried under his arm and tossed it on the ground. Then he lifted the wineskin from around her and threw it there too. Next, he tossed his cloak to form a covering for them to sit on and to keep the rough, large-grained sand off them. Connor turned and tugged the laces of her cloak and lifted it from her shoulders.

"Go. Walk a bit," he ordered, knowing that this small inlet was at least four times the length of his chambers and would give her plenty of space to enjoy.

She looked at him and then at the expanse of beach before her, and she ran, hesitantly at first and then with more speed, down to the water's edge and then along it to the point where the cliffs met the water. The sun glinted off the honey-colored streaks in her hair, and he thought he could see her smile after all. If only it was for him and not this small kindness that he could do for her.

Connor took the reins of the horse's bridle and tugged him along until he got to the growth of trees in the corner of the cliff walls. Tying the reins, he left the horse to graze on the only patch of grass there while he opened the sacks and took out his bounty of food and wine and maps.

The time here was actually just a bluff to give them a

chance to speak away from the keep, where every word and action were observed and reported back to Diarmid or his brother. Even if they were watched from above by Godrod and his men, their conversation would be private. Other than Breac and Agnes, or Dara or Pol when they visited, he trusted no one.

So, he'd put on a farce for them these last few days, imitating his behavior of the last several months when the dizzying need for women struck him and his body and temper raged from the level of lust in his blood. Instead, he felt calmer than he had in almost half a year, and when his blood began to heat, coupling with Moira soothed it.

Strange that no other woman or no amount of women had ever been able to calm the effects of the power building within him before, but taking her to his bed and having her when the need began took away the fierceness and terrible pain and fury that usually plagued him until the full moon and the vision.

Stranger still, bringing her to her release without using his power brought him the satisfaction he thought he'd only dreamed those months ago. A brief moment of the scent used as a means to intensify their joining worked, but more than that interfered with the bond that happened between them and with the feeling of rightness he experienced when reaching his release while planted deep inside her. So far, since she'd not refused him, he'd not put his belief to the test.

Connor walked to the water's edge and watched as Moira walked back and forth from cliffs to water over and over again, making him dizzy just watching her. After ten or more times, she finally noticed him and came running back to him. And better still, she did smile.

"This is a beautiful place," she said, looking around at the beach and the sea. "How did you find it?"

He motioned to his cloak, and he helped her to sit on it.

Handing her the skin of wine, he waited as she drank from it and then took a mouthful, too.

"When I first arrived at Diarmid's keep, I had great freedom to come and go and to roam as much as I wanted," he explained. "Well, as long as my lessons were done first and any work Diarmid wanted seen to. Then I would take a horse and ride and walk for hours. I found this from above and studied the tides and the pattern of them and came here often."

She stared up at him for a moment and then nodded. "So you bring your women here?" she asked. The even tone spoke of no judgment or censure for the behavior, in her eyes—just acceptance.

Damn her! The anger flared quickly, but he was able to put it back before striking out. "You are the first woman—actually the only person—I have ever brought here, Moira," he explained.

Her eyes darkened then, and he wondered what she was thinking. Sometimes she would fall back into the silence of their first days, and he believed that memories plagued her from her past in those moments. But there were other times, like this one, when she seemed to be considering her place with him. Her question was a direct one, when she did speak.

"Did you bring me here to couple?" she asked, reaching for the laces on her gown. "Is that what you wish to do now?" She would be undressed if he did not stop her.

"That would be pleasing, Moira. Anytime I can have you naked in my arms is pleasing, but not now. I brought you here so that we can talk."

She'd rather swive him or pleasure him in some other way, if it was her choice, she thought, as she looked out over the sea again. Talking to him or about him made her think about things she'd rather ignore or dream of things she would never have. So pleasure and mindless passion were safer paths to take.

But, she could only imagine what he'd gone through to arrange this outing, so if he wanted to talk, she would talk.

Moira watched the set of his mouth and the way he clenched his hands and released them, and knew he wished to speak about her. Sighing, she waited, impatiently, for him to begin. When he closed his eyes and shook his head, she worried that it was bad news he had to share.

"I have been searching in Diarmid's collection for the records of my visions," he said.

Of all the things she'd thought of, that was not one of them. "Records? He keeps records?"

"Ranald does. Each month he writes down Diarmid's version of what happened and the names of the people involved. I had never seen them until last week," he said.

She watched as he opened the leather sack he'd brought and took out several sheets of parchment and a scroll. He held them out to her and then must have remembered that she could not read, because he pulled them back. "What do they say?"

He began to read some of the dates, some of them within months of her family's massacre and others well after. He read out names of men, bits of wording that his visions revealed, instructions given in that very formal, almost musical rhythm he used when he was in the power of the visions. She recognized it, even if he did not. Finally, he pointed to a place on the parchment that meant nothing to her until he uttered the words that chilled her blood.

"I think that this is the vision that led to your family's deaths."

The sound of her own breathing grew louder and more frantic in her ears, and the blood pounded in her head and behind her eyes, until she grew dizzy from it. The air became heavy, weighing down on her until she felt herself falling back into the blackness.

The shadow over her moved, allowing the sunshine to touch her face for a moment or two. Then the cold water on her cheeks woke her from her stupor. The Seer helped her to sit up, but he sat behind her, supporting her so she would not fall again.

"Drink this," he said, holding the skin to her lips and lifting it to pour some of the potent wine into her mouth. After three mouthfuls, he took it away. His voice was calm, but she felt his heart race as she leaned against his chest. He still held the parchment sheets in his hand, and Moira decided that hearing the rest of it sooner was better than waiting too much longer for it.

"What did it say? How do you know it is my family?" she asked. She'd told him nothing other than her name, so she could not understand what link there could be in these papers to her family?

She closed her eyes as she remembered telling Agnes her name and that of her parents and their village. Had Agnes told the Seer? Glancing now at the parchments he held, she knew the servant must have reported her words to her master.

"You talk in your sleep, Moira. You yell and you laugh and you cry out about your family when you dream of them," he said softly. "I but listened and searched for what I'd heard in the dark of the nights we've shared."

"Agnes knew," she whispered.

"Did she?" he asked. She wondered if her words would cause trouble for the woman who'd comforted her when she needed it most. "I am glad you confided in her, though I wish it had been me." His gaze softened as she turned to look at him. He sounded wounded in some way by her choice to tell Agnes and not him. "She will keep your counsel well if you have need of her."

Moira wanted to explain how it had happened that day. How the past had poured out of her and how Agnes had shared something about her own past. But something kept her from doing that.

"Do you want me to read the part about that vision?"

She nodded and tried to steady herself for whatever terrible thing this parchment said about her family. He moved it over so he could see it in front of them and began.

"It is the spring of the year 1092," he read. "The visions grow stronger, and Connor cannot yet understand or control them. Today he gifted Skurli from Caithness, who was betrayed by an enemy in Quinag in the north of Scotland. In exchange for his support, Diarmid sent his men north to aid Skurli and help to settle his affairs."

She could not breathe. His words stopped, but the echoes filled her head and the pain of it burned through her. Could that be how it happened?

"Shhh, now," he whispered from behind her, wrapping both arms around her and rocking her gently.

"Then it is true?" she asked, when she could speak. "You gave this Skurli the directions on how to wipe out my family?"

" 'Twas not like that, Moira. I do not remember the vision or the words or the person the power decides to gift. I could not control it then; I cannot control it now the way I would like to."

She pushed out of his embrace then and climbed to her feet. "And that absolves you of their deaths? If you had not . . . if you had . . ."

She shook her head in confusion and walked away. Too many words, too many thoughts and feelings filled her head now, and she would regret or pay for anything she said right now, so she walked. When she reached the end of the inlet and the water crashed up against the thin edge of cliff that sat out farther toward the sea, she stood there and stared out at the dark blue waters and the painfully bright sky.

How much time had passed she knew not, but then he

stood next to her, staring out at the same sea and sky without saying a word. She knew what he wanted. She knew what he'd hoped she would say when he explained the terrible thing to her, but her heart did not have it in it to offer to him. Her hatred of him had fled in these last weeks, along with her need to kill him to avenge their deaths, but there was no place in her heart for forgiveness.

He needed her to say it. Before these visions brought about his end, he needed forgiveness for the terrible cost paid by others for his gift. 'Twas as though her word could give him the peace he sought, not of body, but of soul and mind. But he could read on her face that she could not forgive him for his misguided acts of the past. At least not until one or both of them was dead.

Connor stood there, praying for a word he would not hear, until he could not wait any longer. Turning away, he watched the birds landing on the highest part of the cliff face and then flying off over the sea in search of food.

He'd been wrong again and misjudged her. Thinking that she would accept the explanation offered in the notes and understand he had no choice in the matter, he'd shared what he had found with her. With her, he would pay for the sins of his past forever.

Connor walked back to the place where his cloak lay spread on the sand and sat down once more. She remained unmoving at the water's edge, staring out at the sea as though she would discover something there she needed. An hour passed before she came back into herself and turned to see where he was. The tide, which had remained low, now changed directions, and the shallow pool filled with water more quickly.

When she reached him, he stood and held out a small meat pie the cook had packed for him. At first she began to refuse it, but she finally accepted it and his help to sit on the cloak. The painful silence grew, and he saw that she struggled to chew and swallow the food, so he got to his feet and walked toward the cliffs to give her some peace. Leaning against the rocky wall, he watched as she finished the pie and drank some of the wine. Some minutes later, she turned and faced him as though to speak to him, but instead she began screaming.

"Connor!" she shrieked, as she climbed to her feet and began to run toward him. "Get back!"

Not understanding her warning, he began to walk to her, but she reached him first and pushed him into the wall. The boulder crashed down in the spot where he'd been standing before she screamed out his name. He heard the sounds of a struggle above, and he searched for the origin of it on the top of the cliff. Godrod's voice rang out in warning, calling out to his men and then the body of one of the soldiers fell from the edge and crashed onto the beach in front of them.

Moira stifled the scream that threatened before it escaped, covering her mouth with her hands while trying to catch her breath. "Come," he said, taking her and holding her under the cover and the protection of the sheer cliff wall. If he could not see over the edge of it, someone could not see them tucked in at its base. They waited in silence for some sign of what had happened above to the other soldiers.

The advantage to having but one way onto this stretch of beach was its coveted privacy. The disadvantage, he now discovered, was that, if under attack, there was no other way out. And, in a few hours, the sea would cover the entire inlet as the tide reached its full height trapping and drowning anyone caught here too long.

He kept her in his embrace during those dark minutes as they waited, but he could feel a widening expanse opening between them with each passing minute. Then, Godrod rode onto the beach and ordered them to mount and ride back to the keep.

Connor picked up the leather sack, putting away the parchments and scroll, something he'd not shown her yet, and tossed the uneaten food to the seabirds careening between cliff and sea as he gathered the reins of the horse in his hand. Grabbing the horse's mane, he heaved himself onto its back and held out his hand to Moira.

The sadness in her gaze tore his heart in two as she glanced up at him in taking his hand. With her foot resting on his, he pulled her up behind him and, once she settled and grabbed hold of him, he urged the horse up the path. Godrod followed, leaving the body of the dead soldier there.

"Another attempt on your life, Seer," Godrod explained. "I had two new soldiers in my company who asked to attend you. They stood watch on the edge, but one managed to loosen the boulder and send it over the edge while the other covered his actions."

"The one on the beach?" he asked.

"He pushed the boulder over. Thank God, you were warned before it hit you," the soldier said. The good wishes did not ring true in his voice, and his eyes told another tale. "The other fled, but my men are pursuing him now. Worry not, we will catch him."

He felt her shudder behind him, and he tugged her arms tighter around him as he touched the horse's sides and urged him to gallop. Godrod had been lying, Connor was certain of it. The soldier who fled would be killed when caught to cover up Godrod's own attempts to assassinate them on the beach. Until the other man was caught—and he must be caught before he could spread the news to Diarmid that his brother's men tried to kill the Seer—there was a small measure of safety for him and Moira.

Accepting no attempts to slow them down, Connor gave the horse his head and raced back to the keep.

Chapter Fifteen

That night took years to pass.

Or so it seemed to him.

The edginess returned in his mind, and he felt the fire begin to burn in his blood. 'Twas five days past the new moon, and any soothing effects from coupling with her wore off quickly in the face of their estrangement the previous day. By the time Diarmid released him from attendance in the hall, a performance commanded at each evening meal now, he felt as though his skin were on fire from the inside out.

Breac and Agnes retired for the night, and Moira lay on her pallet, again not climbing into his bed as she had those other nights. They'd spoken very little since their return from the debacle on the beach, for he saw her to his chambers and faced Diarmid's wrath alone. Unsure of how she would react to Diarmid now that she knew his soldiers had come to Quinag to help Skurli destroy his enemy—apparently her father—he thought it best to keep them apart.

Steinar gave some excuses about the attack, which Diarmid seemed suspicious of until Godrod appeared with the second man's head on his sword and appeased Diarmid. But when Diarmid pointed out that he had been against the idea of his

Seer leaving the safety of the keep with his slut, Connor wondered who was truly behind the attack and if it was simply a message to him to obey his lord. Two nights later, he was no closer to finding out the truth.

He lay on his bed, pulling the blankets up and then kicking them down. He turned on his stomach, but that made him remember the way she'd stroked him with her hands covered in warm, fragrant oil, which had become something else between them. He flung himself on his back, but he could still see her face as she'd climbed over his hips and seated him full and deep within her.

A cup of wine did nothing to soothe him. A second cup did not help. Tempted to search for the healer's concoction in his trunk, he cursed and went back to bed. Whatever was between them had held this at bay for four days, but now that it crashed into him from all sides, it felt worse than he'd ever remembered it to be. Ten days remained until the vision, and he knew he could not make it.

At first, while thinking coherently, he understood why she did not come to him. He had brought back the horror of her family's death to her by showing her those parchments and by reading the report of that vision six years ago to her. Only a madwoman would willingly give herself to the man guilty of his sin.

Though she was many things, mad was not one of them.

Later, as the pain pulsed inside and the crazy lust filled his blood, he did not care what her reasons were. He knew she was awake and could hear his torment.

Connor tossed for another hour or two before giving up. He pulled on his trews and threw on his cloak and sought refuge or relief on the walls above. He walked the perimeter of the battlements several times without stopping. A storm brewed in the night's sky, loosening the winds and torrents of rain, but it did not stop him. The guards took shelter in the corner towers, but he stood in the middle of it and faced the angry sky. Lightning crashed through the sky, lighting up the stone wall and sending the guards running.

He dared it to strike him. Standing in the rain, he tossed his cloak to the ground and opened his arms up wide, calling down the lightning. It struck a small building in the yard, sending showers of sparks into the storm. He waited, turning his face up to the sky and trying to draw it to him.

It would be a quicker end than the one facing him. Instead of burning out, blind and insane from the pain over these next several months, his end would come in a flash. The lightning crashed again and lit the battlements again and revealed her presence to him.

She walked to him and stood in front of him, with no cloak to keep the rain from her skin or her hair or the thin shift she wore. The rain soaked through it in only moments and plastered it to her skin with so tight a hold that not even the wild winds tearing around them could loosen it. She took his hand and tried to make him follow her, but he shook free of her grasp and stayed in the storm.

"Seer," she called out to him over the thunder and the pounding of the rain. "You must come inside."

"Leave me be!" he yelled back. He prayed again that the lightning would do its worst, but it touched him not.

"Let me ease your pain," she offered, reaching out to touch his cheek. The rain poured down on both of them as he watched her gesture.

"I do not want your kindness," he spat. Right now he wanted only his death.

"'Tis all I can offer you, Seer."

Even that hurt him. Yesterday she screamed out his name, but now she called him that damned title once more. "My name is Connor."

"I offer you only what I have to give, Seer."

He fell to his knees before her and wrapped his arms around her waist. "Forgive me, Moira. I need your forgiveness." He leaned his head against her chest and felt the burning of tears though they were lost among the raindrops.

She leaned her cheek against his hair, stroking it and pushing it out of his face. "I have none to give, Connor," she said sadly.

He held her like that for minutes while the storm raged around them. Neither one moved; each was lost in their own pain. Then, he climbed to his feet, gathered her in his arms, and carried her down the stairs and back to his chambers. He closed the door and put her on her feet in the middle of the room. He pulled the top sheet from his bed, stripped the soaked shift from her, and used the sheet to dry her skin before she took a chill. He dropped his trews and dragged them over his skin to do the same.

Then he kissed her. He tilted his head down and touched his lips to hers gently, softly, completely. She opened to him, and he slipped his tongue inside, searching for hers. When she touched hers to his, he suckled on the tip of it and wrapped his arms around her, holding her close. He walked her across the chambers, taking a step forward for every step she took back, until they reached the wall. Lifting her once more, he placed her on his bed and followed her down until he covered her with his body.

This time was different. This time they needed something other than hard and deep and fast. This time, their souls searched for something in the joining of their bodies. Connor lifted up and began to kiss every inch of her, gliding down over her breasts and stomach and hips and mons and thighs. He touched her and brought her to release, but neither made a sound.

It was quiet. It was gentle. It was about giving and not simply taking.

And when his body pushed hers over the edge and she fell,

she took him with her. Moira opened her body to him, and he emptied himself into her and accepted what she could give him. She offered kindness, and he took it, praying that there would be space in her new heart for forgiveness before it was too late for him.

"I wanted to die."

Her voice was almost a whisper in his ear as they lay together in his bed. The storm raged outside with a growing violence, but it no longer held power over him. Nor did the rampant need for her, for her gentle touch had soothed his body and soul.

"When?"

"When Diarmid's men . . ." Her voice dropped off, but he needed no more words to explain. Then he felt her shake her head. "I accepted that I would die when I tried to kill you," she explained. "I wanted to die after . . ."

"By the time I brought you back here, something had changed," he said. He'd felt some difference in her, and even Dara remarked on it in her messages to him.

Moira turned to face him now. "I still only wanted to live long enough to kill you."

Connor laughed then. Only Moira would have the boldness or lack of fear to say such a thing. Every other woman bowed and scraped or begged to be in his bed or to share in his wealth and position, but not her. He thought on her words and realized when her change of heart happened.

"On the battlements," he said. "When Breac held you over the side." He met her gaze then. "When faced with it, you knew you wanted to live."

She lay silent for a few minutes, and he thought her asleep, when she spoke again.

"How did Breac come to be in your service? And Agnes?"

"You have won them over, Moira. They regularly reprimand

me for various or imagined slights to you. Agnes suggested that I take you outside," he paused and shook his head, "well-intended, though the result was not what I'd planned for us." He thought about his true hope for the morning at the inlet and shook his head.

"About Breac and Agnes?" she reminded him. Her curiosity was a good sign to him. She was beginning to care about things . . . and people.

"About five years or so ago, I met Breac in the village. They'd just arrived from An t-Oban Latharnach across the firth, and some of the villagers were harassing him for having brought such an old woman with him. Breac took down the two largest of them, and the rest gave him a wider berth. I offered him employment."

"Why? 'Twould seem to most that a man who fights simply over a woman is hot tempered and unreliable," she said.

"Ah, but you saw neither the look in his eyes when she comforted him over his bruises, nor hers when he called the villagers out for their words. It nearly broke my heart at seeing such a love."

It sounded so love struck when he said it, but having never seen such a thing, he'd been intrigued by it. A man and woman who loved so strongly it shone from their eyes. Maybe he simply sensed that he needed them to tether him to a real world while he lived in his made-up one. His world was filled with power and visions, but nothing and no one there could be trusted.

"And Dara and Pol?" she asked.

"Something similar." He'd saved them from exile when they had incurred Diarmid's anger over a small incident that did not deserve such treatment. Connor had never realized that he'd surrounded himself, when he could, with people who understood the importance of love. Ironic, when he considered that he'd never found it for himself. Again, there was another few minutes of silence, and he listened to her breathing grow slower and deeper.

"Do you have sons?" she asked.

"Why do you ask that?" He shifted so he could see her face in the light of the lone candle left burning in the room.

"When a man beds women in the numbers that you do, Seer, bairns usually would follow." Aye, indeed bairns would follow, he thought, if he was a normal man.

"I have no sons, nor daughters either, to my knowledge," he said. "Mayhap another part of the Sith's contrariness for those humans they touch with their power? Give them the drive and the opportunities to create bairns but not the ability? This is less like a gift and more like a curse with the passing of every day." He reached out and caressed her cheek. "And you? No bairns of your own?"

"That I would leave behind while searching for you?" she asked. "Fate has been kind not to grant me bairns, for I will not live to see them grow." He winced at her words. Such hopelessness, but it was a hopelessness he was beginning to understand himself when now facing his own demise.

"I suspect that your wish to see me dead for my sins is not long in coming, Moira." He'd not confided his fears to anyone, and yet he handed the worst one to his enemy.

She sat up then, surprised by his words, and turned to face him.

"Do you plan to throw yourself off the walls then?"

He frowned at her words. "Do you wish to be free of me that much?"

"No. For your death simply brings mine sooner, Seer."

"You called me Connor on the wall," he said, reminding her of her slip.

"A moment of weakness. Why do you think your death is at hand?" Of all the things he could say, that was not the one she expected. "Or do you think that Steinar's assassins will complete their task?" He was out of the bed within moments, standing and staring at her as though she was mad. She shook her head at his lack of knowledge.

"How have you managed to stay alive this long, Seer?" Moira slid to the side of the bed and pulled her shift on. "You have not seen the patterns surrounding your visions. You have not seen the patterns surrounding the attacks on you."

His expression showed he agreed with her. From what she'd seen of his life this last month when close enough to see it clearly, his only concern was surviving the pain and lust the visions brought on . . . and the blindness. They were crucial things to worry on, and she was certain that Steinar counted on those distractions to hide his attempts even better.

The Seer walked around the screen and came back a few minutes later with two cups, wine by the smell of it. He handed one to her and sat on the edge of the bed.

"Tell me of the patterns you see, Moira." His voice was calm and his gaze intent on her.

"Ask yourself this question: who will benefit the most from your death? Not Diarmid, for he sells your services to those willing to pay and keeping you alive keeps him strong and held in high esteem by those who pledge to him. Not those who receive the gift, for they have come to you with a need and you fill it. So, that leaves Steinar, who is so filled with hatred at growing to manhood in Diarmid's shadow, yet is not strong enough to unseat him."

He stared at her in silence so long she thought he was asleep on his feet. Then he shook his head in denial. "You see this?" He laughed a bitter one. "And yet they call me the Seer."

"But I have been seeking to learn everything about you since almost the beginning," she said, drawing her legs up under her. "And I learned to listen."

"And not talk," he finished her words.

"I have stayed alive by watching and listening and being ready to act when the moment comes."

A mischievous glint crept into his dark green eyes then. "So why was I not dead those months ago when I discovered you at my door?"

She shrugged. "I was not ready." The narrowing of his gaze spoke of his disbelief in her words. "I came hoping to get a look at your chambers before the next vision and never expected to find you here alone. My dagger," she paused as he touched his chest where a small puckered scar marked the spot, "was still in my sack."

He drank from his cup and watched her over the rim. "And the next time? Why did you not strike the killing blow?" His face went blank as he asked. "You had me at your mercy then. Why did you not finish your quest?"

It had plagued him for months: She'd forced him to the floor and disabled him with the first strike and her kicks. She had stabbed him once, but not a fatal blow. Then she had hesitated.

"Killing you was not as easy as I thought it would be when I planned it," she admitted. "I was ready, but I hesitated in that lost moment. Then you opened your eyes . . ." She could not control the shudder at the memory of what she had seen in his eyes when the visions burned through them.

"Did you scream? I think I remember hearing a scream," he asked.

"Aye."

She trembled again. No one should ever see the power that flowed out of him when he was controlled by the visions. She shook her head to rid herself of the terrible things she had seen deep in his eyes. She'd wanted to make certain he recognized the identity of the one who inflicted the death blow, to make his last thoughts of the vengeance she sought, and instead she'd found herself being pulled down into the depths of hell.

"Can you feel the fires burning there?" She had her own questions that she'd not dared to ask, until now.

"Yes." He turned away then and walked to the hearth. "It burns without destroying. The pain is like holding your hand over an open flame, but it just goes on and on." He began to reach his hand out toward the banked fire and stopped. "But that is not all of it."

Moira followed him across the chamber. "The other? The lust that fills your blood? It causes pain?" she asked. Lust unfulfilled was like skin that itched without relief. It was not comfortable, but it could not kill you. But what she'd witnessed and heard him suffer was more than that.

He faced her then, his expression grim as he explained the visions to her.

"Once the moon passes through its darkest phase, the lust begins, flowing and pulsing in my blood, something that cannot be denied or ignored. I have tried to, but the pain increases until I feel as though my head is in a vice, ever tightening, without relief. I feel as though my skin and cock are burning from the inside out, and I cannot think about anything but finding a woman and fucking until the lust is satisfied."

"Does it help? Do you need to tup a certain number of times or different women to gain relief?" Though she'd heard some tales about his sexual prowess, stories of this part of it had never been told.

Connor looked at her as though she'd spoken in a strange tongue and then shook his head. "At first . . ." he began.

"Has it not always been so?" she asked. "From the beginning?"

"Nay, at the beginning I could have women when I wanted them. If I did or did not, it mattered not to the power that controls me. The visions grew stronger, and my appeal to women grew."

She laughed then; it surprised both of them. "Those touched by the Sith share in their extraordinary beauty," she said. "Everyone knows that." His body and face were blessed by the Sith: the light coloring of his hair, the strange coloring of his eyes, and the glow of his skin all bespoke the magic and vitality of the otherworldly beings.

"Well, women came to me or I called them as I learned the way, but my bed was never empty."

That much, she'd heard . . . over and over as the tale of his male beauty and virility and body spread throughout the Highlands and isles. A man who could make a woman weep in pleasure, he was called. No woman could refuse, nor would she want to, for to be taken to his bed and loved by him was too much pleasure to bear. Stories spun from a figment of truth into the thing of legends, but she knew the truth from the fancy.

Passion? Pleasure? Desire? Surely there was plenty of those in his bed, but love, she knew, did not enter into this matter at all. Thinking on it distracted her from her purpose now. She needed to know why he thought he would die soon. From his words, he did not think Steinar's plot would bring it about. Nay, he was convinced that the gift would end it.

"The pain? It has been there since the beginning then?"

She wanted to understand what made him the Seer and all that meant. Some part of her looked for a reason to explain his responsibility in the events caused by his gift.

He turned and rubbed his face. He did that when he was tired, spreading his large hands out to cover his face and then sliding them back through his hair. Then he stared at her as though searching for something on her face or in her eyes. The Seer walked closer until she could feel his breath on her face and the heat of his skin. Was talking over then, in favor of tupping?

He took her by the arms and pulled her to him, still staring at her as though trying to decide whether to tell her something or take her to his bed another time. The lightning and thunder crashed outside, shaking the walls of the keep, and he yet held her so.

"No one knows what has been happening to me. Diarmid suspects something but cannot catch me in a lie or prove it. Ranald sees part, but I pay him well for his silence in this. You know the most, having seen it twice," he revealed in a voice so low she struggled to hear his words.

"Not even Breac or Agnes know it all. But I need to tell someone, and I think it must be you," he whispered in a voice filled with need and desperation.

"What is it, Seer? What does no one know?"

"I believe that my final vision will be on Samhain, the end of seven years of visions, and that I will not survive the price the visions demand."

Chapter Sixteen

Connor released her and moved away. Though not the burning edge of desire, a restlessness filled his mind, and he tried to calm himself from it. He had so many things to tell her and explain and discuss that he did not know where to begin. He only knew that he could trust her.

Moira had saved him twice now: once on the beach when she warned him—nay knocked him aside from the boulder's path—and then again tonight on the wall when he'd lost his desire to live and was tempted to put an end to it all. She'd caught him just in time before the despair and pain overwhelmed him.

Though if what he suspected to be coming, a quick fall or the strike by a bolt of lightning might be the easier way.

Nay, there were things he must accomplish before he let the gift burn him out. Planning to be done and reparations to be made for his sins, both those intentional and the ones not of his choice. Most of those involved the woman standing before him—one who had started out his enemy, but whom he believed was now much more than that.

Connor lifted her and carried her to the bed, climbing onto it and placing her across his lap. Her body brought warmth to his; the thoughts of his impending death chilled his flesh. The thought of dying unforgiven chilled his very soul.

"How do you know this?" she whispered to him. Even if she denied it, there was concern in her voice, not just the curiosity he'd recognized before.

"For almost the last year, the visions have become a curse. The first six years, I had no pain, no burning, no uncontrollable urges, and especially no blindness after the visions. Then the month after Samhain was observed, the other things came in tandem with the visions."

He shifted her to sit next to him and pulled the blankets over their legs. The storm's coldness permeated even the stone walls now.

"At first, they were mild, and I even wondered if I'd experienced them at all. I mean, 'tis not unusual for a man in his prime, one unmarried and not having access to the constancy of a wife in his bed, to want more sex one time or another."

Her left eyebrow arched, and he smiled. She was becoming playful and had smiled at least twice tonight and then this. Did she notice it as he did? The urge to touch his mouth there grew.

"Then the blindness began, and as each vision grew in strength and clarity, my own vision suffered. At first, it felt as though I was looking out at night—the shadows covered my sight. Then month after month, the damage has been worse—the blindness lasted twice as long this time as it had the time before. If it increases like that this month and then again next, I will spend every hour of every day blind."

"Blind is not dead," she said. "Even if you lose your sight, you may still have the visions. Do not despair yet," she advised.

"But what if the visions disappear with my sight? What if the gift burns out when my eyes do and I am left with neither?"

That was his biggest fear now: to become a blind, worthless

man in Diarmid's keep was a death sentence. Anyone who held no value to him was discarded, exiled, even killed, and no one would stand in his defense.

"Again," his practical Moira said, "blind is not dead."

"You lived here. Think of anyone here in Diarmid's keep, from sheepherder to the highest in his command, and tell me of one who is impaired. One who is less than able to carry out his duties. Blindness is a death sentence."

Connor leaned his back against the headboard and closed his eyes. There was something more, but he was not certain he could explain it to her. More a feeling, an effect of the visions, that foretold him of death after the final vision. Would she believe him foolish for being convinced by only a feeling, rather than facts he could see or hear?

"Moira, my heart stops when the visions cease. And I believe that when the final vision ceases, there will be no power within me to start it anew."

She could not help herself; she reached out and touched his chest and laid her hand over his heart. It beat strong under her palm, and she felt it for a few moments before meeting his gaze again.

"Have you heard of such a thing, or do I worry for naught?" he asked.

She'd not lied to him yet—not through their time together, in good or bad circumstances, even when she hated him and would have liked to. She'd spoken the truth to him. Now, for the first time she wanted with all her damaged and torn heart to lie.

So deep in thought, she never saw his hand move, so his touch surprised her. He gently slid his finger across her cheek and held it for her to see. Tears. Closing her eyes, she fought them, but her throat burned and her eyes filled with them until they spilled over onto her cheeks and could not be hidden from him.

"You cry for me?" he asked. "After everything you have suffered because of me, you can find tears to shed for me?"

Moira tried to wipe them away, to keep him from realizing what she had that day on the beach. No matter how much she wanted to hate him, she could not. No matter that his words caused events to happen that killed her family. No matter that she sought vengeance against him for most of her life.

He was not to blame.

She shook her head, denying the thought to herself so she could deny it to him. Her heart had searched for too long for the one responsible for her loss. She'd given up everything— her life, her chance to live, her future—to hunt him down, to find his weaknesses, and to kill him. Could she banish all the hatred that had colored her world, her existence, for these last six years now?

From the tears, it would seem that part of her already had.

"So, 'tis true then? What I suspect?"

She inhaled, but her chest trembled and her breath hitched in spite of trying to appear calm. "I do not know this to be true . . ."

"But you have heard? Come now, be the fearless Moira who pummeled me to the floor, but not this Moira with fear written in her eyes. 'Tis not your fate we discuss, but that of your captor, the man who destroyed your family."

If he'd said those words hours or days ago, they may have worked, but now, now that she had faced losing him twice and knew that her empty heart felt fear of such a loss, Moira knew there was no turning away.

"So, Moira the fearless, Moira the avenger, tell me what you know," he said softly. "I would be prepared if I know I face my death on Samhain."

" 'Tis said," she began and paused, trying to form her words. " 'Tis said that when the Sith leave behind a changeling, be it in the shape of a mortal babe, or dog, or cow, or even a plant resembling one in the mortal world, there is only so much Sith magic in such a thing." The tears flowed now, as she gave him his death sentence. "And that when the magic has left, the changeling, be it person or animal or plant, shrivels and dies without it."

She watched his eyes as he accepted the truth, but she could tell it did not surprise him. They darkened in color then, and he nodded at her. Moira could not come up with a word more to ease his fears or convince him there was another possibility, for she'd heard enough stories about Sith magic to know it for the truth it was.

"I may be wrong," she said, trying, it seemed, to convince herself more than him. "You said Diarmid has an extensive collection of books. Mayhap you could search it for more information or other stories that are right?"

"Sshhhh," he whispered, tucking her head under his chin and entwining his fingers with hers.

"What will you do?"

"For now, there is nothing that can be done. I imagine Diarmid would not be happy to learn that he will lose his prized Seer, so I will keep it from him. If you are right about the other matter, mayhap I should alert Steinar of my impending death to save him his efforts and the lives of more of his pawns in the attempts?"

She covered his mouth with her hand. "Do not say that," she warned.

"At least I will not be the pawn in their game as they play for control of Mull and the position of chieftain here." He met her gaze now, and his was clear, with no sign of fear of what was coming to him. "And neither will you," he promised.

"What do you mean?"

"Fear not that I would leave you in Diarmid's control, nor that of Steinar. And I will not allow you to watch my death, in spite of knowing that is what drew you to me." He lifted her face to his and kissed her mouth gently. "I told you that I was keeping you, but what you need to know is that, more importantly, I will let you go," he said. "Now that we have all that spoken of between us, I would think on more pleasant things."

Overwhelmed that he was concerned about her at such a time as this, she understood what he was asking of her now. If she could ease his pain and give him some clarity in his thoughts as he faced his death, it was the least she could do. When she had been distraught and begged him to help her, he had, and there was pleasure for both of them. Now, she would do it for him without him needing to ask her. When she reached over to touch him, he shook his head and stopped her hand before she could.

"I would hold you, Moira. That is all I need now," he whispered.

For a man who liked and needed sex to calm the boiling lust in his blood, his refusal was not what she expected. "I would ease your pain," she said.

"Lie next to me, Moira," he whispered again.

So, she tugged the shift off, tossed it off the bed and slid down next to him. He opened his arms to her and held her close, draping her across his body. Moira reached up and put her hand on his chest again, feeling a strong heart beating there. And although she did not want to believe it, she knew that the story she'd shared with him was true and he would die when the power left him.

And though she had pursued and craved his death for years, she would not be able to bear to watch it now. Her heart, the one that had been empty for so long, now hurt as it opened just a bit to let something stronger than fear or hatred or the need for vengeance in. It had been so long since she'd felt it there, that she could not understand how it came to be.

"'Twas your kindness, Seer," she whispered. "Your kindness made me think about a good life once more."

As she fell asleep in his arms, she dreamed good dreams for

the first time in those long six years. Her family happy and alive around her. Her sister and brothers all grown with bairns of their own. She could see her husband's hand on her shoulder as she nursed her wee babe under his watchful eye. She dreamt of things now impossible, but for those hours she allowed the life that could have been to play out in her thoughts.

The days passed quickly then, too quickly now that she understood what was to be. He spoke of Samhain only a little, and only when Diarmid mentioned it as the anniversary of his birth and announced a celebration for the Seer. Try as he might to dissuade Diarmid, the plans moved forward, with Diarmid already choosing those whose favor he wanted most. Obviously, Diarmid had not heard or considered the stories she had and never seemed to doubt that his Seer would continue on with even stronger visions in his service for years to come.

Connor spent more and more time in Diarmid's company as the visions came closer, but he had been right about one thing: his bed play with Moira kept his pain away. Oh, there was still an edge to him, and if he pushed her hard when they joined, harder and deeper with each passing night, she let him take his ease on her.

The one thing she did not ask him about was his plan to let her go. Moira understood that she was truly Diarmid's prisoner, and, even if Connor willed her to be free, the lord would ignore him and hold her for his own use. If anything convinced her of the futility of thinking she would ever leave here alive or free, Diarmid's visit two nights before the full moon made it clear.

Connor urged her faster, and she moved over him, like a rider on her mount, sliding her hips and the slick place between her legs forward and back, forward and back. Faster.

He teased the nipples of her breasts all the while. She felt each stroke or pull on them deep into her core, and it made her move against his hardened prick. He squeezed the tips more, and she gasped, feeling it in her blood and over her skin. When he reached down and brought her to the fullness of desire with his hand between her legs, her body shook and shuddered and contracted around him as her release began.

With his hands on her hips, he thrust a time or two more, and the seed began to spill deep inside her. He slid his hands into her hair then, gathering her curls and pulling her face down on his so that he could take her mouth as he took her body. She felt his release finish and would have climbed off his hips but for the voice behind them.

"I can think of a better use for the bitch's mouth than that, Connor," Diarmid said with a laugh.

She heard his heavy steps as he approached, but Connor held her in place as the lord of Mull walked around the bed. He touched her back near the place where the globes of her arse separated, and she pulled herself under control to avoid slapping his hand away. When he plunged his finger into the puckered opening there, she shuddered. Connor's body stilled beneath hers, and his glance told of the need for inaction just then.

"Too tight to have been well used. A place you have been neglecting, Seer," Diarmid said, sliding his finger out of her, but drawing it along the skin of her back, tracing her spine up to her neck. He stepped up next to the bed, bringing himself close enough to face her as she yet held Connor deep inside her.

"I told you, Diarmid," Connor said, "I will not share her."

"Why not? She must be a sturdy bitch, or, with the way you wear out women during this time before your visions, she should have been fucked to death by now and you should have moved on to another and another." Diarmid canted his head and looked at them as they sat in the bed. "Anakol's daughters arrived and were sent here. You refused them. Why do you keep only to this one? Is she so different from the others?" He reached for her breast.

"Send them to my farm to provide me pleasure when I visit there, my lord. And Dara would welcome the help."

She could tell from the tone of his voice that it was a distraction—he'd told her of Diarmid's way of finding women, some of whom he never laid eyes on and of whose fates he had no knowledge in his name. He said this to get these newest ones out of Diarmid's clutches. "I will send word to expect their arrival, two days after the vision?"

Connor pushed her off then and climbed from the bed to face Diarmid on his feet. It gave her the chance to put Connor between her and the lecherous Diarmid. Damn him, he noticed the protective move, even though Connor had made it look casual. She did not attempt to cover herself from his gaze, for it would make things worse with a man like this one.

"Not to serve you here?" Diarmid asked as he stared at her body. It made her skin crawl, but she dared not move.

"I told you, Diarmid: she gives me ease. Since she can still walk and breathe and move as you saw so well, I do not seek others."

"You always sought other women, Connor. It was not about keeping one with you; it was about using as many different ones as you could during this time."

Connor stalked away around the screen—trying, she knew, to draw Diarmid away from her—but Diarmid reached out and grabbed her thigh, wrapping his large, strong hand around it, and pulled her to the side of the bed. Tempted to fight back then, she slid along until he lifted her hips off the bed with his grasp. She could not imagine what he was doing until he leaned over and sniffed.

"Ah," he whispered to her, "freshly used cunny." He sniffed again. "Warm and wet and ready for a man's prick."

"Diarmid?" Connor said quietly. "Touch her, and our arrangement is over." Then his voice dropped into a tone she could only describe as dangerous. "Take her, and I will kill you for it."

The battle lasted only a few seconds, for he was the Seer and she knew that to Diarmid she was not worth losing him or angering him over. Diarmid dropped her, and she scrambled back away from him.

Connor held out a cup to Diarmid and motioned for him to sit, in the chair of visions. Apparently mollified by such an honor, Diarmid forgot about Moira and drank the wine.

"You must have had a purpose for coming here. Did I miss your call or not appear as you have ordered?" he asked, taking a sip of his.

"You are different somehow."

"I would think you would be pleased not to have my rages and outbursts disturb your well-run keep, my lord," Connor added for good measure. " 'Tis a simple matter: I slake my raging hunger on her and find ease."

"Only one?" he asked again.

"When she ceases to please me, you will be the first to know."

"I should have killed her," Diarmid said, drinking the last of his wine.

"Worry not, my lord. She but amuses me."

Diarmid's face lost its lust-filled expression and studied Connor for a moment. "Nay, Seer. She has done something to you. There is no edge; there is no anger in you this time." Diarmid put the cup down on the carved flat arm of the chair. "Can you still sense the building up of the power within you?"

"I can," he answered. It was unlike the recent months somehow, but it was there, building stronger and stronger as the full moon approached.

Diarmid beckoned Connor to him. When Connor stood

close, Diarmid leaned over to him. "If she has done something that will weaken you or your visions, I will kill her. I will cut out all the parts of her you seem to like and the ones I think you waste and then kill her."

Connor did not say a word. Diarmid was at his most dangerous when he grew quiet.

"Your value to me is your power of vision, Connor. For it, I forgive much: your impudence, your rages, your demands, that bitch in your bed. But, mark my words well, for if she has done something to you and, by easing your needs somehow diminished your gift, neither of you will live to tell of it."

The lord of Mull pushed Connor out of his way and walked to the door of the chamber, where Ranald stood watching and listening. Diarmid strode out, and Ranald reached in, with a nod, to pull the door closed behind him.

Connor stood in the silence for a few more minutes, trying to feel the power within him, trying to gain a sense of the limits and expanses of it as it pulsed to life. He did not doubt for one second that she had caused a change in him, but it was not the one Diarmid feared. Instead, with her every acceptance of his body into hers and her satisfying the beast that raged within him, she somehow freed the power inside him.

By this time of the month, as the moon grew to fullness, he'd been so caught up in the pain and the desire in his blood that he could focus on nothing else. But this time . . .

He poured more wine in his cup and walked toward the bed, to the woman who had brought death to him when she sought justice for her family, yet continued to give him reasons to live and the desire to control his power.

For the first time ever, he had a better sense of which of those presented by Diarmid had true need as well as a true heart. Of the twelve men Diarmid had presented to him, only one was blameless in the situation he brought to the Seer.

Only one. He could bring the man and his quest to mind just by thinking of him—an occurrence he'd never caused to happen before.

And he would try to cause it to happen this time.

If he only had two more visions, two more months, he wanted to gain what control he could, if he could, before the last one took him. Her movement drew his attention.

"Do you wish to bring other women to your bed, Seer?" she asked. She stood naked and unashamed before him, her body healing and stronger with each day. But it was her heart and soul that were slower to restore.

"Do you wish me to, Moira? Should I seek others to fill your place?" he asked her in reply, without giving her an answer.

For weeks she'd accommodated his every whim and wish of the flesh, without hesitation and without ever speaking of her own needs or desires, only to repay him for keeping her alive. Oh, he could tell what she liked from the way her body responded to his caresses or to his mouth or his cock, but only lately, from the time she saved him from despair during the storm, had he any sense that she wanted to be part of it.

Now was her chance. If she said the word, he would not take her again. If it meant the pain and the fire these last two months, then so be it. Too many had been manipulated into serving him, and it had to end. He walked close enough to see the color of her eyes and watch them as he asked her again.

"Does this," he nodded to the bed, "does it matter at all to you?"

The moment drew out and out until he feared hearing her answer. She lifted her face to him, and he noticed her bottom lip quivered and that she tried to speak once, twice, thrice before words escaped her. But it was not what he expected to hear after all.

"Damn you, Seer," she said in an angry burst, as she pummeled his chest with her fists. "It does matter!" She turned and walked away from him, but stopped and returned to the spot in front of him where she'd begun. "It does matter, and I want to hate you for making it so."

Her fists clenched and released several times before she spoke again. "I do not want you to find others to take my place."

Then she began to cry. He could sense the struggle and the cost to her for such an admission. To surrender all of her hatred, carefully nurtured over the years to keep her focused on her quest and to give her a reason to live, and to begin to accept that she did not want to kill him—nay, that she wanted him instead—was a heavy price on her soul. Only if her heart desired him could she find peace with it.

He knew that, but did she?

Connor dragged her against him, rubbing her back and holding her tightly while she released the tears.

"I told you it would have been better for both of us had you succeeded the first time. I think that trying to live is harder than waiting to die."

He took her to his bed then, but only to hold her near to him. Soon, sleep overtook them, and Connor had dreams of a kind he'd never had before: he saw himself holding a bairn, he saw himself making love to a woman he knew was his wife, he saw a life stretching out for years and years before him. He did not know what the dreams meant, for dreams were signs to those who could interpret them, but he let them come and allowed the hopefulness of them to seep into his soul.

What would it be like to live the life of a normal man?

Chapter Seventeen

September's full moon arrived on a day that was as tumultuous outside as he felt within. Storms rose on the seas and battered the keep and village. The atmosphere among the people was tense, for all knew that their lord succeeded or failed by the Seer's visions. Now it was Diarmid who raged, in spite of the visitors present or his Seer's assurances that all would proceed as usual and another powerful ally would be at his side by morning.

Connor had decided that he would have Moira held some other place during the vision, but Diarmid made it clear she was to watch from her place, chained to the wall. He'd also said he wanted her chained naked there, but Connor convinced him that he would not permit it. Wisely, Diarmid did not make it an issue, but he was testing Connor every step of the way. To ensure she was not trapped when the blindness and pain took over after the vision, he'd hidden a key in her pallet so she could remove the hated collar and chain if he could not.

Then it was the afternoon of the vision, and Diarmid took his place of honor within the room and brought forth those seeking the Seer's help. Connor spotted the man he'd planned to help, if he could control the gift, as he entered the chamber.

This time he did not wait for the power to flow; he looked deep inside and called it forth. When he knew the strength of it, he sat in his chair and glanced around the room. The worry was clear on Moira's face as he nodded to the chosen man to come forward, instead of waiting for others to approach.

He reached out for the man's hand and willed the vision.

Connor felt Diarmid's surprise as he did not lose consciousness this time, but experienced the change from man to Seer awake. His voice was no longer his own, the words tumbling out on their own, and the sight in his eyes left him then as his vision began to rise and move away from the keep in response to the man's request.

The power surged through his body, and he felt as though he were driving a team of unbroken horses, turning and twisting, pulling tighter to direct it and riding it out when it moved in the direction and speed that he wanted. He laughed out loud as he gathered the power and made it work to his will instead of being dragged as it went.

Cadwallen was from Wales, the site of Norman and Viking incursions along with the usual strife between the Welsh princes, and he sought more advice on seeking his place among the factions than he did about destroying this one or that one. Connor saw the faces of those worthy and unworthy to be called friend or lord and spoke quietly to the man about the choices that faced him. This vision was as clear and precise and powerful as the last one, but it lasted longer and he could see and hear the people as he brought them to mind.

Soon, all of Cadwallen's questions were answered, and he released the man's hand. Stepping back, Cadwallen bowed to him and then went to Diarmid to offer his thanks and first pledge of loyalty.

And Connor waited.

Staring across the room at where Moira should be, he could see nothing but the shadows getting stronger and stronger. His voice had become his own again, but he yet waited for the punishment to begin. Ranald clapped his hands, ushering everyone out of the room until he was alone there with Moira. The power waned, and his blood cooled from its heat. The chambers grew darker and darker, and Connor knew he could not stop it.

His heart slowed then; he counted the beats as it did so. Then, when he was unable to fight it any longer, his heart stopped beating, and the darkness claimed him.

As quickly as it happened, it was over, and his heart beat anew. Now only the pain and blindness were left for him to experience, and so he waited.

"Seer?" she whispered from across the chamber. "Seer?"

He sat motionless in his chair, and she could see his eyes begin to change—from the milky glowing of his vision to the complete black of his blindness—until she knew he could see no more. She worried her lower lip with her teeth, and she braced herself to watch him go through the terrible changes and pain as he changed back from Seer to . . . Connor.

It was so much harder, this, for her heart had softened toward him since the last vision, and, may the Fates help her, she cared about him and the torment he would suffer now. But nothing happened.

"Connor?" she called softly. "Can you hear me?"

He opened his eyes then, and the fires burned within them, yet he did not buckle from pain. He tilted his head and turned in her direction.

"Moira?" he said. "Tell me what you saw."

He stood and walked carefully across the chamber toward her, but she noticed that he waited to hear her voice before going farther—to follow it. She thought on what she'd witnessed and realized the differences from the other times immediately.

"You only spoke to one man," she said. "You recognized him without touching his hand. This vision was longer," she added.

"Clearer, more powerful," he added. "There is a key in the back corner of your pallet. Use it to remove the collar and chain."

She knelt down and searched under the covering of the rush-filled pallet for the key. Finding it, she unlocked the collar and let it hang against the wall. He'd not told her of his plan to do that. Moira walked over to him and waved her hand in front of his eyes. He did not respond; his eyes remained burning orbs that could not see.

"There is no pain? How is that possible?" she asked. He startled then, not realizing she was as close as she was.

She reached out and touched his cheek then. The skin was his; the glow was gone. Though she felt bold, she dared not go near his eyes, for even looking at them for too long hurt.

"No pain. I can feel my eyes blazing, but it is a cold feeling and not the fiery pain I have had all these months." He laughed then and reached for her, hugging her to his body and spinning around . . . in relief, no doubt. He stumbled then, and she led him over to the bed.

"Did your heart . . . ?" She could not get the words out, but he nodded.

"For a moment or two longer. I felt the last beat, and blackness covered me." He lifted her hand and placed it on his chest. "But it beats once more."

"How did this happen?" she asked again. "No pain. No burning." His face paled just then. "Do you feel like you will collapse or faint?"

He fell back on the bed, and she guided him onto it. Had the effects just been postponed and not prevented somehow?

"I need to rest," he said. He reached for the piece of fabric that he covered his eyes with, and Moira helped him tie it in place. He laid quietly, and she thought on the other differences in today's vision.

"You controlled it."

"Aye," he answered softly. "We will speak on this later when I can see you and know we can talk without being heard." He moved over and pulled her next to him. "Lie with me, Moira. Keep me safe until I can see you again."

He fell asleep almost immediately. The vision, and controlling it, had sapped his strength, and his body needed rest to regain it. But what had prevented the pain?

Through the hours while he slept, she watched over him. When Breac or Agnes brought food, she fed him. When he tossed and turned, caught in some disturbing dream or another, she gathered him close and held him. And when he spoke in his sleep about his regrets about the past, about the pain he'd caused, about not caring enough soon enough to make a difference, she knew one more truth.

Forgiveness had found a place in her heart, and she wanted to give it to him.

Three days passed before he rose from the bed and stayed out of it, but the blindness was as profound as before. It was not until its tenth day that Connor knew he had not staved off all the effects of the visions, and though he may have controlled them, he had not stopped his spiral downward toward the end.

Moira remained at his side, and he noticed more changes in her as the time passed and she cared for him, even dismissing Breac and Agnes from their duties. She helped him bathe, kept him company, and held him in the darkness when each passing day did nothing to lessen it.

They spoke of the differences between the last months and this one, but the only thing he could pick out that was not the same was her place in his bed. At first, he gave it no heed, but then he thought on it more and realized that, indeed, without the lust raging in his blood, he'd been able to prepare and take control. Though she thought the idea that their swiving had mitigated the effects of the visions on him was daftness brought on by the blindness, he began to think it was part of it.

He'd known there was something different, something important about her and about being with her. What if she was the reason he had no pain? What if she was integral to finding out more? What if the damned Fae planned this too? That the woman who wanted him dead because of his gift could be the one who could help him escape it?

When his sight did not return and the new moon approached, Connor worried. There would be so little time to prepare for the visions on Samhain. So little time to make the arrangements he needed to, and so little time to convince Moira that his next vision would be hers.

Ranald kept his secret this time, but only because Diarmid had been called away to counsel with Earl Magnus of Orkney. Steinar had not the time nor interest in the Seer when his brother was absent, preferring to see to his own pleasures and concerns. So, it gave them the time and privacy to enjoy the newly found tenderness Connor discovered she had for him.

"Moira? Are you done with your mending yet?" he asked.

It was the twelfth day after the vision, only two until the new moon, and though he was beginning to see shadows moving amidst the darkness, he could not see yet. She'd said the fiery appearance was changing, but no hint of his eyes, nor his sight, were present yet.

"Are you bored?" she asked. "I could use you to measure the new trews Agnes asked me to make. Though Breac is much larger than you, I could . . . guess at his size," she replied, her voice getting louder as she approached.

"I do not want you estimating Breac's *size*," he muttered. He held out her hand and brought it to his cock. "Here, feel there, and you will not have to guess."

His cock hardened under her hand, and he smiled as she began to move it along his length, outlining it with her fingers. "Should I get my measuring strings?" she asked, her voice growing husky. "I may be able to tell you your exact size," she leaned over and whispered then. "Or I may have to check it twice to make certain I was accurate."

He did not remember her ever being this playful when it came to their joinings. It would end that way, he had no doubt, but it was always something he initiated and she followed his lead. This, this was unusual.

"Do you need to feel more of it to decide, wench?" he asked, loosening his belt and guiding her hand inside them. When she took him in her hand, he thrust against her palm.

"Mayhap I need a better view of it?" she asked. He could not lift his hips and slide the trews down fast enough, so she tugged them lower.

He waited to see how far she would take this, and he was surprised at her boldness. He felt her breath on his skin just before he felt her tongue move over his length. Connor could not catch his breath since without his sight he had to wait to feel every step she took in this dance of mating. There was a measure of excitement in not knowing what she would do or touch or taste next.

His body was not his own, but hers to command as she kissed and licked and sucked her way along him. His cock received much attention, but there was not a part of him that was neglected before she breathlessly spoke the thing he most wanted to hear.

"Take me, Connor," she whispered, and she climbed over him, her shift and gown long taken off and her naked skin hot next to his.

He swore to all the saints in heaven that he would make this time the best for her. Instead of need driving them relentlessly or his desire being in charge, she wanted this, she'd asked for this, and he would make it good.

He used every ounce of his strength to bring her to release before seeking his own, pushing her over that edge twice before succumbing to her demands to enter her. Then he did as she asked, whatever she asked, slower, faster, deeper or not, with hands and mouth and body. He fulfilled her desires and her demands until she cried out against his mouth as their bodies joined.

His only regret was not being able to see her face, to see the moment when their bodies became one. Connor held her close until her body calmed. The tears on his skin were unexpected.

"Why do you weep, Moira?" he asked quietly. He used his fingers to wipe the tears from her eyes and off her cheeks. Then lifting her face to his, he kissed them away.

"I want to tell you something," she said in a desolate voice. "I did not expect to be able to say these words to you."

What was she planning to say? "Would it not wait until I can look on your face?"

"Nay." He felt her shake her head. "In a way, this makes it easier for me."

"Go on," he urged. "Let me hear your words."

"I have struggled with this for some time now, Connor," she began. Did she even realize that she called him by name now and Seer no longer? "I was wrong to blame you for my family's deaths. I know that you spoke the words, but I know now that you had no control over what you saw or what you said then."

"Do you mean that?" he asked, afraid to believe that the forgiveness he needed from her was so close.

"Sometimes I forget and sometimes the memories haunt me, but I do forgive you, Connor."

Just as though a weight was lifted from his shoulders, the darkness receded as well, and his sight began to return. Connected or not to her act of forgiveness, it was odd timing for it to happen if she'd not caused it. He could not see clearly, but enough to see the glow of something wonderful in her eyes. Her heart was healing, and he hoped he had time to make it whole before he lost the chance.

He kissed her then and enjoyed the moment of holding her and accepting her declaration. 'Twas some time later before either of them rose from the bed to see to their tasks.

Just over two weeks remained until the next full moon and Samhain. And neither of them expected disaster to strike as it did next or in the way it happened.

Chapter Eighteen

Steinar's arrival at the door of his chambers surprised him. He did not ever remember Diarmid's brother seeking him out without his brother's presence, so he did not know what to expect. Connor would have preferred to have Breac in the room, but they'd sent him and Agnes off to arrange for Anakol's daughters to travel to his farm.

In spite of Diarmid's agreement to send them there, Connor had just found out that the girls were still in the keep and under Diarmid's *care*. He had to move quickly, and since his vision was not completely returned, it meant having Breac handle it. So, for now, he must see to Steinar alone. When he opened the door, seeing Ranald at Steinar's back did not comfort him in the least.

"Good morrow, my lord," he said.

Steinar, he knew, enjoyed being called "lord" though he had not the right or title to it . . . yet. If anything happened to Diarmid and Steinar could present himself as the man most capable of taking control, his claim as chieftain would be upheld by the Earl of the Orkneys and isles. A good thing for Steinar and those who supported him, but a bad thing for anyone in places of authority or privilege placed there by Diarmid.

A bloodbath would follow Diarmid's death, as Steinar cleared his path of anyone he deemed a danger.

Connor knew he'd long been in that group.

Steinar swaggered in, glancing around the room, his eyes lighting first on his chair and then on Moira. He nodded at her and studied him before he spoke. "My brother said she is to be chained at all times, Seer. Why is she not?"

"Lord Diarmid does not extend his control to what happens in my chambers, my lord," he answered. "She cannot serve my needs chained to the wall."

Everyone in the keep knew that Diarmid did what was needed to keep his Seer pleased. A matter such as an unchained woman in his room was not something he would bicker about.

"Still," Steinar said. "She was dangerous enough to try to kill you, and almost succeeded. I would see her secured while I am here." Steinar nodded to Ranald. "Chain her."

Connor knew better than to object and give Steinar any reason to question his loyalty or his actions. He did take his eyes off the dangerous young man as Ranald ran to do his bidding, and Moira did not fight Ranald. Once the chain clattered against the wall, Connor nodded at Steinar.

"Diarmid bade me watch over you while he is away, and I am concerned that you have not been at table since your vision. Nearly two weeks spent only in this room," Steinar said, walking around the chamber, inspecting the tapestries, the luxurious carpets on the floor, the large bed, and the slave now chained to his wall. "Cadwallen yet remains, waiting for the opportunity to thank you for the vision he was granted."

"The visions tire me, my lord. Diarmid knows it takes some time for me to regain my strength." Connor tilted his head, watching Steinar's movements with the outer edges of his eyes, the only parts that yet worked. "If it pleases you, I will join you at table this day."

"You are alone here?" he asked. "Where is that manservant you keep? What is his name?"

Connor did not doubt for a moment that Steinar knew every detail it was possible to know about Breac, Agnes, and anyone else who served him, rather than Diarmid, in this keep.

"Breac is seeing to some errands for me, my lord, and should return shortly. Have you need of him for some task?"

Steinar stood behind him now. "Ah, he is taking Anakol's daughters to your farm, is he not? They were a lovely show of gratitude from Anakol for the vision he received. Lovely," he repeated. "You should have tried them when they first arrived, Seer." He laughed then, and it sent shudders through him. Steinar turned toward Moira again, and Connor held his breath. "They will most likely be a disappointing thing to a man of your tastes now."

"So, my lord, I will see you at table," he began.

Steinar seemed to accept the dismissal, but then he turned back and grabbed Connor's arm. "This month, I want the vision, Seer. Not one of the weaklings Diarmid wishes to bow and scrape before him. Me."

"I do not decide who is gifted, my lord. Surely Diarmid has explained it to you," he offered.

"Diarmid has explained things to me and others have as well. I know the secrets you keep from my lord and brother and suggest that I need the vision in order to keep those facts away from his view."

"I know not of what you speak, my lord," Connor said. What could he know?

"There is the fact that your servant is making arrangements to spirit your love slave away from here."

"Not spirit, my lord, ship. I have need on my farm, and she is strong."

"There is the gold you have been hoarding."

"Almost all of that has been through Lord Diarmid's generosity," he insisted, believing he could explain any claim of Steinar's.

"Ah, I do not think you will be able to explain this one, Seer, for the information I have says that the Seer is," he paused, and Connor saw movement to his right and turned to face Steinar there.

"Blinded by the visions," Steinar finished, from just in front of him. Startled, Connor stumbled back to move away.

"If my brother knew, he would begin to doubt that your visions will continue much longer. I see"—he laughed at the play on words—"no reason to inform him as long as I am the recipient of the next vision."

Connor decided it was better to placate him now, for his vision was weak, as Steinar had demonstrated by his tactic of tossing something to feign movement.

"I can only try, my lord."

Steinar clapped him on the back and motioned to Ranald to go. "'Tis all I ask from my brother's loyal Seer."

Connor thought the threats were over and he could avoid the meal when Steinar called out as he left.

"Cadwallen has mentioned not only his beautiful daughter, but his strong, young son, both of whom he would offer into your service in thanks. I will tell him you accept them."

The door closed, and Connor swore bitterly. He searched around a bit and found his cloak. He hit a bench he could not see as he turned back to find the door. It was like walking on a moonless night; the shadows were stronger than the clear parts of his sight still.

"Where are you going, Connor?" Moira asked.

"Get that off your neck and stay quiet. I must find Cadwallen and warn him to leave here."

"Please wait for Breac to return, Connor," she said, as he heard the chain hit the wall and saw her form move in the shadows. "Wait for him to accompany you."

"I know these halls well enough to make my way, Moira. I will be back before Breac returns."

He went to her and kissed her mouth before leaving. Then, he opened the door, nodded to the guard, and walked to the stairway that led to the main floor.

He never made it.

It was several hours later when they found him unconscious at the bottom of another stairwell, the same one where Gillis had perished.

He had played it to perfection. Obviously guilty of not only the secrets he'd accused him of, but many more, the Seer had decided to take matters into his own hands. Unfortunately for Connor, Ranald's information about the Seer's blindness was correct. With explicit instructions not to kill him, yet, his man had caused Connor to lose his balance and fall into the stairway.

The situation was set up just the way he liked to see it—either way, he was the victor. If the Seer did die, Diarmid suffered. If the Seer did not die, he would be injured enough not to be able to have a vision next week. If the Seer did have a vision, he would be the recipient of it. His standing would improve, and Diarmid's would weaken.

Now, all he needed was Diarmid's return to put the final piece into action. His next target would be his half brother. He'd decided that it would be easier to simply remove him from this equation than to fight him for the position.

With his Seer gone, Diarmid's allies would scatter, and Steinar would take over.

Nothing caused by the vision ever hurt this much.

Connor tried to open his eyes, but his head screamed in pain every time he tried. His arm hurt, his leg throbbed, and his back spasmed with any attempts to move. Even his face hurt.

He could hear whispered words swirling around him, but he did not hear the one voice he wanted: Moira's. Connor drifted back into the darkness and waited until he felt stronger and could try again. The next time he woke, the room was darker and he could open his eyes, but still the one person he wanted to see was not there. Finally, the third or fourth time he woke, he called out her name.

"Moira?"

"I am here, Connor," she said in a shaking voice; then more whispers surrounded him.

"Stop that damned whispering, and tell me what is happening," he ordered.

'Twas Breac's voice that answered now. "Lord Diarmid is on a murderous rampage. He is searching for those responsible for your injuries."

"I fell?" he asked, unsure of what had occurred.

"Pushed, more likely, considering your visitor just prior," Breac answered. "Moira said she told you not to go."

Now Connor answered to his servants?

"Where is she?"

"Diarmid has been here several times since he arrived back, and 'tis safer for her to remain . . ."

"Chained?" he finished.

"Aye."

"I am sorry, Moira. Breac, help me up," Connor said as he struggled to sit up.

The room swam around his head, and colors and sounds followed it for several minutes. Agnes gave him some brew that smelled like pitch but settled his stomach and eased the dizziness. Through it all, Moira said not a word.

Then when he would have gone to her side, he heard the door slam open against the wall. Diarmid charged in, and came around the wooden screen looking for him. Steinar followed a few paces behind. A look of concern floated on his face, but Connor saw the truth in his eyes.

"What happened, Connor?"

"I fell, my lord," he said. "A bit of clumsiness, 'tis all."

Breac and Agnes stood back, forming a wall in front of Moira, keeping her out of sight as much as they could.

"He said his visions had taken his s . . . strength, brother." Steinar nodded grimly then. Connor caught the suggestion in his stutter—a warning to him.

"Still weakened by the last vision, Connor? Over two weeks?" Diarmid asked, forgetting that he demanded Connor speak of that to no one.

"My lord," Connor began, glancing at Steinar, to remind him.

"I found him unstable on his feet when I came to invite him to table," Steinar said. "Cadwallen wished to say his farewells, but the Seer had not been out of his room since his visions."

"The healer has been here to treat me," Connor said, pointing to the variety of bottles and jugs and powders on his table. "Agnes is following all of her instructions, my lord. My strength will return, and I *will* be ready for the visions."

Diarmid appeared content for the moment, but he shook his head then. "I will put more guards on your door. And since you cannot come to table to meet my guests, I will bring them here."

"Very well, my lord," he said, ready to agree to anything to get rid of all of them.

Diarmid took another look around the chamber, so upset by the possibility of losing his Seer that he said nothing about Moira. A welcomed first time for that. Then, with a wave to Steinar, he left, calling out orders for more guards at the door and down the hall.

"The quiet is good," Connor said, as he moved to the edge of the bed. "The ringing in my ears is lessening as well."

"You could have been killed."

Moira's voice was different, and he watched as Breac and Agnes moved away so that he could see her. Her face was a ghostly white, and her eyes looked huge. She looked more angry than upset, and he waited as Breac unlocked the collar.

"You daft, damned man, you could have been killed," she repeated. His servants were fighting not to smile at her words. He dismissed them with a wave of his hand.

"Breac, wait," he said. "Did you get them to the farm?" He'd only just remembered Breac's task when he'd had the accident.

"Aye, they are safe."

Connor nodded, glad at least for now. He listened as his servants left, and then he walked over to Moira. She stood, twisting her hands in front of her, but once more he sensed her anger.

"Would you have mourned my death, Moira?"

She narrowed her eyes when she looked at him then, but she said neither aye or nay to his question. He was pushing her, he knew it, but time was short and he hoped that her heart was open to him now. Forgiveness was the largest step she needed to take. The next one could not be as far or as difficult.

He hoped.

It had not been difficult for him, for once he watched her begin to be the person she should always have been, he began to fall in love. Then, when each time she chose him over another choice, he knew it deeper inside himself.

But he could not and would not ask her for the declaration he was now willing to make to her, for it would bind her to him and he would not be here to honor such a bond.

She took the first step, and then he met her halfway.

"Next time, you need to listen to me," she ordered.

"Next time?" he asked. Did she realize what she said?

"You know he plots your death, Connor. Give him not the chance to succeed in it."

"My death approaches quickly, Moira."

She flinched at his words. "Do not say that to me," she whispered. "I cannot think that you are right in this."

"Honor my wishes in this. Follow my instructions, and all will be well," he said. He would allow her to believe what she would, but make all the preparations and plans he knew he must have in place.

He stepped back as she raised her hand to his face, not certain of her intent, but she laughed then and touched a spot on his chin that hurt. Leaning closer, she kissed it.

"Where else does it hurt? What can I do to ease your pain?"

The words had meant something else for so long now between them that his cock answered her question, readying itself to be eased. She looked at his groin as his trews tented and shook her head then. "Do you never tire of such things?" she asked.

"With you? Nay, Moira. I will never tire of you, as long as you give yourself to me willingly. I will not force you to come to me or use false reasons between us."

She kissed him gently on his mouth, and he winced as his torn lip pulled. "I will not force you either, Connor," she said, making light of his injuries in a way he knew she did not feel.

She led him to the bed and helped him undress. They spent the night comforting each other, and by the time the dawn's light crept into his room, she admitted that she would mourn his loss. But every time he tried to speak of his love, she stopped him.

"After Samhain, we will speak on such matters."

"After Samhain then," he said, knowing for certain that he would not be there to tell her.

* * *

The next days passed both too slowly and too quickly for them. Diarmid brought his guests to meet Connor, encouraging this one or that one as the one to choose. Connor flexed his powers over those days, testing them, using them in small ways, and then deciding who would receive the last vision.

He kept Breac busy, and began moving things from his chambers back to the farm where Dara and Pol could use them. His strongbox held gold accumulated over the years, and he divided it so that both Moira and those dependent on the farm would be cared for.

Moira watched in silence, seeing more than he wanted her to, but never saying a word about the things he did. The day before Samhain, he brought out the map he'd found to show her where her village had been and how to return to that area. Such sadness filled her eyes that he rolled the parchment back up and put it away.

They spent what time they could together, and each time they joined, Moira seemed a bit more frantic, as though realizing their time was coming to an end. She would not allow him his words of love, and when he asked if she could receive his last vision, to give her peace about the past, she became so upset that he had to swear not to do so.

It mattered not, for he had already made his decision; he only waited for the rise of the moon, just after midnight on Samhain to carry out his plans.

The irony struck him again when he realized that as his powers were ending, he'd learned more about using them since meeting her than he had since they began more than six years ago. And if not for Moira forcing him to see the reality of his life, the misuse of his gift, and his need to make reparations, he would have never even tried.

The night before Samhain, when Diarmid brought the last few men to meet him, the unexpected happened, and he was able to "see" some parts of Diarmid that he'd never known before: the most important thing he learned was that not only was Diarmid aware of Steinar's plans and his shadowy manipulations, but he was pulling the strings to bring Steinar down.

And he enjoyed informing Steinar of that when he came to remind Connor of his demand. Word would spread by dawn that Steinar had broken with his half brother and had been exiled from Mull and the surrounding isles.

Finally, midnight approached, and everything that could be done had been put in place. Now, there was nothing left to do but wait for it all to play out to its conclusion.

Chapter Nineteen

She woke to discover him sitting by the hearth, staring off at nothing. Climbing from the bed, she realized that midnight had passed and it was Samhain, the day when the veil between the Sith world and the mortal world was at its thinnest and the Sith were able to walk the earth.

"Sleep, love," he said softly, and she felt compelled to do just that, in spite of her curiosity about what he was doing and her fear that something was about to happen. Sleep dragged her away, and when next she opened her eyes, the faint light of dawn pierced through the darkness and through the open window high in the wall.

"Connor," she whispered. "Are you here?"

He walked around the screen and stood by the bed. Something was different about him. Something was dangerous about him. His eyes had changed somehow, but it was the look within those eyes that took her breath away.

"Aye, love," he said, climbing onto the bed and peeling the bedclothes back to expose her naked body to his sight. "I am here."

The first touch of his strong hands encircling her made her

shiver in anticipation of what was to come. She moved closer and opened her legs to let him in. With little prelude, for her body had prepared for him at the sound of his voice, he filled her emptiness with his flesh. Spreading her legs, she urged him in deeper and felt his hardness touch her womb and swell, filling her to her core and taking her breath away.

He did not move, but only remained there, while he kissed her mouth gently, tasting her and stroking her with his tongue until she ached for more. He took her mouth and then began to take her body for his own. Slowly, so slowly she nearly screamed out a protest, he slid back until she felt the emptiness, and then he filled her at such a pace that she nearly impaled herself on him.

"Hush now, Moira," he whispered as he slid in to fill her once more. Then, leaning back on his heels, he lifted her until she rested on his thighs. She only realized how this position opened her more fully to his touch when he slipped one finger into her cleft and touched the sensitive spot there even while his manhood filled her channel. She arched against it, swelling and throbbing until she could feel the tension pulling her from inside. And, damn him, he stopped moving his finger and only held it there as her body pulsed around it. Her release was close, but he did not allow it yet.

She closed her eyes, enjoying every touch, every stroke, every caress as he bent forward and teased her with his mouth and his tongue and his hands. He brought her close to release two—nay three—more times before he called her name and met her gaze with those eyes that spoke of something more than human within him. Staring into hers, he moved closer and thrust deeper and deeper still until she moaned out her pleasure at the cascade of sensations moving through her body. From inside her core, through her hips, through her womb, to her heart, she ached for him, and she began to match his movements so that they moved together toward that moment when she could let go of restraint and revel at his flesh possessing her.

Then her breath caught in her chest, her body surrendered to his, and she lost everything of herself as somehow they merged and melted into one being.

No longer a quest and a searcher.

No longer a seer and an enemy.

No longer man and woman, Connor and Moira.

Just one body that breathed together and one soul that began and ended in each of them.

She wrapped her arms around him and held on as he thrust himself into her flesh and spilled his seed there. Wave after wave of pleasure and heat shot through her as her body shuddered around his, spasming on and on around him until she drew out the last drop of his release.

Moira collapsed in his arms, overwhelmed by the connection she'd felt between them in that moment and unable to understand how it could be that way between them. Connor kissed her mouth so softly it made her cry when he lifted away from her.

"I love you, Moira," he said, putting his finger across her lips. "Deny me not the chance to say that to you."

Her heart filled in that moment, but she could not find the words to say what she found there. The tears flowed freely now as he slid from her body and climbed off the bed.

"Come to me, my Moira," he said, as he walked away from the bed.

Confused, she slid off the bed, wiping her eyes so she could she her path around the bed and then around the screen. He sat in his chair now, but it was somehow not Connor there—it was someone more than Connor. He had become the Seer right before her eyes.

His release still pulsed through his body, and he could feel some part of her remaining in his heart and his soul. They had touched just then. They had joined more than just their fleshly bodies in that moment of ecstasy and passion. Their souls had touched. Their hearts had touched.

Somehow her need for justice still burned deep within her, for he could feel her soul cry out for it even now. It gave him the strength to give her that one thing she would never ask for herself: a vision to see the truth of her family's destruction.

He knew that she would never heal and never be free of the past until she knew all that had happened, and now, as his last vision, he would try to give her what she needed so that she could move on with her life after he was gone.

He would give her the truth.

She watched him as he held out his hand to her, and he thought she might refuse to take it, but she moved ever closer until she stood before him, much as she had the first time he'd joined with her. She leaned over and put her hand in his, and he closed his fingers around hers, holding her and willing the power to flow, instead of waiting for it to happen.

The shock of it took his breath away, and he heard her gasp as she felt it, too. It moved like fire through his body and into hers, filling her blood as it filled his. Soon he could hear her thoughts and see her memories. He'd never moved back through time before, but it was necessary to show her the truth.

"Take me back, Moira," he ordered. "Take us back and show me how it was then."

He, they, watched a scene unfold before his eyes: the days and years peeled away, and the Moira who held his hand was only a girl now. The brightness of the day was so strong it hurt his eyes, but it was her voice that he heard as she called out to her family.

"That is Eibhlin, my sister, carrying the bucket from the well. Look! My brothers, Cailean and Dòmhnall, are chasing her now!"

The girl, younger than Moira, had long blond hair that curled around her bright face. The boys, twins, had the darker coloring of eyes and hair, but the shape of the chins and noses bespoke their relationship. The children passed by her, and she laughed out at their antics.

Moira turned around and watched them run to the cottage on the lane where they lived. She followed, as did he, and she opened the door on an argument between her parents. Shaking her head, she pulled the door closed. He could feel her discomfort over witnessing the exchange, and her hand grew cold in his as he heard the angry voices spilling out.

"Moira lass, come with me," he told the child, and then he leaned back and brought them both high into the sky soaring over the village below. She laughed in childlike joy as he moved them through the air faster and faster until the winds pushed against them and the sun warmed them. The Quinag hills separated their village from the higher mountains, and from their place high above he could see the whole of the peninsula where their town lay. Connor turned in one direction and then another looking, searching for something, until he saw a group of men approaching from the east.

"Connor . . . I cannot do this . . ." she stuttered.

She said his name in her own voice, and he felt the fear within her growing.

"Be strong, my Moira," he said. "You need to find the truth. Hold me tight, and all will be well."

Some of this was familiar to him from the time he called it forth for Skuli, but Moira and her siblings had not been part of that vision. Now he remembered seeing only her father's role, which he knew she would see next.

They slowed then, and Connor brought them to stand just outside the group of men, some Norse from the look and sound of them and others from Diarmid's lands. Seumas, son of Neacail and Moira's father, of Quinag, stood arguing with the man called Skuli of Caithness.

"You betrayed me, Seumas. If you wanted out of our deal, you could have walked away with nothing more than some gold lost. Instead you sold your honor behind my back. Did my brother pay you more?"

"Your brother is the rightful earl; you should honor his claim to Orkney," Seumas said, but Skuli cut off his words.

"My claim is stronger and has been upheld by the King of the Scots, and you swore you would fight at my side if the king named me earl here." Skuli drew his sword and held it out in front of him. "You sold your honor and your word to my brother. Your honor is broken, your word no good. All in Caithness and Orkney will know you cannot be trusted."

Skuli lifted his sword and would have cut off Seumas's head had not Seumas called out an offer of gold. "Your brother's gold is in the village. If you let me leave here alive, I will tell you where I have hidden it."

Moira shook as she watched her father betray himself and their family, selling his honor for gold and their lives for his. "No, Papa," she cried. "No."

Connor lifted them up and away, and they could see the Norsemen heading for their village and hear the screams. They flew then, moving over and ahead until they could see the men catch up with her father and take their vengeance out on him, leaving him hanging from a tree as a sign to others of the cost of treachery.

Now, he felt Moira fall into his arms, and he brought her back the way they'd come, through the years and months and days and hours until she was once again the woman he loved. She sobbed in his embrace for a long time; the terrible truth that her own father had brought death to her family and village would be hard to accept. He watched as she stood and stepped away from him and as the brightness in the chambers began to fade.

"That was some trick—that could not be the truth!" she cried out. "Did you make me see that believing that I would accept it and condemn my father instead of you?"

"I wanted you to see the truth, so that you can have peace and live your own life now," he said, every word he spoke draining him of energy. "You deserved to know."

"I told you I did not need to see it," she pulled away and shook her head. "I did not want to cause your . . ." Now a look of terror entered her eyes, and he knew she was seeing his end.

"Connor, do not leave me," she screamed. "Connor . . ."

The room faded, and he felt a coldness pierce his eyes now, draining his sight even as the power seeped away, draining his life. He tried to reach out to her, but his heart slowed and slowed until he felt the last beat.

And then nothing more.

He'd sworn not to do this, and now his death was on her soul after all. He'd sworn to fight the last vision, to try to prolong the power until he could learn more about it. And in the end, he'd called down the vision for her to seek the truth she needed.

Connor was dead.

She fell on the cold floor in front of him and wretched uncontrollably. He could not be dead. He could not be. She'd wanted his death for so long, but not like this. Not now, not now that she'd accepted his love. Not before she could tell him . . .

She looked at him, his body reclining in the damn chair of his visions as though relaxing, much like the first time she'd joined with him, here, in this room and in that chair. She shook her head, not believing it.

He was right. He was right. His last vision would bring his death, and he'd called it forth for her.

Why?

Why?

So he could make her believe something he suspected? He showed her a scene that could not have happened the way they saw it from above. She'd felt younger when she took his hand and heard him speak in that voice. The one he used during his visions, when someone else sat in his place and spoke his words.

What could she do now? She looked down and realized she was naked. Running to the bed, she found her shift and pulled it and her gown on quickly.

He could not be dead.

He could not be.

She needed help. Wanting only to shake him until he woke, she felt her heart pounding in her chest and tried to think of the right thing to do.

Moira ran to the door and told the guard to find Breac. Then she went back and placed her hand on his chest. His chest did not rise, and no heart beat beneath her palm now.

But, his face looked at peace. For the first time since she'd met him that small furrow did not form between his brows. She touched his mouth and felt the heat of his body changing to cold.

She slid to the floor, grasping his hand, and she sobbed.

Minutes later, or longer she knew not, Breac entered and stood over her.

"He is dead, Breac," she said, wiping the tears with the back of her hand. "He called the vision, and it killed him, as he thought it would."

Breac did not seem surprised by what he found. Without a word, he moved around the chamber, gathering clothing and other things.

"Breac, he is dead," she repeated.

"I know, Moira," he answered, coming to stand behind her. "He told me to tell you farewell."

She turned to look at him, but he placed his arm around her shoulders and held her chin in his hand. Then, he leaned her head back, and before she could do anything to stop him, Breac poured some foul brew in her mouth, pinching her nose until she swallowed it down.

The room spun and grew dark, and she stumbled back against him.

"Breac?"

Connor had promised not to turn her over to Diarmid if he died. Was this his way of taking her with him in death? Moira forced her eyes to open and took one more look at Connor. Somehow she knew it would be the last one.

The darkness swelled then, and she fell away from it all.

Chapter Twenty

An t-Eilean Muile (Isle of Mull), five months later

The voyage around past Skye and the lands of Lorn was much different from the last one she took to reach Mull. That one was carried out in secret, as she hid her intentions and her identity, and this one was in a well-made boat sailed by experienced men hired to see her . . . home.

When Connor had died, she'd thought her life was over. Waking from the concoction given to her by Breac, she found herself well away from Diarmid's keep and his lands. His last orders to Breac, before giving him his freedom, were to take Moira to safety and give her her life back. Breac gave her Connor's last words and a chest of his gold to ease her way.

And it had.

For the first time, she controlled her life.

It took weeks for the grief to lessen enough for her to think about a future. Then it took more to figure out how to find out if his last vision had been true. Her heart ached when she tracked down the truth and found she'd been wrong to doubt him or his love in the end.

The sun came out from behind the clouds now, and the sea

breezes carried the boat along the coast, south toward Mull and Connor's farm. Well, as Breac had explained, it was Pol and Dara's farm now, given to them on his death. He'd told her that there would always be a place for her there if she did not find what she was seeking in the north of Scotland.

The wind tugged her hood, and she let it drop to her shoulders so she could enjoy the warm weather of this spring day. No one would know her now, for she'd used the juice of some berries to darken her hair and she used her real name once more.

Moira of Quinag.

One of the sailors called out to her, and she turned to watch them approach the small, wooden dock. If she closed her eyes, she could remember leaving this place to go back to Diarmid's keep, to face her certain death and the wrath of the Seer. Instead she'd discovered a man imprisoned by the terrible power that controlled him.

And now she'd found a reason to live in spite of his death.

The boat bumped up against the dock, and one of the men climbed out, tying the boat to a spike there. When it was secured, he helped her out of the boat. Walking onto the shore, she watched as the cart came over the hill to fetch her.

Standing there, she tried not to think too much, but memories flooded back at her. Somehow she'd thought it would be easier than this to return to his lands. Wiping away the tears, she walked up to greet Pol as he pulled the cart to a stop before her. He jumped down and came around to greet her.

"Dara is glad that you decided to visit," he said, nodding to the men who stood waiting at the boat. "Secure the boat and use the horses to come to the farm," he called out to them.

Several horses and another cart were always kept here for use in traveling back and forth to the farm some miles away through the coastal hills. She had already explained it to the men when she hired them, asking them to stay at the farm for a few days while she made her decision. Pol helped her into the cart, her bags were tossed in the back, and soon they had crossed through the first line of hills along the path that would take her . . . home.

She'd known she made the right decision when she stepped off the boat, but she wanted to speak to Dara first and make certain of her plans. Somehow bearing Connor's child and raising him or her among the people he loved seemed the right thing to do. They would keep his name and memory alive and teach her son or daughter about the father he would never know, just as she would teach him about her family.

They would remain alive in the memories and hearts of those who loved them forever. Her only regret was never having the chance to recognize that she loved Connor or to tell him of her love before he died. If only she had realized what he was doing and the price he would pay. If only . . .

She wiped more tears away. It seemed all she did lately was cry, but according to one midwife she'd spoken to, that was to be expected in a woman carrying.

Moira did not speak much along the way, and Pol must have realized there was little she could say then. They rode in companionable silence, the miles flowing by quickly. By midmorning, the farm came into view, and she straightened on the seat, watching it grow closer and closer. When they reached the house, several people stood waiting for her.

Breac and Agnes and Dara.

Pol helped her down, and Dara reached her first, throwing her arms around her and hugging her. The thickening waist and stomach between them was noticed quickly.

"It cannot be," Dara exclaimed. "Yer carrying?" Dara looked at her closely, rubbing her hand over Moira's stomach as though she could tell something by the size or shape of the growing bump there. "'Tis Connor's?" she asked in a whisper, before the others came close.

"Aye," she said with a teary smile. "'Twould appear that neither of us was barren after all."

From the symptoms and what she remembered, she could only think that it had happened that last, magical time that they made love. It had been different from every other time they joined, in some way she could not say and she was sure that this bairn was the result of it. She'd not known for some months, and then she'd refused to believe it for she'd never been caught before in all those times and all those years.

But, that last time they loved . . . it had been a true joining of bodies and souls, and somehow the fates, or the Fae—she knew not which—had granted her this piece of Connor to keep with her. She rubbed her hand there and was gifted with a flutter of movement beneath her palm.

Breac and Agnes reached them, and Dara shared the news with them. Agnes stood quietly at her side, touching Moira's belly and smiling at her as though she always knew it would happen. Breac, well, he tried to say something, but would end up just shaking his head at her, stunned into silence by the news.

"Are ye feeling well, Moira?" Dara asked as they walked toward the house. "Any of the sickness or dizziness?"

"I am well, Dara. Strong as an ox and just as stubborn, I think," she said.

"Will ye be staying here then?"

They reached the gate to the house, but Moira was not ready to go inside yet. Now that she was here, more than anything she wanted to visit a place Connor had spoken of those months ago. A meadow where he'd promised her he would perform every sort of wicked delight for her pleasure. She smiled even now, just thinking about the place.

"I think so," she said, with a nod. "I think it would please him to have his child born here."

Dara turned away then, as though unable to speak of Connor, but she grabbed Moira's hand and squeezed it tightly.

"Connor told me of a meadow near the sea. Is it close enough for a walk?" she asked.

Dara looked past her to Breac and Agnes before answering her. " 'Tis a fine day for a walk and 'tis not too far or hard to find."

Within a few minutes, with a skin of watered wine and a sack filled with bread and cheese, Moira headed up the path toward the place Connor had promised to bring her on a fine spring day. She did not fight the tears then, but let them flow as they seemed wont to do. The mile or so along the path took little time, and she followed Dara's directions off the path, through the trees to the meadow.

She held her breath as she passed the stand of trees that separated the path from her destination, and the view of it was well worth the effort to get here. Already the warming temperatures hastened the growing season here and covered the field with a mix of soft grass and spring flowers. Turning to see if he'd told her the truth, she spied the hill that he had claimed was an entrance to the land of the Sith.

The small rise was just as he'd described, and she began walking toward it. He'd claimed that much as he would like to tup her here on the soft meadow grass, with the flowers all around them and the sun shining down to warm her naked skin, he could not, for fear that the Sith would come out of their burrow and steal her away to their lands.

They had driven each other to madness with words that day, but now seeing it as he'd said it would be made her heart heal a bit. She thought she heard soft laughter as she passed on her way to look out at the sea, but she could see no one around in the meadow. She was walking toward the sea when she saw someone, a man, sitting nearer the edge of the cliff.

Dara had not spoken of anyone else being here, so Moira

called out to the man, who sat on a rock with his face turned toward the sun, much as she liked to do on such a day.

"Sir?" she called as she walked closer. "I do not mean to disturb you. Dara did not . . ." She stopped then, as he lowered his head.

With the distance still between them and his face yet turned away, Moira had the feeling she'd met him before. Mayhap another unfortunate victim of Diarmid's cruelty taken in by Connor? She stopped and spoke again.

"My name is . . ."

"Moira."

Her body reacted before her mind did, for how could someone explain speaking to the dead except that her mind had fled? Her hands trembled, and her body shook as it recognized the voice.

"Moira? Speak to me," the man said.

It could not be. It could not . . . be.

She was running before she knew it, and she screamed out his name. "Connor! Connor!"

He turned then, and she saw the face of the man she loved, the father of her bairn. She reached him and stopped directly before him, waiting for him to look at her. But when he did look in her direction, it was with eyes that were empty and unseeing.

He was blind.

The air around her felt heavy upon her, and her senses began to spin until she could feel herself falling. Grabbing his cloak, she tried to stay on her feet, but the shock of seeing him, seeing him alive, overwhelmed her and she lost the battle, sinking into a faint at his feet.

The first thing she noticed was the sound of the ocean pounding against a nearby shore. Then she felt the strong arms around her, holding her tightly against an even stronger body.

A body that breathed and a heart that beat.

Moira opened her eyes and found herself on Connor's lap and in his embrace. She reached up and cupped his cheek in her hand.

"You are alive? How can that be?"

If she was dreaming, she did not want to wake from it, for there were words that needed saying between them. In the moment when he died and she was overwhelmed by the truth of her father's treachery, she'd hated him for revealing it to her. And that bitter moment had haunted her these last months when the depth of her love became so clear.

"You were dead—I felt your chest. Your heart stopped beating." And she cried. The tears came out in a torrent, and the questions also, flooded out in a stream as she tried to understand. "How did you live? How did you escape from Diarmid?"

He reached up and put his finger to her lips, shushing her. His lips warmed her skin as he touched them to her forehead, and she fought the urge to simply lie back in his arms and forget the last time she'd seen him. Pushing against his chest, she leaned back and searched his face. She spoke his name softly now, still not believing that he was real and not imaginary.

"Connor," she whispered, clutching his shoulders and breathing in his scent. "They announced your death. They blamed it on me. If you lived, why did you not summon me to your side?"

He took her face in his hands, drew her close, and kissed her until she stopped trying to talk. When he lifted his mouth from hers, he explained the plans he'd set in place in case his worst fear was realized.

"I told you of my fears, Moira. I knew the power would end in my death and made arrangements to get you out safely," he whispered, never pausing in kissing her face as he spoke. "I gave you my word that you would be safe and swore Breac to the task." He leaned away then. "I could not risk telling you about it. Diarmid shows no mercy to those who defy him."

Moira trembled then, her body and soul remembering the cost of her own defiance against Diarmid's plans. Connor held her closer.

"I know how Breac got me away—he told me the whole of it when I woke miles and hours away from Mull. But tell me how you survived that vision. How is it that you still live?" she asked, letting the strength of his arms surround her. "How can it be?"

"Breac returned once he had smuggled you out and got Diarmid's permission to bury me here on my lands. As he was wrapping a tarp around me, I woke." A sad smile touched his face. "I could not explain how I lived; I only knew that my sight was gone. My eyes," he rubbed them then, "see nothing."

"Maybe in time?" she asked, thinking on how his sight would return after his visions. "Do they pain you?"

Moira reached up to touch his eyes then, but stopped. They were open, but never focused on her. The green coloring was gone, replaced by a white, hazy layer that showed no sign of changing back to what it was.

"Nay, no pain now. Only a piercing cold and darkness," he said. "I did not send for you because I did not want to tie you to a blind man. Your life had been stolen away from you because of me, and I wanted you to have a chance at a new one without the burden of my care."

"You are alive, Connor—that is all I could ever have wanted. Alive! Power or not, sight or not, alive." She shook her head at his words, but realized he could not see her gesture.

"Do you remember the time after your heart stopped? How did you make it begin anew?" she asked, sliding from his embrace to stand before him. Laying her hand on his chest, she felt the strong pulsing of his heart, pushing blood through his veins and giving him life. "How is it that you live?"

Connor smiled then and shook his head. "I know not, Moira. I only know that I felt the last beat and fell into the darkness and then later my heart beat again and I woke. I know not if it was part of the Fae gift or curse or something else." He reached out his hand, and she guided it to her face. "I wonder if I was really dead or simply deeply unconscious."

"Nay," she said, shaking her head. "I felt your chest. There was no breath there and no heart beating. I watched you die . . ."

She could not help the way her own breathing hitched as she spoke of it. The terror and horror of witnessing it flowed once more through her. And the regrets with it.

Moira kissed him again and let him feel the love within her flow to him. "And I should have believed you," she whispered. "About my father and his . . . his . . ."

"Hush now, my Moira," he soothed.

But the regrets still haunted her. Now she had the chance to set them straight. She stepped nearer and pulled his head down to her, kissing him.

"I love you, Connor. I love you," she whispered against his mouth. "I should have told you before Samhain. I was a coward and could not admit it to you. But, I do. I love you."

She would have said it again and again, but the sound of laughter surrounded them. Looking around, she saw no one. Then a glimmer of light appeared between them, and the fairy hill, expanding taller and wider, became an opening of some kind through which a man stepped out.

"Connor," she said, clutching his hand in hers. "There is a man . . ."

"Not a man," the stranger proclaimed boldly in a musical voice. If the tales told true, he was not mortal at all. Could he really be a Sith?

Though she thought she might have already fainted, Moira tried to understand what or who she was seeing. He looked like a prince, with his regal bearing, beautiful robes, but it was his eyes that shocked her: they were the exact same green as Connor's. His every movement and word caused the light around him to rival the sun's; shimmering waves poured off him as he walked toward them.

"Moira tell me," Connor said, tugging on her hand.

She'd already forgotten that he could not see what she was witness to. "He is . . . a Sith," she finally forced the words out.

His smile warmed her, and he stepped closer now until she could have touched him. She wrapped her hands around Connor's arm now, holding him tightly, as the creature spoke.

"I am Sith," he said, "and would share what we are called with you, but it is incomprehensible to your human minds and tongues." He reached out his hand toward her, and Moira shuddered.

"Fear not, mortal. Our touch will not harm you."

And it did not, for it felt much the same as Connor's had felt when he held her hand during his vision, the heat passing from him into her and . . . it was just the same.

The Sith laughed then, and it moved the trees and grass and even the air around them with its power. "You have already been touched by our magic and lived, woman. He is part of us," the Sith said, pointing at Connor.

As if to make his point, he touched Connor's cheek, and Connor's skin glowed as it had during his visions. His face changed, and his eyes . . . his eyes glowed with power and sight as they took on their usual dark green color.

"Moira," Connor said. "My eyes . . . I can see once more!"

Connor looked around the meadow and could see the greens of the grass and plants, the pinks and reds and yellows of the flowers bursting into bloom, the blues of the sea and sky, and the light of the sun and the Sith standing before them. But more importantly, he could look once more on the face of the woman he loved. The face of the woman . . .

His gaze dropped lower, taking in her form, and his heart

nearly stopped again, for she carried a child. His child, it had to be!

"A bairn?" he asked in a whispered voice. "A bairn?"

He shouted her name and took her in his arms and swung her until she screamed and laughed and cried all at once. It took several minutes before either of them could speak a word, for all he could do was hold her and place his hand over the place where his child grew within her body.

Apparently the Sith felt ignored, for the clouds raced across the sky, covering the sun and making his glow the only thing lighting the day now. Connor turned them to face him.

"So, Sith, is this just to remind me of how much you have taken from me? Will my sight go when you do? Will I spend the rest of my days in the darkness and never see the face of my child?"

For years he'd lived with their gift and then with their curse, and through it all, he'd never lived his own life. If he had to be blind, he could accept that, but he would not have this Sith interfering with the rest of his life. "Or will you and your kind continue to twist my life for your amusement?"

"Your sight is restored," the Sith said quietly. "And the other as well."

Connor felt it then, the power, the visions moving deep inside him, waiting for him to call it forth. No longer servant to it, but master now. "Do you expect my gratitude then, Sith? I would rather face a life of blindness than be burdened by your gift."

His anger spilled out in his words, and he felt Moira tremble next to him. Wrapping his arm around her, he knew she would accept him blind or sighted, but he did not want some power that would forever control his life.

"Take it back, Sith."

The Sith stared at him with those eyes that glowed, and then he laughed once more. Connor heard the laughter and re-

membered hearing it before . . . hearing it in this same meadow . . . on his seventh birthday when the first vision happened. "You were here?"

"I cannot take back that which is part of you, Connor. You
were not a changeling," he said, staring at Moira as though he
knew she'd carried those tales to him. "You are Sith, and you
are mortal."

Connor felt the world under his feet shift as he grasped the
truth of it. It explained so much, but prompted many questions.

"My mother?" he asked. "Where is she?"

The Sith's face darkened then, as did the sky above them as
though in fear of the Sith's anger. "She betrayed me."

"Tell me my past, Sith," Connor commanded. He needed
to know how he came to be and what awaited him after the
Sith was gone.

"She did not catch me, woman," the Sith said, looking at
Moira, "I caught her. She was a daughter of this isle and spent
many a summer's day in this very place. I caught her, coming
to her in the day and the night and giving her my love."

Connor noticed that the Sith now referred to himself as a
separate being from the rest of his kind.

"I took her to my lands," he said, nodding at the fairy hill,
"and we spent many months there together. I gave her everything," he said fiercely, "but she was not happy and asked to
return to her mortal world and the man she'd been betrothed
to before I found her. She refused my love and found her way
back here on that Samhain night twenty and eight years ago as
you count time."

The Sith turned from them then and nodded at the place
before them, and Connor could see it as it happened. He thought
only he saw it until he felt Moira clutch as his hand and watch
as he did.

A young woman appeared, pushing her way out of the fairy

hill. She was huge with child and stumbled out of the ground, holding her belly and moaning against the pain of her impending birthing. She kept looking behind her to see if anyone followed, and then she began to run toward the path.

But she did not make it, falling to the ground as her pains struck. When she looked over her shoulder before gaining her feet once more, the Sith stood there on the fairy hill.

"Do not leave," he said. "I gave you my love." Connor did not think the Sith were capable of such mortal emotions, but he could see and hear both the love and the pain as the Sith spoke.

"Come back with me now." He held out his hand to her, but she turned away, trying to run.

"I cannot live with you. I do not love you," she said, gasping for breath as another pain struck. She howled in pain but still turned away. "Let me go!" she screamed.

The Sith's rage and pain exploded then: flashes of light and waves of heat pierced the night's sky as he lashed out at the woman who'd betrayed him.

"They are mine," he said, pointing at her huge belly. "They are gifted." Something flashed from his hand to the woman's belly, and she screamed in pain. "But cursed for your betrayal, for when they use their Sith powers, their mortal lives will suffer. Their powers will grow, and their mortal bodies will suffer. When their powers peak and end, they will wither and die."

"No!" she screamed. "Please! Do not make my bairns carry the punishment for my sins against you," she cried out, pulling herself up onto her knees and reaching out her hand to him. "Spare them, I beg you!"

The Sith approached her and crouched down in front of her then, placing his hand on her belly for only a moment. Connor could not describe the look on the creature's face as he felt the bairns inside her womb.

"They will be taken from you, for you are not worthy to

raise them. They will not know of their powers or the source of it, and you cannot tell them or the Sith will strike you all down," he commanded.

She began to crawl away as though to escape his sentence, when he shook his head at her and waved his hand. Four others appeared around her, holding her and keeping her from running.

"Unless they find true love, given and spoken by one called their enemy, their Sith nature will destroy their human one, and they will live in our world forever. If they find that true love given and spoken, before their powers end, their mortal nature will control their Sith side."

Connor did not move as they heard the words declaring his fate. The scene sped up, as Moira held on to him, and they watched the woman give birth to three bairns, all boys, and as each was born, one of the other Sith took the babe and disappeared. When the birth was done, the last Sith faded away, leaving only the woman and this Sith alone.

The Sith shook his head at her. "You will not find what you seek with him. You will suffer this loss and more by refusing what I offered you. Only one of the three can help you find the happiness you seek."

"No," the woman keened out. "No more!"

"I do not curse you, Aigneis," he said softly now. "I only see what the failure of your mortal heart will cause for you."

Moira felt her own tears flow as she watched the Sith walk to the fairy hill and fade into it. The vision of that Samhain night faded, too, until it was the present day and the sun shone overhead. She wiped her face and turned to Connor as the words made sense.

I had children, but they were taken from me.

"Agnes," Moira whispered to Connor. "She is your mother."

The Sith's eyes glowed then as he turned to face them once

more. "That was your past, born of betrayal, half Sith, half mortal. I did not give your sight back to you, Connor," he said, nodding at her now, "Moira did." The Sith's gaze softened then as he smiled.

" 'Twas a piece of your heart and soul left behind in him that saved his mortal life that day, but your love, given then but spoken today, that freed him from the curse laid on him in anger."

Just as on that day long past, the Sith glimmered across the meadow to stand near the fairy hill. "Wait," she called out to him. "What will happen now?"

The Sith laughed then, and all the clouds that had gathered in the sky blew out to sea in an instant. Did he even know his powers here in the mortal world?

"Your lives will be as they should be, Moira," he said. Looking at Connor, he smiled. "Your Sith powers now bow to your mortal will, Son. Use them as you desire, and they will serve you well."

Connor took a few steps toward him and called out a name, one she did not understand and could not repeat if held to the sword. But the Sith understood it, and it bound him to Connor for that moment. Only a Sith's name spoken by one fully mortal had the power to bind him completely to their will.

"And my brothers? What of them?"

"They followed their own paths, Connor. While you were facing your test, they faced their own."

"You know them? You know if they lived or died?" he called out, for the Sith began to fade until only the slightest glimmer remained in the air over the fairy hill.

"I know them," a voice said, as it spread all around them. "As you may, in time."

A moment later Moira knew they were alone, and she turned to Connor and saw that his eyes still glowed, but now with love for her. He lifted her head and touched his mouth to hers. She opened to him as she wanted to, as she needed to, now and for the rest of their lives.

"You had the true power, Moira. You saved me," he whispered against her mouth. Lifting his head, he smiled. "Come, we have much to plan and much more to celebrate."

"Can we visit here again, Connor? You promised me. . . ." She let her words fade and let him remember their talk about the grass and the sun and the sea breezes.

"We will find a new place, Moira. One of our own that no one can find, and then I will lay you down, strip off your clothes and . . ."

He whispered such wicked promises in her ear that her body shuddered and heated in anticipation and in memory of other times when he brought her such passion. Then, he stepped away and laughed as she stumbled. "But not here."

She took the hand he offered, and they turned to the path that would take them back to the life they would live. Together. But, a woman stood there watching them.

"Go to her, Connor. Let her greet her son for the first time," Moira said, releasing his hand and watching him approach the woman who had paid for her inability to love the Sith prince by losing her children.

He stopped a few feet away from Agnes, and Moira could tell they were speaking. She held her breath, waiting and waiting until he opened his arms to Agnes and she fell sobbing against his chest. Moira tried to control her own tears and gave them a few minutes of privacy to begin their bond as mother and son.

She wondered if the Sith, Connor's father, would be angry that Agnes would find forgiveness from Connor. She could not see him, but she heard words, spoken in a language she did not understand, swirling softly around in the air, teasing her with his answer. Then the words surrounded her and were spoken in her tongue.

"Only the love of a human heart is stronger than the power of the Sith. 'Tis why I coveted it so much and sought it in the mortal world."

Connor released his mother then and held out his hand to Moira and she rushed to join him. Agnes hugged her, and they cried as they walked back to the house.

They had much to do and time enough ahead of them to do it. The bairn would come in four months or so and change their lives again. Hope swelled in her heart, and the life she'd never allowed herself to think on now awaited her.

A man who loved her enough to die for her.

A child created out of that love.

A life filled with memories of loved ones.

And she walked toward that life, hand in hand, with the man she loved with her whole heart and soul.

Epilogue

Oidhche Shamhna (Samhain night)

"Are you certain, Moira?" he asked her again. Well, for the eighth time that day, if he told the truth. "Mayhap we should leave things as they are."

"Aye, Connor, I am sure." She reached up and touched his cheek softly as they watched the moon rise high in the sky and shine down its light on the meadow where he was born.

The air over the fairy hill had its own glow as midnight approached, and the force keeping the Sith within it weakened. Words and laughter floated around them, and she nodded at him to begin. He changed then, into the Seer, and she could feel waves pouring out from him as he spread his power out over the isle and the seas, searching once more for the brothers he'd lost those years ago.

From the things she'd discovered about Samhain, she knew this was the one day when Connor's powers were at their strongest and the best time if he was going to find those he sought. And in this place, with the land of the Sith so close, she hoped he would succeed where he had failed before.

The bairn fussed in her arms, as though he felt it too as his father used his otherworldly powers this night. Holding Aidan close to her heart, she rocked him back to sleep.

Minutes passed, and then Connor shook his head.

"Nothing?" she asked.

"Only a stone keep and the sea," he said, shaking his head. "And that could be anywhere in the isles or on any coast." He let out a loud breath. "No matter how hard I push it out, I cannot find them."

Laughter rang out then, and Moira saw the shimmering light over the fairy hill glow stronger now. The same Sith stepped out of it and walked toward them. She calmed her thoughts and brought to mind the name that Connor had taught her over these last months.

When the sounds swirled inside of her, she concentrated and plucked all the bits of sounds together. Then she spoke them out loud, calling out the name of the Sith. He stared at her, regarding her with that strange glow in his eyes, and then he bowed to her.

"What is your wish, human?" He walked closer until she thought he might touch her and then stopped. His glimmer floated around them in the air, like tiny fireflies of all colors and sounds. "But have a care, for only the foolish try to control the Sith."

"Tell my husband of his brothers," she said, her voice shaking as she spoke. Connor's hand on her shoulder gave her courage.

"That is your command, woman?" the Sith asked. "You control far more power between you than he needs to answer that question."

Startled, she glanced at Connor, who seemed to be conversing with the Sith without uttering a word. The knowing smile on his face told her he knew how to find them.

"So, is that your command?" the Sith repeated.

"Nay," she shook her head. "That was my request. That you give him your blessing is my command."

She lifted the blanket away and held the bairn up so the Sith could see him. "I would have Aidan know his father's kin."

The Sith reached out for her son and then stopped and shook his head. "You would trust him to me?"

"I would trust his father's father to hold him and give him a blessing," she said.

Though her words were bold, her stomach ached in tension now, for handing her child to the Sith could be dangerous. She could feel Connor's strength and moved closer, holding her son, their son, out before her. The Sith took the bairn, who awoke and stared up at the creature who had the same green eyes as he did.

Moira fought the need to grab the babe back and waited for the Sith to know her son. But when he brought the child to him and smelled him, she laughed.

"He smells human," the Sith said, disdainfully. He closed his eyes and touched the babe's head to his, and then he smiled. "But he is Sith."

Connor's father turned toward the moon and then faced the fairy hill as he spoke in that other language and laid his hand on her son. The air around them swirled, and the moon grew brighter as he held the child up and called out his name in Sith. The name that would give someone power over him. The name that was his Sith blessing.

"He is gifted," the Sith said, as he handed the bairn back to her.

"Gifted?" she asked. "I did not ask you for that." Now fearing what this would mean to her son she turned to her husband. "Connor?"

"'Tis well, love. Gifted, but not cursed."

The Sith laughed, and then her son laughed, too.

"Go home, for you have much to do this night before the moon sets."

Apparently Samhain was the time of greater power, and now Connor must know how to use it. Moira nodded at the Sith and began to turn away when he faded. Words spun in the air around them as he went. Another name floated waiting to be heard. Connor smiled as he heard. "My name," he said.

"Send him to me in his seventh year, and I will train him." the Sith said.

Moira shook her head, for she was not certain she wanted to lose her son to the Sith. Connor gathered her close and shook his head. "As his father, I will train him in his gift when the time comes."

He hurried them back to the house, and Moira fed the babe and wrapped him tightly and placed him in his cradle. Agnes had followed her into the small room and offered to sit with him until he slept.

"Go now, Moira. Connor awaits you."

Moira could feel him—she could feel the pull of his blood within her and the heat of his passion when she opened the door to their room. She'd barely closed it when he pressed against her and began undressing her.

"I need you, wife," he whispered, kissing her neck and then her face as he turned her and tore off her shift. "I need you," he repeated, pressing the length of him against her stomach and rocking into her. His mouth moved down over her skin to kiss the sensitive tips of her breasts and then down and down until he knelt before her. When his mouth touched the curls on her mons, she arched and trembled so much she thought she would fall.

Connor leaned her back against the door and lifted one of her legs over his shoulder. The cool air of the chamber, for the autumn winds blew now through the opened window, touched her between her legs and chilled her before he used the heat of his mouth and the touch of his hands to make her throb and shiver.

She thought she would scream as her arousal flowed through her and her wetness met his tongue. He licked and sucked the aching folds until she dropped her head back and could do nothing but feel his desire as it grew stronger and stronger.

He moved slowly then, soothing rather than inflaming, and then he stepped away and stood between her legs. Lifting her hips, he placed her on his erect manhood and helped her to slide down him, taking every thick inch of him within her. She gasped at it; the friction there caused the muscle to spasm around his length, making it difficult to breathe or think, so she did neither. When he was fully sheathed, he carried her to their bed and laid her there.

"Moira," he whispered in that way that made her blood heat.

Climbing higher between her legs, he used the bed beneath her to steady her body as he claimed her again. Thrusting deep, he drove her to madness as her body became his to move, to touch, to fill, and to satisfy. The moment began, and she felt the ripples of pleasure moving through her as he brought her to her peak. He took her hands in his and spread them out at her sides then.

"Moira, look at me." He compelled her to open her eyes, and she saw that his were changing, from green to that glowing color as his power filled him. He thrust in once more and then withdrew. She opened wider and waited for him to take her completely. As her muscles contracted and her body wept its release, his seed flowed into her even as the heat of his power did, and Moira watched as he lifted her and they flew.

She could not tell if it was the present or the past, but the sky was bright now as they passed over the sea going north. Endless miles and then a tall, stone keep and a chamber. She could see the man's face, so like Connor's, and he looked at them as they paused there.

"Duncan," they said together with their one voice.

Then they were flying, north again as the air turned bitterly cold and the Norse isles came into view. Again, they did not recognize the isle or the town, but they kept moving until they reached the sea and followed the edge to a place where the sea caves opened. The man stood at the cave's entrance and watched as they passed. His resemblance to Connor and Duncan was uncanny.

"Gavin," they said.

They laughed out their joy, as they were no longer flying but back within themselves as her body clenched around his flesh and wrung out those final moments of pleasure from him.

They remained joined for some minutes until their breathing calmed and Moira could think on what they'd just done. Together.

"Your father told you how to do that?" she asked, remembering the shared unspoken words that had passed between them earlier.

"Nay, love," he said kissing her mouth one last time before he left her to lay at her side. "He only reminded me that my powers are stronger on the day of my birth."

"Samhain?"

"Aye, Samhain. Then I remembered that our joining gave me the power to call the vision from within, and I thought I would try it again."

She laughed then and touched his face. "It worked."

"Duncan and Gavin," he repeated.

"Could you tell if we were seeing them in the present or the past?" she asked.

He rolled then, tucking her beneath him and settling between her legs once more. "I could not," he said as he slid his prick inside her gently. "But . . ." he began to thrust deeper and retreat and again.

"But?" she said as he moved within her again.

"The moon has not set, and there is time to try again."

She pulled his head down to kiss him and waited for him to thrust again. When he did and the change came into his eyes, she whispered against his mouth.

"Call forth your visions, Seer," she commanded, using the name his father had called him. "Call forth your visions."

And like a storm, their passion surrounded them as their love made his power go farther and wider and clearer in search of his kin. When he found the answers they sought and lay replete in each other's embrace, the truth they discovered was more important than any vision could reveal.

For they knew now that the love of a human heart was stronger than any power of the Sith.

Try DATING OUTSIDE YOUR DNA, the latest from
Karen Kelley, out now from Brava!

"Lyraka is different."

Roan crossed his legs. "I've heard that crap before."

"She's not full-blooded Nerakian. Her father is an Earthling."

He raised an eyebrow. Okay, Joe had his attention. "I didn't know there were any half breeds old enough to train, but it makes sense they would mate. The ones I've run across make no bones that they like a good roll in the hay."

"Now you're being crude," Joe admonished.

"Just stating facts. Chocolate and sex are the only things they seem to care about."

"That's not true and you know it."

Yeah, he did, but he'd been in a particularly foul mood since Joe told Roan that he wanted him to stay at the training center a little longer. Now Joe was giving him this new assignment. Roan wanted to get back into field work and out of training. He was starting to feel trapped, and that didn't set well with him.

A leg injury he'd sustained a few months ago had kept him on the sidelines. The doc still wouldn't release him for full duty even though Roan felt fine. He had a feeling Joe was behind some of it.

"Train her, and I'll get you the release you've been wanting," Joe said.

"Are you serious?"

"Yes."

"She must mean a lot to you. Is she that good?"

"You can't imagine." Joe handed Roan a manila envelope. "This is everything I have on her. I know it's not much, but read it tonight."

Roan was still skeptical, but believed Joe when he said he would get him the release. Hell, he'd do just about anything to get back to active duty. He didn't believe there wasn't more to training this chick, though. "What's the catch? There has to be something wrong with her."

Joe shrugged, a little too casually, if you asked Roan.

"Like I said, her abilities are different, stronger than the average Nerakian, but she needs to learn discipline and control."

She was half Nerakian and half Earthling, how strong could they be? He assumed she was a warrior so he wouldn't have to actually do that much. A few weeks of his time and he'd be back getting his hands dirty. He could handle that.

"Okay, it's a deal. When do I get to meet her?" He'd known Joe for quite a few years. At one time, Joe had been a kick-ass agent, but when the elite force was formed, Joe had taken over recruiting people who had the potential to be the best of the best. Roan knew it took a lot to impress Joe. So yeah, he was curious.

Joe beamed. "You get to meet her right now." He pushed a button on his intercom. "Go get Lyraka and ask her to come in."

A few minutes passed before the door opened. Roan didn't move from his chair. Nerakian women were beautiful, but it hadn't taken him long to realize they had strange ideas about things.

And they took everything literally. He didn't have that much patience when it came to explaining every little detail. Women from Earth were more to his liking. They knew the score. He slowly turned in his chair, expecting to see a beautiful woman.

There were very few times in his life he'd ever felt as though the wind had been knocked out of him. This just happened to be one of them. She didn't look like most Nerakians. Each one's appearance was different. Warriors were darker: dark hair, dark eyes, dark clothes. Healers had long blond hair and usually wore green flowing robes, and man, were they a pain in the ass. He'd only met one, but that one had been more than enough. Each Nerakian had a different look that immediately said what their role on Nerak had been.

But this woman was different. God, was she different. His heart had already begun to pound, and the palms of his hands to sweat just looking at her. She was a walking, talking billboard of every man's sexual fantasy—him included.

How the hell was he going to train her?

Some relationships burn WITH EXTREME PLEASURE, so go out and get Alison Kent's newest Dragon One novel today!

He stilled in the act of scrubbing the day's sweat from his face and waited to see if Cady had something to say, or if she'd only come for the facilities because she couldn't wait. He didn't want to make her uncomfortable if she had.

But she didn't say or do anything. Best he could tell, she was standing unmoving just inside the door. And since his clothes were in a pile somewhere near her feet and his towel on the edge of the sink, he needed her to do whatever it was she'd come to do and get out.

So he nudged her. "First my truck, and now my shower. Is nothing sacred?"

"Sorry," he heard her mutter. "The TV wasn't working."

What the hell? "You came to get me to fix the TV? Did you try calling the front desk first?"

"No. I mean, the TV works fine. It just wasn't . . . working. As a distraction." She groaned beneath her breath, the sound giving off an emotion he hadn't heard before. "I needed a distraction."

She had dozens of channels broadcasting more distracting crap than a person could need in a lifetime. She wasn't making any sense. And he wasn't exactly comfortable here with the situation.

"You're looking for a distraction? In here? Where I'm bare-as-the-day-I-was-born naked? Cady, Cady, Cady." He clicked his tongue. "You devil."

"It's not like that."

"Then what's it like, boo, because you coming in here saying you need a distraction kinda leads me down that road." He stared at the shower curtain where he could see her shadow on the other side. It was the strangest way to be having a conversation, not one he was exactly good with.

The water was beating down on his shoulders as he stood with his hands at his hips, keeping his secrets out of sight the same way Cady was on the other side of the cheap white vinyl keeping hers.

His were of a physically personal nature; he didn't hang it out for everyone to see. But her own package of mysteries was obviously pretty damn heavy. After all, it had sent her seeking refuge in a steamy wet bathroom when she had a perfectly comfortable bed to hide out in.

King leaned into the spray, rinsed the shampoo from his hair, the soapy water from his face, neck, and chest. He was clean and ready to get out, but he was also butt naked, and she was standing between him and his towel.

Except standing wasn't exactly the right word. Even through the curtain he could see her nervous movements, pacing, rocking, leaning over the sink and talking into her hands instead of to him.

He'd had enough. "Cady, either talk to me or get out so I can get out."

"I can't go back out there."

Then talk it was. "Because?"

"I just can't. In the city, I felt safe. The incident with Alice aside," she added. "In the city, I was just another nameless person in the crowd. It was easy to stay out of sight, lost, bland, blending in."

She was not bland. She was anything but. "And somehow that all changed with me taking you home."

"That place is not my home."

No, but it used to be. She had a lot of history there. Was standing out now what was bothering her? "You think the gossip mill is all churned up with tales of your face meeting your mother's fist?"

"It's not the tales and the gossip that scare me."

Scared? That's what she was feeling? He would've thought something like rejected, dejected. Embarrassed. Any one seemed more in order. "Then what scares you?"

"That after all these years, they're finally going to catch me. And kill me when they do."

Okay, now this was getting spooky weird, but the thing about feeling safer sharing a room? If she thought someone was after her, it made sense. Made him glad, too, he'd kept his gun close. At least until he knew more.

Like whether she had a real reason to be frightened. Or whether she was some kind of schizo whack job. "They? Who is they?"

It took her several seconds to respond. He sensed her move again, lean back against the wall beside the door. "I don't know their names, or even who they are except for being friends of the guys who went away for Kevin's murder."

Real enough. So far. "And you think they're after you?"

"They've been after me since the trial."

There were a dozen things he wanted to ask, all related to wondering why she was still living here in this part of the country when she had no ties. Why, if there was a legitimate threat, had she not found out who *they* were and filed a restraining order?

But her fear was immediate, her need for a diversion urgent

enough to bring her in here while he showered. He ended up asking, "And you think they're here? Now?"

"I don't know. It's just . . . When I looked out the window, I saw a truck idling behind yours, then rolling forward slowly and stopping as if searching for our room. Or searching for me."

He didn't want to discount what she was feeling, or ignore what she thought she'd seen. But he'd been the one driving, and nothing about the traffic around them had struck him as strange or hostile.

No, he hadn't been on the lookout for a tail or had any reason to be, but those early years behind bars had left him with a good pair of eyes in the back of his head.

As far as he knew, they were still working, and they hadn't seen a thing. "I'm sure it's nothing."

She bit off some not so nice words. "You're sure I'm hallucinating? Is that it?"

Women. Twist and turn everything a man said. "No, I'm sure you saw what you saw."

"But until you see it for yourself, then it doesn't count."

"I didn't say that either."

"You didn't have to. You don't believe me."

What he believed was that they weren't going to get anywhere with this barrier between them.

He shut off the water, grabbed his wet rag and held it with one hand in the most strategic of locations, then whipped the curtain out of the way and met her gaze.

The hooks clattered the length of the rod, and Cady jumped, her eyes going wide as she took him in in all of his Garden of Eden glory.

Then a smile teased one corner of her mouth upward, and a knowing brow followed suit. "Nice fig leaf."

He glared, moved his other hand to his hip to secure the terry cloth from both sides. "I can't talk to you when I'm naked and you're not."

"Are you saying you want me to take off my clothes?"

That hadn't been the response he was after, but now that she'd brought it up . . . "If you're not up for doing that, then I'm going to put mine on. You can stay and watch, or stay and help, or you can turn your back until I'm dried off and dressed. And we can pick up this conversation then."

She'd lost a bit of her smirk during his speech, and though she hadn't run screaming out of the bathroom, he wouldn't be surprised if she turned and did.

He wasn't much to look at as it was, but dripping wet and naked save for his terry cloth fig leaf—the rag itself growing wetter with all the dripping going on—he could scare the chocolate out of an M&M candy shell.

So it left him feeling strangely naked and vulnerable when she was slow to reach for the handle, and even slower to open the door, leaving him behind with an expression he swore was tinged with regret.

And don't miss Cynthia Eden's ETERNAL HUNTER, in
stores next month from Brava . . .

She reached into her bag and pulled out a check. Not the usual way things were handled in the DA's office, but . . . "I've been authorized to acquire your services." He didn't glance at the check, just kept those blue eyes trained on hers. Her fingers were steady as she held the check in the air between them "This check is for ten thousand dollars."

No change of expression. From the looks of his cabin, the guy shouldn't have been hesitating to snatch up the money.

"Give the check to Night Watch."

At that, her lips firmed. "I already gave them one." A hefty one, at that. "This one's for you. A bonus from the mayor—he wants this guy caught, fast." Before word about the true nature of the crime leaked too far.

"So old Gus doesn't think his cops can handle this guy?"

Gus LaCroix. Hard-talking, ex-hard drinking mayor. No nonsense, deceptively smart, and demanding. "He's got the cops on this, but he said he knew you, and that you'd be the best one to handle this job."

Erin strongly suspected that Gus belonged in the *Other* world. She hadn't caught any scent that was off drifting from him, but his agreement to bring in Night Watch and his almost desperate demands to the DA had sure indicated the guy knew more than he was letting on about the situation.

Could be he was a demon. Low-level. Many politicians were.

Jude took the check. Finally. She dropped her fingers, fast, not wanting the flesh on flesh contact with him. Not then.

He folded the check and tucked it into the back pocket of his jeans. "Guess you just got yourself a bounty hunter."

"And I guess you've got yourself one sick shifter to catch."

He closed the distance between them, moving fast and catching her arms in a strong grip.

Aw, hell. It was just like before. The heat of his touch swept though her, waking hungers she'd deliberately denied for so long.

Jude was sexual. From his knowing eyes. His curving, kiss-me lips, to the hard lines and muscles of his body.

Deep inside, in the dark, secret places of her soul that she fought to keep hidden, there was a part of her just like that.

Wild. Hot.

Sexual.

"Why are you afraid of me?"

Not the question she'd expected, but one she could answer. "I know what you are. What sane woman wouldn't be afraid of a man who becomes an animal?"

"Some women like a little bit of the animal in their men."

"Not me." *Liar.*

His eyes said the same thing.

"Do your job, Donovan. Catch the freak who cut up my prisoner—"

"Like Bobby had been slashing his victims?"

Hit. Yeah, there'd been no way to miss that significance.

"When word gets out about what really happened, some folks will say Bobby deserved what he got." His fingers pressed into her arms. Erin wore a light silk shirt—and even that seemed too hot for the humid Louisiana spring night. His touch burned through the blouse and seemed to singe her flesh.

"Some will say that," she allowed. Okay, a hell of a lot would say that. "But his killer still has to be caught." Stopped, because she had the feeling this could be just the beginning.

Her feelings about death weren't often wrong.

She was a lot like her dad that way.

And, unfortunately, like her mother, too.

"What do you think? Did he deserve to be clawed to death?"

An image of Bobby's ex-wife, Pat, flashed before her eyes. The doctors had put over one hundred and fifty stitches into her face. She'd been his most brutal attack.

Erin swallowed. "His punishment was for the court to decide." She stepped back, but he didn't let her go. "Uh, do you mind?"

"Yeah, I do." His eyes glittered down at her. "If we're gonna be working together, we need honesty between us."

"We need you to find the killer."

"Oh, I will. Don't worry about that. I always catch my prey."

So the rumors claimed. The hunters from Night Watch were known throughout the U.S.

"You're shivering, Erin."

"No, no, I'm not." She was.

"I make you nervous. I scare you." A pause. His gaze dropped to her lips, lingered, then slowly rose back to meet her stare. "Is it because I know what you are?"

She wanted his mouth on hers. A foolish desire. Ridiculous. Not something the controlled woman wanted, but what the wild thing inside craved. "You don't know anything about me."

"Don't I?"

Erin jerked free of his hold and glared at him. "Few things in this world scare me. You should know that." There was one thing, one person, who terrified her—but now wasn't the time for that disclosure. No, she didn't tell anyone about *him*.

If she could just get around Jude and march out of that door—

"Maybe you're not scared of me, then. Maybe you're scared of yourself."

She froze.

"Not human," he murmured, shaking his head. "Not vamp."

Vamp? Thankfully, no.

"Djinn? Nah, you don't have that look." His right hand lifted and he rubbed his chin. "Tell me your secrets, sweetheart, and I'll tell you mine."

"Sorry, not the sharing type." She'd wasted enough time here. Erin pushed past him, ignoring the press of his arm against her side. Her body ached and the whispers of hunger within her grew more demanding every moment she stayed with him.

Weak.

She hated her weakness.

Just like her mother's.

"You're a shifter." His words stopped her near the door. She stared blankly at the faded wood. Heard the dull thud of her heart echoing in her ears.

Then the soft squeak of the old floorboards as he closed the distance between them.

Erin turned to him, tilted her head back—

He kissed her.

She heard a growl. Not from him—no, from her own throat.

The hunger.

Sure, he made the first move, he brought his lips crashing down on hers, but . . . she kissed him right back.